Shane pulled Rina into his arms, resting his cheek against her hair. His uneven breathing stirred the loose tendrils of curls.

"What am I going to do with you?" he whispered, his voice tight with an unfamiliar emotion.

Her breath stopped for a moment, and she nestled against his chest.

"What do you want to do with me?" The question slipped out, and she waited impatiently for him to answer.

"This."

At once he took her lips in a demanding kiss, slipping his arms behind her slight body and drawing her up against him. Rina went willingly, luxuriating in the loving closeness.

"Ah, Rina."

Her heart skipped a beat at the promise his words held. A liquid heat started slowly burning at her thighs and flowed upward. Sunlight dappled around them, turning the shady spot into a hidden cocoon— a piece of paradise. It seemed like they were locked together in a world of their own, unseen and suspended in time.

The sweet quiet of the clearing enveloped them, the only sound their own breathing and the hypnotic call of the whippoorwill. Shane gently kissed her, tasting her mouth, reveling in its sweetness.

His hands moved, caressed, making her feel things she'd never felt before . . .

Taylor—made Romance From Zebra Books

JOYCE ADAMS
GAMBLER'S LADY

ZEBRA BOOKS
KENSINGTON PUBLISHING CORP.

ZEBRA BOOKS are published by

Kensington Publishing Corp.
475 Park Avenue South
New York, NY 10016

Copyright © 1994 by Joyce Adams

Zebra and the Z logo Reg. U.S. Pat. & TM Off. Heartfire
Romance and the Heartfire Romance logo are trademarks
of Kensington Publishing Corp.

First Printing: April, 1994

Printed in the United States of America

To Sueann, Shelia, Carol, & Judy—the best critique group anyone could ask for—thanks for seeing the good and the bad, and to my agent, Beverly Wadsworth for helping make my dream come true.

Thank you all.

One

Arkansas—1868

Things were too quiet.

As Rina Taylor dropped the armload of kindling into the bucket Pa used for a tinder box, danger prickled the hairs at the back of her neck. She slapped her dirty hands against her too-snug breeches, giving a nervous glance around the clearing. It felt as if the hills were a-holdin' their breath. A fine layer of dust floated up then resettled over her legs, bespeaking the August dryness in the hills.

Tossing back her silvery-blonde hair, she wiped the sweat from her forehead. With her other hand she scooped up the long-barreled shotgun propped against a stack of cut wood, then turned her back to the dilapidated lean-to and scanned the wooded area rimming the clearing.

To her right, Pa's favorite still with its soot-covered kettles cooked up another batch of whiskey. The fire underneath burned just right. No problem there.

But then a scuffling sound to her left caused her to spin around, and she was stunned to find herself looking directly down the barrel of a six-shooter held in gnarled hands.

"Now, missy, you let go of that there shotgun real easy now."

Rina forced her gaze away from the barrel pointing at her and up to the man behind it.

Nolan Gant. She mighta known. Bowlegged and bewhiskered, Pa's worst competitor and life-long enemy looked a lot like a leprechaun in one of her brother Lucas's books. Except meeting up with Nolan Gant didn't bring anybody good luck. He was ornery as a badger and crookeder than a barrel of black snakes. Rumor in the hills whispered that the old man was deadly when crossed wrong.

Fuming, Rina let the shotgun drop into the dirt at her feet. "Hell and damnation," she muttered under her breath.

"That's where you and that batch of whiskey are going to if'n you don't tell me the recipe."

Pa's whiskey recipe was secret and legendary. Old Nolan had been after it since before she was born. He was an addle-brained fool if he thought she'd turn it over to her pa's worst enemy just to save her own hide.

"Not likely." She planted her hands on her hips and faced him squarely, an arrogant tilt to her chin.

"You may do as you darned well please around these parts, but I'm the one with a gun."

Rina told herself that Nolan was just a scrawny, puny old thing *She could lick him if she tried*. All the same, he brought to mind a polecat stretched full length, all sharp teeth and claws a-ready.

Pa'd be right furious if word got around the hills that Nolan Gant had got the drop on her. She'd never hear the end of it. Pa was right proud that his only daughter was more than a match for anybody—man or woman.

It was plumb embarrassing, and Rina racked her mind for a way out. Used to having her own way, she hated to be thwarted. Surely Nolan was up to no good; she could feel it without even looking at him. He'd come here to do more than ask for the recipe.

One glance back at Pa's whiskey still proved her suspicions right. A pile of pine cones nestled beside the fire. Old Nolan was likely as not gonna blow Pa's favorite still to kingdom come.

"Now you just stay put." Nolan circled her warily.

Stepping backwards, careful not to take his eyes off her, he stopped when he came up against the copper pot. He kicked another cluster of pine cones into the fire under the big pot.

Rina stepped forward. "Nolan Gant! You get away from Pa's still."

He answered her with a caw of laughter that reminded her of a pair of fighting blue jays.

She tried another tactic, knowing Nolan Gant's

puffed up pride was known through the hills. If she could just feed that. "You're smart enough to know that fire's hottening up too fast."

Another raucous shout of laughter answered her. Anger raced through Rina, making her throw caution to the wind. She weren't no good at flattering anyhow. She was too prone to honesty.

"You blow Pa's favorite still, and he'll send you to meet your Maker," she stated flatly.

Her threat had no effect on the old coot. He swept it aside as if it had been a pesky fly.

Damnation. She scanned about her for something to stop him with, and her eyes lit on a fist-sized rock.

"Look out!" She screamed the warning, anticipating his next move and getting ready for it.

The instant Nolan turned to check the fire, Rina grabbed up the rock, wound her arm once for the throw and let the rock fly. It landed upside Nolan's head with a thunk. The pistol in his right hand flew into the air and landed in the bush several feet away. He staggered backwards a step, stunned.

Before he could recover, Rina grabbed up her shotgun from the ground and faced him down. The comforting weight of the gun reassured her. She could outshoot 'bout any man in the county. And most of them knew it. Pa had seen to that. If there was one thing besides whiskey-making he was good at, Ben Taylor could spread the word faster than a hoot owl.

Nolan swore a blue streak. He even found a

cuss word or two Rina hadn't heard yet. She suspected he made them up. He rubbed the side of his head and swiped away a streak of blood. The red stain caused her a pang of pity, hounded by guilt. She hadn't really meant to hurt him none, only stop him from blowing Pa's still into the next county.

"Nolan Gant? You all right?" She stepped forward.

He took advantage of her movement and kicked another cluster of pine cone backwards into the fire. Damn fool, she thought, he was likely to blow them both to kingdom come and then some.

"Nolan Gant! You kick those cones right outta that fire, you hear me." Rina stopped and leveled her shotgun on her adversary again, all traces of pity buried. "That fire's hottened up so much that the whiskey's ruined anyhow."

As he hesitated, she rested her finger on the trigger. "I'll blow those boots right off your feet lessen you do it."

Grumbling, he gave in and thrust a pile of singed pine cones out into the dirt, never taking his baleful gaze from the gun barrel pointing at him.

He paused, and she added, "Now, some more."

He shifted his weight back and forth. "My feet's gettin' hot."

"Not near as hot as they're gonna get."

The air fairly turned blue with his cussing, but he kicked out two more piles of smoldering cones and woodchips before he faced her again. His whiskered face was mottled red with anger.

"I'm done," he challenged. "But I'll be back. Never you fear."

Nolan sauntered with a bowlegged stride across the clearing. He couldn't resist a parting shot. "You don't scare me none, missy."

"Well, maybe this will."

Rina took aim and squeezed the trigger. A deafening blast roared through the quiet clearing. Shotgun pellets landed right where she'd aimed—between Nolan's bowed little legs.

He yelped and jumped clear off the ground, then whirled on her.

"Nolan! I catch you back here, next time I'll aim higher," she shouted.

He turned and lit a rag for home, his bowlegs carrying him as fast as they could. Rina's throaty laughter followed him, in spite of the fact that she knew he wouldn't take this humiliation lightly.

At the edge of the clearing, Nolan wheezed to a stop and turned around. Safely out of gun range, he raised his fist and shook it at her.

"You'll regret this, missy. I swear it," he yelled over the distance. "I'll see piney-roses on your grave before winter's out."

His threat echoed across to her, carrying a real menace she'd never heard in his voice before. It gave her the all-overs. A shiver set in along her spine, and easing her gun to the ground, she rubbed her hands over her chilled arms.

He'd make her pay.

Nolan Gant paced the deck of the riverboat. Muddy water churned and he turned away from it. He hated the river. Hated making this trip. Another thing he owed Rina Taylor for.

The last two days on the boat had him feeling as caught up as a possum in a snare. He'd dared not go into town before he left and chance the folks' scorn. Rina Taylor had surely been to town bragging. That meant he couldn't go near there until the talk died down some.

Oh, he'd make her pay for all she'd done. Just wait and see if he didn't.

The only good thing that'd come out this trip so far was that he'd picked up word of a man ripe for a job. Any job.

Word on the riverboats was that a Southern gambler named Shane Delaney would do anything a shade either side of the law for money. Nolan liked that in a man. He needed him a little crooked, or he'd never hire on. But not too crooked or he might turn on him.

Nolan belched and scratched his belly. Felt like it was eating its way through to his backbone. Damn, how he hated parting with money for vittles when he'd much rather steal them. Tasted better that way, too. He checked the setting sun and figured it was about time to mosey down toward that fancy dining room. Sure to be some easy pickings there.

He grinned, showing dark-stained teeth. Yep, things was sure looking up. This Shane Delaney sounded like the man he needed to do in Rina Taylor. Yep, and time would tell.

New Orleans

Shane Delaney urged his horse on. *Damn, time was running out.* He had to get to the auction before it was over.

The late afternoon sun beat at his back. It had been a long, hot ride. Both yesterday and today.

The hot, humid wind tore at his waistcoat, but he ignored it. The packet of money in his pocket was secure; he'd seen to that. Soon, very soon, Belle Rive would be his again. *If* he made it in time.

Reaching the city, he galloped through the streets, mindless of the curious stares and indignant shouts his haste garnered. All that mattered was being in time.

"Sold!

Shane galloped up in time to hear the auctioneer's shouted proclamation. He reined his horse to a stop at the outer fringe of the auction. Pain, as sharp as a blade, knifed through him at the word.

Too late. Too damned late.

He swore in disgust. He was hot, damned angry, and sore from days spent in the saddle. When he'd got word of the upcoming auction, he'd been two hard days' ride away. He'd ridden day and night, until both himself and the horse had to stop. That stop had cost him Belle Rive.

He swung to the ground and looped the horse's reins around his saddle horn, not waiting to tether the horse properly. Hand on his gunbelt, he strode forward.

"It's too late. Let it be." Brad Weston clasped him by the shoulder and turned Shane away.

Instinctively, Shane reached for the Colt .45 nestled in its holster on his hip. He caught himself in time, stopping short of drawing on an old friend.

"Let go." Shane said the words with calm determination.

He'd known Brad Weston since before the war, and he had no inclination to cross his friend.

Brad released him, but moved to stand in front of Shane. "It's no good. You're too late."

"Who bought it?"

"A Northerner. Name of Simon Cooke." Brad nudged his hat back with a thumb. "Shane, he bought it fair and square."

"Since when is losing your home fair?" Shane met his friend's remark with an icy stare.

Shane took a step forward, but the next words stopped him.

"It went high. A lot higher than we'd thought it would."

Shane whirled around to face him. "How much?"

The answer made him purse his lips in a low whistle.

"Man wanted it real bad," Brad pointed out unnecessarily.

Shane's spirits sank. No way he could carry out his alternate plan of offering the new owner an instant profit to sell it back to him. The packet of cash in his inside pocket fell far short of the selling price his friend had quoted.

He was about to turn away when he spotted Mary Ellen Dupre, her dark glossy curls perfectly styled, not a strand out of place. His fiancée—ex-fiancée, he reminded himself harshly. When he'd returned home from the war to find Belle Rive lost for back taxes, Mary Ellen had tearfully relayed the news of their broken engagement. She'd said her papa wouldn't let her marry a penniless ex-Confederate officer.

Shane followed her hungrily with his eyes. The memories of the times spent down by the riverbank with her naked beneath him taunted him, urging him on.

He strode toward her. He wasn't penniless now, not like three years ago. If he had another six months, he'd even have enough money to repurchase Belle Rive and give the Northerner a handsome profit.

"Shane!" Brad Weston grabbed his shoulder and hauled him up short. "It's no good."

"I'm only going to talk to her."

"There's something you better know first."

Shane froze, more at his friend's tone than his

actual words of warning. Turning slowly, he faced him.

"What?"

"Miss Dupre has engaged herself to Simon Cooke."

Shane stiffened in defiance at the news. "No."

He'd known Mary Ellen was driven by her desire for money and a return to the old way of life. But to marry a Northerner for it?

Maybe the whispered stories that circulated about her at the saloons were true. No, he couldn't believe that. She was Mary Ellen Dupre, the woman he'd thought of for so many years as the perfect lady for his Belle Rive. Now it looked like he'd lost them both.

"The wedding is set for two months from now—"

"Like hell." Shane stiffened. It left him so little time.

"Let her go. She never was any good. You were the only one who couldn't see it. All she ever wanted was to be mistress of Belle Rive," Brad said.

Shane swung and barely stopped his fist from connecting with the other man's face. He lowered his arm slowly and released a frustrated sigh. It was an old argument, and one neither man had a hope of winning. Brad Weston had taken a dislike to Mary Ellen years ago, and nothing Shane could say would ever seem to change that.

"I'll let that pass." Brad stepped back and locked stares with Shane. "But you're looking for trouble. It'd be best if you left town for awhile."

His friend was probably right, Shane admitted. There was nothing here in New Orleans for him now. At least not until he had the additional money he needed. And the best place for him to head for it was back to the riverboats and the gambling tables, but thirst clawed at his throat.

"Mind if I have a drink first?"

"Of course not, Shane. But in the mood you're in, be sure and steer clear of the occupying Yankee soldiers."

Shane nodded.

"You want company?" Brad offered.

"Not today."

"Be careful, huh?"

"Aren't I always?"

Shane caught his horse's reins and swung into the saddle. His first stop would be the livery, then the saloon. Both he and his horse were in need of a drink.

The saloon was crowded when Shane entered. From the looks of it, the place promised to be rowdy by nightfall. Suited him just fine. He'd welcome a fight.

He got a bottle and a glass from the bar. His money was more than good enough here, even if it wasn't good enough to repurchase Belle Rive. The lush land of his plantation home haunted him, and he poured the dark liquid in the glass. Raising it to his lips, it was gone in a long swallow. The whiskey burned its way down his throat.

He poured another glass, grabbed the bottle,

and headed for a card game going on at a back table set against the wall.

"Got room for one more?" Shane asked, watching the card game from the side.

He casually scanned the table, sizing up the gamblers. From his experience, only one looked serious. Or professional. The pale, blond man to his left laid down five cards and raked the pile of money toward him.

Shane recognized him immediately. Roger Chastain. It had taken only one game of cards played over a year ago to make him permanently remember the crooked gambler sitting at the table. Chastain had obviously run into a streak of bad luck; both his trademark diamond stud pin and his gold and diamond ring were conspicuously absent.

One lean man stood to his feet and glared at the winner. "Chastain, either you're the best I ever met or a damned good cheat."

"Care to repeat that?" The man called Chastain slid one hand under the table.

Two other men stood to their feet, shook their heads and left the saloon. The other man backed away and joined them.

The blond man flicked Shane a glance. "Seems there's plenty of seats available. You got the money?"

Without waiting for Shane to answer, he scooped up the scattered cards and began to shuffle them.

Shane tossed down a wad of bills and straddled the chair. "Seems I have a seat, doesn't it?"

Shane smiled; he was in a fit mood to welcome pitting his skills against a cheat like Chastain.

The cards and whiskey flowed with evenness as the evening progressed. Players came and went, but Shane and Chastain remained at the table.

Shane kept a watchful eye on his opponent. Although Chastain had been playing it fairly straight, Shane knew it was only a matter of time. He'd learned to spot a cheat before he ever sat down to play, especially a desperate cheat. He'd had to learn—to survive. And Chastain had the look; no matter how well he hid it, the greed and desperation showed through. He'd never known a greedy man who didn't give in to the lure.

Gradually the cards' luck changed, and Chastain began to win. More, and more. *Gradually,* as if testing Shane out. Shane watched the game, keeping his own bets low. With enough time—and he had all night—he'd set Chastain up and take him for all he had.

He hated a cheat. He viewed them with the same disgust as he did the greedy Northerners who came and bought up homes that had been held by families for generations. Like they'd snatched up Belle Rive as soon as the fighting was over. Before he could even get home from the last battle.

Shane shook off the memories, took a long drink of whiskey, and called Chastain's poker hand. Another win. The last man to join the game swore. Middle-aged and balding, he'd lost heavy, and seemed determined to lose even more.

During the next hand, the man pulled out a piece of paper. His hands trembled as he scribbled out the note giving the deed to his home in place of cash. Shane longed to stop him, but he knew it wouldn't do any good. Taunted by Chastain, the man couldn't back down. And Shane knew he'd lose. Chastain was sure to hold the winning hand again.

There was only one thing Shane could do to stop it—call Chastain for the cheat he was.

Damn. He had no choice. He couldn't sit by and watch a man's home stolen away from him. It looked like the man wasn't going to sit by either. The damn fool was likely to get himself killed unless Shane did something.

"You sure you want to lose your home to a cheat?" Shane asked in a casual tone that belied his attentiveness.

In an instant the relaxed atmosphere of the game became charged with deadly tension.

"What?" The man grabbed back the note as Chastain reached for it.

Ignoring Chastain's icy stare, Shane added, "If you check his vest, you'll find a holdout. From my estimates, there's one card left in it. Right, Chastain?"

The flash of metal in Chastain's right hand gave Shane enough warning. He shoved the table, knocking the derringer to the floor.

As Chastain lunged, Shane surged to his feet

in a deft sidestep movement that left the other man grabbing empty air. Cursing, Chastain turned around and swung, but Shane ducked his blow and sent a sharp upper cut to the other man's chin.

Although Chastain's head jerked back from Shane's blow, he quickly recovered and plummeted his fist into Shane's stomach. Gritting his teeth, Shane fended off the next strike and landed a series of blows in return.

Chastain's nod alerted him to someone behind him, and Shane moved to the side. But it wasn't enough to dodge the bottle the man was swinging at his head.

Sharp, searing pain drove Shane to his knees, and above him he heard Chastain congratulate his partner on the sneak attack. Then Shane slumped to the floor in a heap.

Two

Shane Delaney opened his eyes and blinked against the sunlight streaming through the barred window in the vermin-ridden jail cell. Groaning as pain pounded through his temples, he dropped one arm gingerly over his eyes.

The prior evening came back to him in full detail. The card game gone sour, the speed with which Chastain had drawn his gun, and the fight. It had been quite a fight.

Flicking aside his ripped shirt cuff, he turned his head only enough to check out his cellmate.

As loud snores assured him that Roger Chastain was still out cold, his own aches faded. Chastain had definitely gotten the worst end of the fight. A smile lifted the corners of Shane's mouth.

He'd had the drop on the low-down cheat, then Chastain's partner slugged him from behind. All in all he considered himself lucky that he hadn't been shot in the back. It had turned into quite a brawl. He flexed his shoulder muscles, working out the kinks. He'd be willing to bet Chastain was a hell of a lot sorer than him.

Nothing Shane hated worse than a cheat. He'd made his livelihood with a deck of cards, skill and lady luck. Not once in these past years since the war ended had he ever cheated. Not even when his desire to own the plantation again raged within him. He'd own Belle Rive again. And soon. All he needed was one more good job.

Scuffling footsteps alerted him and he sat up, turning to face the cell door. Prepared for whatever might come.

What came to the door was a gaunt man with bowed legs and a scrubby beard. Shane met his sullen stare with a challenging one of his own.

"You Delaney?" Nolan Gant poked a finger through the bars and squinted, studying him.

"Maybe. Maybe not. Who wants to know?" Shane challenged.

The little man rocked back on his heels, scratched his stomach, and looked Shane up and down.

"Dress a mite too fancy fer my tastes."

Shane raised his brows but refrained from answering the man.

"But it probably draws the ladies like flies in the summer." The scruffy little man grinned, showing dark-stained teeth.

Shane remained silent, waiting for the man to either say what he'd come to say or go away.

Instead he looked Shane up and down. "Yep,

24

you's that Delaney fella right enough. Purty. And fancy duds. Yep. You's him."

Shane turned away, casually checking on his cellmate. Roger Chastain was snoring. Totally oblivious.

"Heh, fella. I got a job you might be interested in. If'n you can bother yourself to turn around." Irritation flavored the words, hinting at the little man's self-importance.

Shane did need money. Last night's card game had been sorely disappointing. The fight had put an end to any chance he'd had of winning a few hands of poker.

He turned back, trying not to appear eager. "Say what you have to say. I don't have all day."

The man laughed. "Looks like time's all you gots right now."

Shane clenched his jaw, and leaned casually against the bars to the side of the cell. "Go on."

"Name's Nolan Gant. Me and my boy, Billy, gots us a real good business back home."

Shane doubted the truth in that comment. His expression showed his disbelief.

Nolan raised his chin, jutting it forward. He reached beneath his shirt, fumbling around, and pulled out a large wad of money. Shane nodded concession at this.

"I gots one problem. That's where you comes in, Delaney. I need something from my neighbor, and you're likely just the man to get it."

"Go on." Shane crossed his arms across his chest, waiting.

"I needs their secret. All you gotta do is sweet talk it outta a girl."

"What?" Shane straightened up, jerking away from the cell bars.

"Now keep yer pants on there, fella. Leastways fer now." He laughed and slapped his thigh. "A fine fella like you shouldn't have no problem with a hill gal like Rina Taylor."

Shane narrowed his eyes on the laughing man.

"I gots a picture of her. One a them miniature painted picture things."

Shane didn't answer.

Nolan searched his pockets and finally pulled out the tiny picture his son had stolen about three years ago. He thrust it through the bars at Shane.

"Here. See fer yourself."

Shane took the framed picture from the man's grubby outstretched hand. As he casually looked at it, the image caught and held him fast. He barely heard the old man's voice droning on.

"She's a real looker. Cain't tell much by that miniature thing. It was a couple a years back, too."

Shane stared at the picture. The old man was right—Rina Taylor was a looker. He could see that even though the image had faded as if it had been handled and rubbed repeatedly. The features were faint, but he noted eyes the color of a deep emerald stone. In contrast, her hair was a pale, silky cloud framing unflawed skin. But it was the eyes that held him—trapped him. They seemed to sparkle and invite from the flat surface. Calling to him.

The woman in the picture brimmed with a love of life. He thought he saw a hint of the devil in her smile, but not enough to be sure he wasn't imagining it. Or wishing for it.

Shane cleared his throat, trying to return to normal. It didn't work. She still held him tight.

"Tell me about her," he demanded.

Nolan thought hard, knowing the man in the jail cell wouldn't take no for an answer. He tried to remember how his boy had gone about her that one summer, then let the words flow, like a snake slipping up on a field mouse.

"Not too tall. But all woman, you hear. Even though she's small, she's no child. Long legs like one a them fancy racing horses hear tell of back East."

Shane had a disturbing vision of those legs wrapped around his waist. He leaned back against the cell bars, trying to dispel the fantasy.

Nolan mistook Shane's posture for disinterest. "I aims to pay real good."

"How much?" Shane asked.

He waited to hear what his visitor considered "real good" before making up his mind. Rina Taylor interested him—more than interested him, but reclaiming Belle Rive came first.

The sum Nolan named caused Shane to inwardly grin. It would supply the last of the funds he needed to repurchase Belle Rive, and in time before the wedding. He'd be able to give the new owner enough of a profit to ensure that he'd sell it back to Shane. By the end of two months, Shane intended to own his home again. Outwardly, he shrugged off Nolan's answer, seemingly unaffected.

"And you gets her too, if'n you want," Nolan added with a smirk.

When that didn't draw a visible response, Nolan fell quiet. He stared at Shane for several seconds before adding, "And I'll pay what it costs to get you outta here, too. Today. And pay your way to Possum Hollow, Arkansas," he said grudgingly.

Shane glanced across at Chastain. He'd stopped snoring, but appeared to be asleep. His old friend Weston had warned that it would be healthier if he departed New Orleans for a while, he told himself, and he wouldn't mind being gone when Chastain came to. The man was vengeful as the devil himself. And Shane had seen to it that Chastain hadn't added a drunken man's deed to his stack of winnings.

He'd let many things pass, but he hadn't been going to sit still and let him steal the man's plantation. Too many homes had been lost these past years, he thought bitterly.

He stared hard at Nolan Gant. He didn't trust the man one bit. "What's the job?"

"Sweet talk her pa's recipe outta the gal."

"Recipe?" Shane asked in disbelief. "All this for some biscuits?"

Nolan chortled and slapped his thigh. Once he

finally fell silent, he glanced furtively around the jail. Then he pulled a small bottle from his hip pocket. Leaning forward, he uncorked it and waved it back and forth at Shane until he was sure he'd gotten a good whiff.

"Whiskey. Best this side of the Mississippi," Nolan grumbled in a low voice. "Damn it all, it belongs to the Taylors."

He shoved the bottle through the bars at Shane. "Jus' try it. See fer yourself."

Shane took the bottle and wiped the neck of it with his torn shirt cuff. Raising the bottle to his lips, he took a sip.

The whiskey had been aged and tasted smooth and rich with the kick of a good, strong mule. The old man knew his whiskey.

Shane nodded his approval and handed the bottle back through the bars. "That's some fine whiskey."

"And I plans fer it to be mine. You interested in the job?"

"Half my money now and half when the job's done," Shane stated flatly.

"Half when you gets to Arkansas and the rest when I gets the recipe."

Shane nodded his agreement. "Done."

He glanced back down at the picture in his hand and smiled.

When his friend suggested he lay low for awhile, Shane Delaney couldn't have anticipated that within the week he'd be spread out on his belly peering through the heavy undergrowth that rimmed a tiny clearing. Arkansas in August wouldn't normally be his first choice.

The only enticement was the money secure in his pocket, half payment he'd received from No-lan Gant that morning. Not the sole enticement, he admitted, as the memory of Rina Taylor's picture taunted him, with a special lure of its own.

He shooed away a mosquito buzzing near his ear, then refocused his attention on the clearing. There *she* was. A slow, lazy smile edged his lips, and he rested his chin on his palms.

He'd bet Brad Weston would get a chuckle out of this, but would be more than willing to trade card hands in a breath. Shane grinned, settled himself better in the dirt, and watched.

She was bending over again, showing him the sweetest backside he'd seen since he'd last visited Della's house of pleasure in New Orleans.

She straightened, flung her hair over her shoulders, and bent back over. Shane almost groaned aloud as the lower part of his body responded, tightening his pants. Curls the color of rich corn-silk rippled and brushed across her backside, teasing, swaying with her every movement as she fed the fire beneath the sooty kettles.

He clamped down on the gut-wrenching urge to replace the curls' caress with one of his own making. He shifted uncomfortably, reminding himself why he was here.

In spite of the admonition, his gaze returned

to the seductive sway of her hips. Curiosity teased him. Over the past quarter hour he'd yet to see her face clearly. Had the face in the miniature Nolan Gant had shown him been only a figment of his imagination? Or was Rina Taylor as alluring in the flesh?

The way his luck had been running the past two months, the face that belonged to that delicious body in thigh-hugging men's pants probably looked like the horse he'd won in a poker game last month. He'd given the scrawny thing back to the poor man since he figured the man needed the horse worse than he did.

He sighed as she reached over and picked up a long-barreled shotgun. It appeared she was the only guard, but she had a decided fondness for that shotgun. She'd probably let him have it with both barrels if he stepped out of hiding. Even he didn't believe for a moment that his Southern charm could overcome lead. No matter what he'd been told in the past.

Shane continued to watch as she shifted the gun, then propped it against the stack of split wood before turning her attention back to the large copper kettles. If he wasn't mistaken, Rina Taylor was mixing a batch of the best whiskey this side of the Mississippi. And it appeared to be about done.

She leaned over again, waiting for the first drops of whiskey to run out of the end of one pipe.

Rina wiped the sheen of sweat off her forehead,

her thumb smearing soot from her cheek along into her hair. She lifted the heavy mass of curls off her neck and blew a stray tendril from her forehead. The fire had hottened up real good. Pa would be right proud. She'd be willing to bet the latest dime novel she'd bargained from her brother that this was her best batch ever.

A whisper of sound tickled her ear. Listening a second, she recognized it as a nearby squirrel, then shook her head, brushing the noise off like a disturbing fly. She wasn't afeared. She knew these hills better than just about anybody, and she could *feel* when something was wrong.

Rina cocked her head and listened again, concentrating on picking up any uncommon sound. Silence. Damn, now it felt too quiet, as if nature were a-waiting for something about to happen.

Something didn't quite feel right.

Rina shoved back the tumble of curls with one hand and scooped up the shotgun once again with her other hand. Arms wrapped about the gun, Rina scanned the brush surrounding the clearing. Cocking her head to one side, she waited and listened.

A long minute later she heard it—a rustle in the undergrowth to her right. Two-footed or four-footed, she couldn't rightly tell which yet, but something was out there.

Rina pressed the butt of the shotgun tight into her shoulder and took a cautious step forward. She rested her finger on the trigger.

"Whoever you are, you show yourself," she ordered.

Silence. It was as if the entire woods was holding its breath, waiting. *Well, she wasn't.*

A brief flash of movement caught her eye. She gripped ahold of the gun and started forward.

She hadn't taken more than a couple of steps when an angry hiss of steam from the kettles warned her. She whirled back around to the whiskey. It couldn't be happening. She'd checked everything twice. Damn that sneaky Nolan Gant. She knew that polecat was at the bottom of this.

"No!" she shouted, as if it'd do any good.

A low rumble shook the ground beneath her feet. That sound meant only one thing. Pa's favorite still was getting ready to blow and there was no stopping it.

Rina took off at a dead run for the woods that rimmed the clearing. Seconds later, a man in dark clothes charged at her from the side of the clearing.

"Get down," the man shouted.

A split second later, he dove for her. The force of his impact discharged the shotgun and knocked Rina backwards. Thankfully the shot went wild over their heads.

"Dammit, woman!" he yelled in her ear as they both tumbled to the ground.

He landed atop her, shielding her with his body. Moments later an explosion ripped through the hillside, sending pieces of wood and copper sailing high into the air. They rained down in a hail of thuds around them. Above her, she heard a thunk, then the man jerked and swore.

Rina opened her eyes and stared into a pair of the most comely, bluest eyes she'd ever seen in her life. A sigh left her lips. Black hair dipped low over his forehead, and he was dressed in black pants and coat. Dark as Satan's sin. And likely just as dangerous, she thought.

A loud crack from the tree above them jolted her back to the danger seconds before pieces of copper tubing, wood chunks and embers fell from the overhanging branches.

Rina flinched, squeezing her eyes tightly closed—as if that action would make the debris land anywhere but on her. Above her, the dark stranger swore.

She snapped her eyes open just in time to meet his for a second before his eyelids closed, and he collapsed atop her. His full weight pushed the breath right out of her. She gasped in a breath of air.

"Hey. Hey, you." She pushed at his wide shoulders. No matter how hard she shoved, she couldn't seem to move him a bit.

Where had he come from? And what was he doin' here?

As she turned her head to look at him, his cheek rasped against hers. The beginning growth of whisker felt funny to her, and she moved her cheek again, testing the feeling. Oddly enough, it seemed sorta pleasant. She jerked herself back from the thought.

"Mister?" She pushed against him again.

His breath warmed her neck and stirred the loose tendrils of her hair. It tickled and she swiped at her neck.

"Hey!" she shouted in the ear now nestled beside her cheek.

The man laying atop her didn't stir a bit. She drew in a frustrated breath.

There was no doubt about it. The stranger was out cold.

Hoping she wouldn't hurt him further, Rina pressed both hands against one of his shoulders and shoved. It worked. His heavy body rolled to the side, and he flopped over onto his back, lying motionless.

Oh, damn. What had she done now? He could be dead for all she knew. Then she remembered the pleasurable feel of his warm breath on her ear. If'n the fella was breathing, he was alive. Suddenly an unexpected mixture of hope and relief flooded over her.

Rina raised herself up on her knees and leaned over him. She rested her head against his chest and held her breath, listening. The steady beat of his heart beneath her ear assured her he still lived, and she raised her head from his chest.

"Well, it's good to know you're still alive, mister," she said more to herself than to him.

She looked over at Pa's favorite still. Or at what little was left of it. There wasn't enough left to try to save anything. A-lookin' at the twisted scraps of wood and metal gave her the all-overs.

Nolan Gant had nearly had his wish of putting piney-roses on her grave. She coulda likely as not been a-lying in that charred, smoking pile.

The stranger likely had saved her life. That explosion had been more potent than she'd expected. Likely it coulda even thrown her a-ways. What had made it blow?

"Stranger, you either got mighty good timing or mighty bad." *And she intended to find out which.*

If'n he had something to do with the still blowing, he'd almost got himself killed saving her. And that sure didn't make a lick of sense.

She glanced back at the still, torn between trying to do something about it and staying with the injured stranger. Sighing, she turned back to the stranger.

Sure seemed like she owed this stranger her life. She sat back on her haunches and looked him over. Only a smattering of blood lay on his fancy white shirt. He wasn't from around these parts, that was for sure.

Gingerly she reached out a hand and touched the ruffle on his shirt. Instead of making him look womanly, the shirt made sure that anyone a-looking knew he was all man. She'd seen pictures in a book once of clothes like this. They'd belonged to a Southern gentleman, she recalled, or had it been a gambler?

What was she doing? Rina pulled herself up sharply. She should be checking the stranger for injuries, not admiring his clothes. Likely as not he was a smooth-talker, just like the one her ma ran off with. The last man in the world the Taylors wanted in their lives was *that* kind of man, Rina reminded herself. Look at what it had gotten her ma. A whore, the townsfolk had called her, in hushed whispers.

Forcing herself to pay close attention to what she was doing and not let her mind wander away to painful memories, Rina set to checking the stranger. She prodded at his shoulders. Finely muscled, they appeared free of harm. She slid her hands down each of his arms, pausing to prod gently now and then. Just to be certain, she ran her fingertips back over the bones of his arms up to his neck. His arms were powerful strong under her hands.

"Those are mighty fine arms." She glanced back up at his face. "Fiercely handsome," she said under her breath.

Swallowing the lump that formed in her throat, she unbuttoned his shirt and parted the edges, pushing it away to expose his chest. A thin scar marred the smooth skin just below one shoulder. She knew an old knife wound when she saw one. She'd treated enough of them.

"Wonder how you got that, stranger?" Her question went unanswered, just as she'd expected it would.

Her fingers trailed over the white streak again, and she stared down at him, her thoughts becoming all jumbled. He didn't look much like a common fighter—not that she questioned for a minute his ability to take care of himself in a fight.

He'd be a man *well* able to take care of himself, she'd reckon. She trailed her fingers back across the scarred skin, wondering what kind of man he was to have a knife wound. Usually common folks got in knife fights, not fiercely handsome, fancily-dressed men like this. The skin was warm under her hand, and she recalled the feel of his body atop hers in the moments before he'd been knocked out. A strange warmth came over her, and she ran her hands across to his other shoulder—checking for injuries, she told herself.

Shane knew he must be dreaming. Soft, gentle hands were smoothing back and forth across his chest. A woman's hands. Or an angel's. He wasn't sure which.

A sharp memory of the explosion jolted through his brain. He remembered tackling the woman, then the whiskey still blowing up, followed by pain and blackness. Fingertips skimmed across his skin, leaving behind a honeyed warmth. This must be heaven. And he sure liked his particular angel.

He lay unmoving under her ministrations, enjoying the soothing touch. When he couldn't stand not knowing if he'd died and gone to heaven or not any longer, he opened his eyes a crack and peered through his lashes.

A vision of silken blonde curls reminiscent of pale moonbeams draped over his angel's shoulders and tickled his chest. He had a flash of memory of eyes the color of an emerald stone. He blinked his eyes, and the vision came into focus. Rina Taylor in the flesh. He snapped his eyes shut, squeezing them tightly closed.

Rina froze as she thought she felt him stir beneath her touch. She stared at his face, but his eyes remained closed. She continued her task, running her hands across his broad chest, looking for anything that needed tending to.

The dark mat of hair slowed her exploration, and she found herself rubbing her fingertips back and forth across the pelt.

"Feels kinda like petting a cat. Only better." This sent a tingly feeling through her that she'd never had before.

She forced herself to stop it and ran her hands down over the smooth skin covering his ribs, checking for broken ones. So far she hadn't found anything broke.

She told her unconscious patient so. "Leastways you're lucky nothing's broke. It'd sure be a shame to see somebody like you laid up for a spell."

She slid her hands lower, across his flat stomach and downward. The skin under her fingers seemed to be heating more the lower she went. She dared a glance at the stranger's face.

His eyes remained closed, but something looked different. Had his lips tipped up slightly before? She stared hard at his face. His eyes were still closed—too tightly closed.

Why, his eyes were scrunched up the same way

that her brother's used to be when he was playing possum!

As her fingertips accidently brushed across the bulge in his pants, she swore he moved beneath her hand. She snatched her hands away as if she'd been burned.

"Lordy."

Rina quickly tucked her hands in the pockets of her breeches and sat back on her heels. Embarrassment burning her cheeks, she looked around the clearing at the trees and green grass—anywhere but at the stranger.

A few moments later, she sneaked a peek at him. He lay still and unmoving. Tentatively, she reached out a hand and touched his arm. He didn't so much as stir, and she released a deep sigh of relief. She musta imagined that he was awake.

Three

Shane forced himself to remain as still as death under Rina's touch. He didn't dare so much as flinch. It practically killed him to do so. Her hands were soft and gentle, but his body was beginning to heat under her searching hands.

He really should let her know he was awake and conscious. But her touch was so enjoyable. No harm in waiting just a little longer, was there?

Rina gulped in cleansing draughts of the fresh mountain air. The stranger lay deathly still. Maybe she'd imagined that part about his eyes being all scrunched closed. He looked normal enough now.

She glanced around to make certain no one had seen what she'd been a-doin' to the stranger. Her cheeks still burned with shame. But there was no one around to see them. Thank goodness.

Thankful that no one's eyes censured her, Rina returned to her task of searching out the stranger's injuries. As quickly as she dared, she checked his legs, rubbing her hands down his muscular thighs and calves with haste. They sure seemed fine enough. Her fingers tingled as she pulled her hands away. She scrubbed them up and down her breeches, hoping to shoo away the peculiar feeling.

Nothing broken. No bad cuts that she had to worry about stopping bleeding. Sighing with relief, Rina sat back on her haunches. Must be that he was hit on the head from a piece of wood or that tree branch that fell. In that case, she'd have to get him down to the cabin and tend to him. She couldn't just leave him out here where a bear or any animal could come upon him.

"That'd sure be a waste, mister," she murmured. "Nothing doing but I'll have to take you home. Pa's gonna have a fit."

All her common sense told her to steer clear of the stranger. But he was hurt. Pa always said, "Rina, gal, trouble with you is you can't resist any wounded critter."

Pa was right, as always. She looked the stranger up and down. He was tall. She'd bet well over six foot, stretched out. He'd be a heavy load to haul down to the cabin, too. She glanced toward the narrow trail.

Rina bit her lip in concern. Returning her gaze to him, she stared hard. He was staying out plumb cold for what seemed like a mighty long time.

Gently raising his head, she ran her fingers through his thick dark hair. It lay close against the back of his neck, brushing the collar of his shirt.

"It's purely sinful a fella should have hair that purty," she said without thinking as she trailed her fingers through the dark waves.

As she grazed the back of his head, a moist stickiness warmed her fingers. When she drew her hands back, they were covered with blood.

"Lordy," she gasped.

Rina wiped her hands down her thighs, then pulled her shirt out of her breeches. Bending over she caught the edge of the material with her teeth and tore off a wide strip.

Carefully she raised his head and placed the center portion of the strip of cloth at the back of his head over the cut. She leaned low over him, pressing his face against her breasts as she wound the makeshift bandage around his forehead.

His breath became hot between the valley of her breasts, and Rina drew back. She coulda sworn she felt him stir against her—kinda nuzzle closer. She leaned her head back as far as she could and looked down at him. His eyes remained scrunched closed.

As she continued to stare at him, she thought she saw his lips twitch. She snatched her hands back, letting his head drop back. Instinctively she reached out and caught him in the next breath and lowered his head to the ground.

Shane had been resisting the urge to press a kiss against her softness when she pulled back.

"Mister?" Rina called out.

When he didn't answer, she leaned closer, placing her hands on her hips. *The scoundrel was awake. She'd bet her next breath on it.*

"I knows you're awake now. My brother used to scrunch his eyes that same way when he was a-playin' possum, trying to get outta doing chores."

Shane opened his eyes and pretended to look befuddled. It wasn't hard to do. His head hurt like hell.

"Well?" Rina practically shouted.

"Shh," he ordered, holding his head. He blinked several times and sat up.

The world around him spun and tilted at a crazy angle, finally resettling itself. Damn. First he'd been cracked over the head at the poker game, and now here.

"What happened?"

"That's what I wanta know. What're you doing here?" Handsome or not, he had no call being where he was.

Just how much had he heard her say? How long had he been laying there awake? Now she wished she'd dragged him down the hill trail—by his feet. Well, almost, she admitted.

"What're you doing up here, stranger?" she repeated. "Hill folks don't cotton to strangers poking round where they don't belong," she warned.

Shane had to think fast. He'd had an excuse all thought out before he'd come here, but his mind drew a blank. Damn. It must be the blow on the head he'd just received.

He tried to come up with an answer she'd accept. He knew she'd never accept that he'd got lost. Or that he'd been admiring the beautiful scenery.

He shook his head, trying to clear his brain. It was the wrong thing to do. Shards of pain shot through his head, and he closed his eyes against it.

"Hey, mister, are you all right?"

"No, I'm not," he snapped. "My head hurts like hell."

A pang of guilt pricked Rina. He had gotten himself hurt trying to protect her.

One glance at her guilt-stricken face, and he immediately repented. "I'm sorry for yelling at you," he apologized.

Looking at her made the pain recede. Odd, how she had that effect on him, he thought.

"I never did say thank you for saving me," Rina looked away from him, embarrassed at the intensity of his gaze. "If'n you think you can get up, I'll help you down to Pa's cabin. I can tend you there."

A smile brushed Shane's lips before he schooled it away.

"Just until you can get yourself all mended and ready to go back to the place you're staying at," she quickly added.

"Of course," he answered.

He levered himself up and stood to his feet. He swayed, unsteadily. Rina grabbed him with both hands. She drew one of his arms around her shoulders.

Shane dared a glance back to the whiskey still. Or at least back to where the still had been. The only thing left was a pile of rubble and a soggy puddle. He might as well go with her. He wasn't going to learn anything about the Taylor's secret whiskey recipe here.

Nolan Gant ducked back behind the tree and cupped his hand over his mouth. He choked back the laughter that threatened to spill out. Wouldn't do to give himself away by laughing out loud now. Things was going better'n he had even hoped.

His sabotage of old man Taylor's still had worked jus' fine. Yep, crimping those coils way high up, where nobody could see them was a right good idea, Nolan congratulated himself. It had built up to enough trapped-up steam for a right good explosion. Sure threw *her* and his man together good, too.

He recalled seeing the fancy riverboat gamblerman laying atop Rina, protecting her, and a wide grin split his face. Couldn't a' worked better if he'd tried.

It looked as if Rina Taylor had more than her hands full with his fine Southern gamblerman. Yep, she had more than she could handle, that much was sure.

"I sure picked him right, didn't I?" he whispered over his shoulder to his son.

He didn't expect no answer. Billy was likely still mad as could be at him fer bringing a man into *her* life. His boy would jus' have ta accept she weren't fer him. And there weren't no way that a fancy gent like Delaney would settle for a gal like Rina Taylor who wore men's breeches. But that gamblerman would work out jus' fine anyways. He'd get Nolan what he wanted.

Nolan clamped his other hand over his mouth, and his body shook with suppressed laughter. Yep, it was jus' a matter of time. All he had to do was wait, and Shane Delaney would bring him the Taylor recipe.

He watched the two of them until they were out of sight. When he knew they were far enough away so not to hear, he laughed aloud.

"Yep, Billy, all we gots to do is wait. It won't be long now," Nolan assured his son. "That there Taylor secret will be ours."

He glanced to his right, and the laughter was replaced by a frown.

"I don't want to hear you defending her kind. How many times I told you that gal's no good?"

Nolan turned back to stare across the clearing. He didn't need to look into Billy's brown eyes to know he was sulking. He rubbed a hand back and forth across his sparsely-stubbled chin, remembering the bitter as gall argument he'd had with Billy over her.

He patted his pocket, wishing he hadn't finished up his last cigar over an hour ago. He thought about searching around for the butt, see if there mightn't be a good puff or two left on it, then discarded the idea. It weren't worth it.

"No damn good," he muttered. "And I don'ts want to hear another word from you about her. You understand me, boy?"

Silence was the only answer. He took his son's lack of response for agreement and smiled.

"Come on, Billy. Let's get on home. I'm so hungry my stomach's rubbing my backbone. And it's talking right loud to me." Nolan laughed and patted his belly.

The silence continued. That was *her* fault too. Things had never been right between him and his only boy once Billy took a shine to her. Nolan closed his mind against the memories of the things he'd been forced to do to stop his Billy from mooning over that gal. The memories continued to tear at him like the sharp talons of a chicken hawk. It was all her fault. He'd only done what he had to do.

And now he was doing what had to be done.

The last traces of humor vanished as hatred narrowed Nolan's eyes. Yep, soon he'd have their whiskey secret, and there wouldn't be no reason to keep Rina Taylor living no longer. He'd have to give some thought to jus' how he wanted to see her die.

* * *

Rina tugged Shane's arm more firmly about her shoulders. "Better let me help you. The path's pretty steep, and it's a far walk."

Right now the walk couldn't be long enough to suit him, Shane thought. Rina Taylor was a surprise in more than one way. Beneath the man's shirt, his hand felt her finely-boned shoulder and the softness of her skin. As he uncurled his one fist, his fingers brushed the top of her breast. She may have seemed tiny, but underneath the mannish clothes was a shapely woman.

Shane glanced down at the top of her head. Her hair shimmered in the sunlight. Bright strands of silver and pale gold glimmered, blending together. He stared, mesmerized. There was *something* about her—more than mere outer beauty, although she certainly had beauty—that pulled at him, drew him.

Rina took a step forward. When Shane didn't move with her, she nudged him in the ribs. "Ready?"

As he felt his body stir in response to her soft body and her question, he resisted telling her just how ready he was. Instead he swallowed down his desire and took a step forward toward the trail.

He left his arm where she'd placed it, smiling to himself. She felt small and delicate under his weight. And womanly. He tried to hold back as much of his weight as he could, afraid she'd crumble under the load. Her outward aura of bravado hid a wealth of tenderness and gentleness. And, he suspected, a little vulnerability.

Within minutes, he realized he needn't have worried about her; she proved stronger than she looked. He stumbled over an exposed tree root, and she caught him, straightening him back up. His hand slipped from her waist to slide down to her hip. He felt the gentle sway of her walk under his fingers. No harm in leaving his hand there, was there?

Rina promptly shifted his weight, grabbed his wrist, and yanked his hand back up to her waist.

"Now, you just leaves it there, you hear me, stranger?" she ordered.

Sighing, Shane left his hand where she'd placed it. It wasn't a bad location to have his hand resting after all. She had a tiny waist underneath the baggy shirt and man's breeches.

He couldn't help comparing her to Mary Ellen Dupre. Although Mary Ellen's waist had been small enough laced in a corset, she was a bit plumper than the young woman he had his arms around at this moment. He could tell by the feel of the gentle curves beneath his fingers that Rina didn't have on a corset. Did she even know what one was?

Jerking himself up at the thought, Shane missed his step. His toe caught on the edge of a fallen log. In the next instant he lost his balance and stumbled, pulling Rina along with him over the log. They landed in a heap of arms and legs with Rina sprawled across Shane.

As she started to scoot off him, Shane caught her tight with one arm, stopping her movements.

She glared down at him a moment, then propped her elbows on his chest, before she spoke. Her simple question wasn't the order he'd expected.

"You never did tell me what you're doin' up here, stranger?" Her voice had a faintly breathy quality to it, like she'd been running up a hill.

"The name's Shane Delaney."

"Oh." Her lips formed the word, tempting him. She didn't know what had happened to her voice or her brain. Neither one seemed to be working much at the moment.

"And you?" he asked in a low voice.

His voice was low and seductive, tempting her, calling out to her. She stared down into his eyes. They really were the purtiest color of blue she'd ever seen. Kinda like the sky on a clear summer day, or like a rare colored, specially deep blue wildflower she'd once found and woven into a crown of blossoms.

"Your name?" Shane asked again, a smile tipping the corners of his lips.

Oh, he had a powerful smile. Rina made an effort to find her own voice. He really was the mostest charmer she'd ever met. She answered, "Rina Taylor."

"Rina." Her name was a soft breath of sound on his lips. It made her feel funny all over.

Shane waited for her to say his name. For some unexplainable reason he wanted to hear how his name would sound coming from her softly-parted lips. Would she say his name with the same faint accent she gave most of her words? It flavored her speech like a hint of spice in a fine meal. He waited in vain.

"You never did say what you was doing here," she reminded him, nibbling on her lower lip.

Shane resisted the urge to pull her to him and kiss those delectable lips she seemed so intent on tempting him with. He forced down the need to taste her sweetness. He didn't want to scare her off.

She wiggled backward, and he spread his hand across the back of her waist to stop her moving. Without knowing it, she was pushing him almost beyond endurance. Her movements had caused her shirt to ride up, and her bare stomach pressed against his equally bared skin. His white shirt hung open, draping on either side of him, still left unbuttoned from her earlier exploration for injuries.

He suddenly remembered to answer her question. "Would you believe I got lost?"

He felt as if he could easily get lost in her gaze. What was it about her that drew him so strongly? It was almost as if he'd found something that had been lost. Something he'd been searching for a long time. He brushed the foolish thought aside.

"Nope." Rina shook her head emphatically, and her hair brushed back and forth across his chest.

The motion and the soft tickle almost knocked the breath out of him. He cleared his throat and said, "I was looking for a job?"

"Liar." She laughed down at him.

He gave her a wickedly sly smile. "I was looking for the woman of my dreams."

"Ha!" She burst into laughter.

As she started to roll off him, Shane caught her waist and held her to him. Rina's laughter died in her throat to be replaced by a lump. It felt like a big lump of sugar caught, 'cause it sure seemed to be a-meltin' with the heat, running down her throat and into her stomach like warm sweet syrup.

Rina stared into his face, unblinking. Her lips parted in an "oh" that Shane couldn't refuse, even if he'd tried.

Shane moved one hand up from her waist to the back of her head, to catch his fingers in the waves and curls of spun golden hair framing her face. Gently, ever so slowly, he drew her head down closer to his. Her sweet breath brushed his face. Above her lips, he saw her eyes widen, then fasten on his own gaze.

"Oh," she murmured, a look of guileless wonder on her face.

"Oh," he answered back.

She knew what he was about to do. Hadn't Billy Gant tried to steal a kiss from her? She'd blackened his eye good for that. As if she'd ever have let a Gant touch her. However, this time it felt different. Her stomach was all a-bunched up, and it was hard to draw a breath.

Instead of striking out, she stared wide-eyed down at Shane. Inches apart, their breaths mingled in the short space separating their lips.

Shane increased the gentle pressure of his hand, and her lips came closer.

He anticipated the feel of their lushness against his own lips. His mouth went dry with the thought. She would be sweet. So sweet.

"My stomach's all disquieted," she said, a puzzled expression on her face.

"Maybe this will help," Shane offered.

He gently drew her head down to his until her lips lightly touched his. He brushed his own lips back and forth across hers in the faintest of kisses, almost afraid he'd scare her away.

Rina held her head perfectly still for a moment, then moved the slightest bit closer to Shane. He groaned against her mouth and deepened the kiss.

She kissed him back, but held her lips tightly closed. He ran the tip of his tongue back and forth across her lips. She moaned and mewed like a small kitten, wiggling closer to his body. Returning his mouth over hers, he lengthened the kiss.

She melted into his embrace, and Shane tightened his other arm around her tiny waist. All pain, all thought vanished as if it had never existed. There was only the moment.

Rina raised her head and touched her fingertips to her lips in wonderment. "My." She smiled at him.

Shane returned her smile and drew her head back down toward his.

"That didn't settle my stomach a bit," she teased, an imp of mischief in her bemused gaze.

She leaned toward him. Shane anticipated the coming kiss. It would be deeper, sweeter than the one before.

A rustle of movement in the underbrush to their right froze them both for a moment. As silence enveloped the woods, all sound, all sight was forgotten. Brushed aside. Rina dipped her head toward his, and Shane waited in anticipation.

At another rustle of sound, Shane shifted his gaze. Out of the corner of his eye, he thought he detected a movement.

Before he could move another inch, he felt the press of cold steel against his cheekbone. He was familiar enough with the feeling to know exactly what it was—a gun.

Slowly, Shane turned his head and stared up into the long barrel of a shotgun.

"Fella, if you wants to live to draw another breath, you'll get your hands off my daughter."

Four

Considering their position and the state of undress he'd been caught in, Shane estimated that he had about thirty seconds left in which to talk his way out of the mess he found himself in.

Shane knew he should say something, defend himself, but his brain didn't seem to be working properly. Splinters of pain shot through the back of his head. The words wouldn't come, and the world around him tilted at a crazy angle again. He blinked his eyes against the threatening blackness that seemed intent on enveloping him.

As the world righted itself, he refocused and turned his attention back to the man with the shotgun. One look at Mr. Taylor's set face, and Shane figured he was as good as dead.

"Pa! What in blue blazes do you think you're doing?" Rina stared up at the man without the slightest hint of embarrassment.

Shane had to admire her courage. The lady had it in spades.

Rina wiggled off him and jumped to her feet, brushing at the leaves and twigs on her clothes. Giving a nonchalant yank to her shirt, she pulled it down into place and tucked the ripped edges into her breeches.

"Is that any damned way to greet the man who jus' saved my life?"

"Rina, don't swear." Ben Taylor said the words in a tone that showed he'd recited them often enough for the words to become a habit. And to have been ignored more times than a person could keep track of.

He took a menacing step closer to where Shane lay. "Now see here, mister—"

Shane knew he should stand and face the man, but right now he was doing good just to remain conscious as the pain increased its tempo with each shouted word. Rina sidestepped quickly, blocking her pa's aim.

"Pa? Did you hear me?" She planted her hands on her hips. "I jus' told you he likely saved my life!"

"I heard ya. That's why I ain't shot him yet."

"That's good. And your still's gone," she announced. "Blown to kingdom come."

Her pa swore mightily and stared off into the distance toward the clearing. His scowl deepened when he turned back to Rina.

Above Shane, Rina and her tough as cowhide father continued arguing. Shane stared up at the wiry man. His skin was tanned by the sun and looked as wrinkled and tough as leather. The diminutive Rina faced him down, giving every bit as good as she got. He resisted the impulse to laugh.

As they continued to shout at each other, Shane knew his presence had practically been forgotten, but he wasn't willing to draw an irate father's attention and possibly his gunfire as well by interrupting them. He grimaced as a fresh wave of pain assailed him and remained silent, fighting to keep aware of what was going on around him.

Something tickled his cheek, and he brushed it aside with his hand. His fingers came away wet and reddened with blood. Oh, damn.

"Breeches again." Ben Taylor shook his head in an obvious sign of disapproval. "Dagnamit gal, why don't you ever wear a dress?"

"They's uncomfortable. And those petticoats are too bundlesome fer—"

"Rina! A gal never mentions *that* sorta thing in front of any fella. Much less a stranger," he added in a near shout.

"Yes, Pa," she said to mollify him.

"*If* I agree to take him to the cabin, will you wear your dress tonight?"

A long stretch of silence followed.

"Rina?"

"Hell's bells—"

"Don't swear. Will you wear the dress or not?"

"Okay. But I don't have to like it."

"You'll—"

Their voices seemed to echo in Shane's head, ricocheting and pounding through his skull. The worse his head hurt, the brighter the dappled sunlight seemed to become. His brain ordered him to close his eyes against the pain.

He fought the pain and brightness as long as he could, then closed his eyes and let the blessed cool blanket of darkness and quiet sweep over him.

"And what happened to my still?"

"It blew—"

"I know that. I have ears. Now, what in the blazes were you doing when—"

"I was checking things—" When she saw the disbelieving look he threw her, she sputtered, "Don't you go a-giving me that look. You knows I'm the best around at making your whiskey. I *know* what I'm doing. It weren't my fault."

"Now, Rina—" he attempted to placate her rising anger before her temper blew as high as the still. His daughter might be slow to anger, but one might oughta head for cover when she did.

"If'n you wants to know what I think, it was Nolan Gant that had something to do with it."

"And what about him?" He pointed at Shane with his shotgun.

"If'n it had been his fault, he wouldn't risked his life to save mine. Now would he?"

"Not likely," he admitted grudgingly.

Pa glanced down at the stranger again and swore. "Dagnamit. Looks like he cain't answer us this minute. He's plumb out. Now we're gonna have to carry him down." He lowered his shotgun and shook his head.

"I told you he got hurt a-saving me," Rina defended Shane.

"We'll get him down the trail as soon as I check my still."

He turned away, stopped and looked back over his shoulder at her. "And you keep yer distance from him till I get back. You hear me?"

"Pa!"

"Keep yer distance."

"Pa, we can't leave him a-lying there. We gots to help him. Now."

"Oh, all right. I'll come back up and check things out later. Let's get him down to the cabin."

Shane awoke to cool quiet. He relished the peace and silence a full minute before he remembered why he was here. *Rina!*

Where was he? And where had Rina disappeared to?

The pain in his head had receded to a dull ache. He forced himself to peer through half-opened eyes, not quite ready to face bright sunlight yet. Instead his eyes met shade. No, not shade, but the underside of a roof and the inside of a building.

Instead of the hard, rough ground, he lay on a soft feather bed. It cradled and soothed his body almost as well as Rina's touch had in the clearing.

He blinked and slowly took in his surroundings. To his left stood a large oak table in what appeared to be a kitchen. He seemed to be in the

center room of a three-room cabin. The only fur-
niture in this room consisted of a high back rocking chair sitting beside the hearth, and the single
bed he laid on.

Gingerly he turned his head to the side. Another room stretched off to the right. It was probably a bedroom.

A stir of movement from the side of his bed
caught his attention, and he froze.

"So, you're awake?"

The masculine voice came from just above and
behind his right ear. Shane jerked and turned his
head.

"How're you feeling? I sure imagine your head
hurts some. You'll probably find yourself feeling
swimmy-headed over the next few days."

A slim, studious-looking man leaned low over
him. He wore a rumpled white shirt and a black
silk bow tie. This was definitely not his angel.

"But that will pass. You received a pretty fair-
sized hit from the looks of it," he kept talking,
chattering on, ignoring Shane's questioning
glance. "Rina said that you'd—"

"Rina?" Shane asked for her without thinking.

"Sorry, outlander. Her and Pa are busy right
now. You'll have to make do with me."

Shane raised himself up on one elbow, grimac-
ing at the pain the movement brought.

"And who the hell are you?"

The young man laughed good-heartedly. "I figured there had to be something special about you
for Rina to insist you be brought here. Pa's mad-

der than a wet rooster about it, too." He stuck out his hand. "I'm Lucas Taylor. Rina's brother."

"Brother?"

Shane noticed the resemblance in the bold green eyes almost the same shade as Rina's.

"Sure enough. Older by three years, too. That part always makes her mad. She said your name's Delaney. Glad to meet you." He pumped Shane's hand up and down briskly, then let go.

Shane stared at the man. He spoke with a cultured voice that the other two Taylors had lacked. Shane found he missed the soothing sound of Rina's voice.

Shaking his head, Lucas immediately began the same type of poking and prodding as Shane had endured under Rina's hands.

"Don't worry. I'm the doctor over in Blueberry Bluff. Have been for the last two years." He held up his hand to forestall any questions Shane might have, and continued on. "Blueberry Bluff's the nearest town. You can't really call Possum Hollow a town. It's more like a stop in the road." He chuckled.

As Lucas examined him, Shane looked the other man over. He could see the resemblances between Rina and her brother, and the subtle differences. Lucas Taylor had the same color of green eyes as Rina, except his lacked the imp of mischief hers continually held. Lucas's hair was a dark blond, where Rina's hair was the pale color of sunlight.

Lucas continued telling him about the merits

of Blueberry Bluff. And Shane swore the "doctor" never paused to take a breath. He'd never met a man who talked that much.

"You're going to be a mighty nice shade of black and blue here in about another day. Looked as if you took more than your share of hits when Pa's still blew. I fixed up several cuts on your back, too."

Lucas picked up a basin of blood-stained water and headed in the direction of the kitchen.

"Thank you," Shane said before he could leave.

"No, I want to thank you for saving Rina," Lucas mumbled the last, in an embarrassed undertone and hurried from the room.

This surprised Shane. He didn't think the talkative doctor could be embarrassed by anything. It seemed a trait the Taylor family shared.

"Pa says thanks too. Even gave you his bed." Lucas stepped back into the room. "He laid down a pallet over there for himself." He jerked his head to the space in front of the hearth.

"Rina went back to the clearing a little while ago with Pa to check on the still." Lucas returned to the side of the bed. "She stayed with you until I got here."

So, Rina had stayed with him. Shane closed his eyes to think this over. Thank goodness the doctor didn't expect, or allow, any verbal responses to his tirade.

However, Lucas's sharp mind missed very little.

"Don't worry about being so tired," Lucas explained for Shane's benefit. "You lost quite a bit of blood from that crack on the back of your head. But you'll be fine. Just need lots of rest."

Shane raised his hand and felt the new bandage across his forehead.

Lucas moved his hand away. "It's just fine. Leave it be."

He stepped away from the bed, but returned with a chair. Sitting, he leaned back and studied Shane.

"Seems like you've had quite a day, outlander. Pa's pretty upset. This is his second trip back up to the still since they brought you down." Lucas paused, rubbed his chin, and added, "But it seems you're in the clear about that. Pa found fresh footprints and a hunk of old Nolan Gant's cigar in the brush. He's hopping mad. Swears he'll get even with Nolan for this one. They've been feuding since before I was born."

Shane let the words wash over him. He knew it wouldn't be of any benefit to try to interrupt the good doctor. He'd bet Lucas Taylor would either ignore his words or trod right over them.

Lucas paused, then continued, "They found a bundle of your things and brought them back down." He motioned to where the bundle sat on the rocking chair.

"Thanks—"

"Rina and Pa are still arguing about what you were doing up there. Wouldn't care to let me in on the secret, would you?"

Now that the pain in his head had dulled, Shane's mind operated with its usual quickness, and he remembered his original planned-out answer.

Lucas crossed one foot over the other and waited for Shane's response.

"It's no secret," Shane shrugged off Lucas's curiosity.

"Umm?"

"I work the gambling tables on the riverboats."

"A gambler, are you? Yeah, you have the look of one," Lucas put in.

Shane raised his eyebrows. He didn't know if the observation was good or bad.

"Word travels along the Mississippi, and I heard about the Taylors' whiskey. I decided to check it out for myself, and if it's as good as I heard, and we can make a deal, then I pick up some extra money by reselling it to the boat owners."

"You'll have to deal with Pa."

"I plan to. So, how good is it?"

"Better than anything you ever tasted." Lucas grinned in pride. "It's so good that old Nolan Gant's always been after Pa's whiskey. Even stole a barrel once to sell. It made Rina spitting mad, barely stopped her from going over there after him. You see, that was her best barrel of the year. She'd been mixing—"

"You don't make the whiskey?" Shane interrupted.

"Me?" Lucas looked at Shane like he'd just said something hilariously funny.

"No. Pa hasn't let me near the still in over five

years. It seems I have a decided knack for making the *worst* whiskey in the hills."

Shane stared at him in disbelief.

"It's the truth. Pa says it was all the book learning that ruined me." He shrugged and laughed. "It doesn't seem to have hurt Rina any."

"She can read?" The instant the words were out of his mouth, Shane regretted them.

Lucas brushed the question aside without taking insult. "Of course. Mr. Mossman, the teacher over in Blueberry Bluff, taught us both. I'm sure you've already realized that Rina can be, ah . . ."

Lucas paused. He was finally at a loss for words—for the first time since Shane had opened his eyes to find him looking him over. A smile teased Shane's lips.

"Determined, that's the word for it," Lucas announced. "Pa says it's just cursed stubbornness."

Shane let the smile spread to a grin. Yes, Rina Taylor was *determined*.

"Always had to learn everything I did. So she reads, writes, does the doctoring here in the hills when nobody else is around."

"She's a doctor?"

"Rina? No. But she's the closest thing to it around here when I'm over in Blueberry Bluff. You're lucky I was coming for a visit today. Not that Rina didn't do you right."

Shane blinked in confusion. Didn't the man ever pause to breathe?

"So, she also makes whiskey?" he asked, trying

to get the doctor back to talking about the Taylor secret.

"Yeah, Rina inherited the talent from Pa. Everybody says I got Ma's softness. What there was of it."

The last words carried a harshness that Shane hadn't heard in Lucas's voice up until then. He refrained from asking any further questions on the subject. For now. It didn't have anything to do with the recipe.

He listened, gathering together what information was useful and sorting out the rest. The overly-talkative young man was a wellspring of information. From him, Shane learned that Rina was not betrothed, or involved with anyone. He smiled at that bit of fact.

Lucas leaned forward and patted his shoulder. "Well, I got to be getting back to town. And there's a mighty pretty little lady named Milly that I want to see before then." He winked down at Shane.

"You're in good hands here," Lucas continued. "Go ahead and get some rest now. If you do that, then you'll probably be well enough to leave here in a couple of days," he announced.

His proclamation startled Shane. He didn't have much time to find what he needed.

By the next afternoon Shane felt well enough to be restless and bored in the cabin. He'd slept the sleep of the dead—restful and deep. He'd awoke without the pain in the back of his head, and the dizziness had disappeared as well.

He refused to believe that the vile concoction that Rina made him drink after Lucas left had anything to do with how he felt today.

What had she said? "That it'd help get his blood a-pumping better'n before."

Smiling at the memory of the words, he tossed off the light covers and slowly stood to his feet. Only the faintest trace of unsteadiness remained. He chalked that remainder up to Rina's "potion."

Shane headed for the kitchen, deciding that would be the logical place to start his search for anything that might deal with the famous Taylor whiskey recipe.

Several jars filled with varying colors of mixtures caught his attention. He proceeded to unstop each one, checking the contents and being careful to replace it in exactly the same spot he'd removed it. Apparently he'd happened upon Rina's "doctoring" potions. He suppressed a shiver at a particularly vile-smelling jar and set it back.

After carefully and methodically searching the cupboards and small nooks and crannies the room held, he came up empty-handed.

It seemed that logic had nothing in common with the Taylors. Now why didn't that fact surprise him in the least?

Trying to keep his ears attuned to the sound of anyone approaching the cabin, he circled the center room and checked it over. The room was clean and practically dust free, a fact that surprised him. Rina didn't strike him as particularly good at the womanly art of keeping a home.

Finished with the room, he turned his attention to the last room with relief. His body was beginning to ache and offer up a variety of complaints, not the least of which was a returning headache. To quote Dr. Lucas, he was feeling "swimmy-headed."

The instant Shane entered the small room tucked away at the far side of the cabin, he knew it was Rina's bedroom. The room held the faint, pleasing scent he realized he associated with her. It seemed a mixture of flowers and a tinge of spice.

A grin crept over Shane's face. That definition described Rina exactly. Sweet, delicate, with a hint of spice.

He made a cursory sweep of the room. A feminine, delicately-stitched coverlet spread across the bed. He couldn't believe for an instant that she'd made this. It seemed as far distant from his version of Rina's bed as possible. Lace bordered each square detailing tiny clusters of lilacs, the purple blooms and green leaves bright against the milky white lace.

Shane reached out his hand and trailed a finger along an emerald green leaf. It reminded him of the color of Rina's eyes as she'd stared down at him in the moment before their kiss.

He sighed with a strange sense of regret. Turning away from the bed and its too-tempting reminder of the woman who slept in it, his gaze fell on a pair of breeches kicked in the corner. He grinned. Rina—part hoyden, part "doctor," part whiskey-maker. All woman. Too tempting.

In the other corner a shelf of books drew his attention. He crossed over to read the titles. *Kid Hollander and the Great Stagecoach Robbery, Kid Hollander Takes His Gun, The Gunfight at Cimmaron.* The list continued, all with similar titles. Shane grinned. Not exactly considered proper reading for a young lady. But then, Rina Taylor couldn't exactly be called a proper lady either.

As he reached out for the last book on the shelf, the crush of leaves underfoot sounded from outside. Shane spun around. Damn, someone was coming. And coming way too soon.

He rushed for his bed, hoping against hope to make it back there and safely under the light covers before whoever was coming got inside. He couldn't be found searching the cabin—especially Rina's room.

Shane had almost reached the foot of the bed when the door swung open. He stared at the doorway with a sinking feeling of dread.

For an instant the bright sunlight haloed behind the person, making it impossible to make out their features. Then Rina's voice rang out sweet and clear, across the short distance between them.

"Hell's bells! What on this green earth are you a-doing up?"

Shane did the first thing that came into his

mind. He faked an attack of weakness. He swayed unsteadily on his feet, weaving back and forth.

"I . . . I . . ." he spoke slowly, hoping to dig himself out of the situation he'd gotten into.

"Why you can barely stand up," Rina admonished him, her hands planted on her hips. "What—"

Damn, she was beautiful, Shane thought. "I was thirsty," he blurted out.

"Well, let me get ya back in that bed, and I'll get ya a drink."

Shane stared at her silhouetted in the doorway. The sun at her back emphasized the curves he'd merely brushed against or dreamed about. She practically took his breath away. A first for any woman.

He took a step forward, and Rina rushed across the room to help him at the same time. In her haste to reach him before he could fall, she used too much force. Her small shoulder collided with Shane's chest, knocking the breath out of him.

Shane struggled to regain his balance, leaning backward, then forward. He failed and lurched forward, trying to stop himself.

His full weight caught Rina, knocking her back against the foot of the bed. The edge of the mattress caught her behind the knees, causing them to buckle under her.

Letting out a startled yelp, Rina caught Shane's forearms. She sat down on the bed with a whoosh, pulling Shane along with her.

He landed atop her, having just enough time

to brace part of his weight with his arms. He stared down into her wide-eyed gaze.

His first thought was that her eyes were the same deep emerald as the flowers' leaves on the coverlet that lay across her bed. Temptation clawed at him, demanding his acquiescence. Common sense ordered him to get off the bed and the woman under him.

As the surprise turned to laughter in her emerald gaze, it caught at his heart and held him fast. He couldn't have moved if his very life depended upon it.

Temptation became a living, breathing thing, demanding an answer.

He gave in, lowering his head. He could feel her breasts pressed beneath his chest, her hips cradled beneath his.

"Stranger—" she began in a soft, breathy voice.

"Shane," he interrupted.

"Shane," she whispered his name.

"Humm?"

He could feel the moistness of her breath against his lips. Her own lips were only a heartbeat away from his.

She stared up at him and slowly licked her lips before speaking.

"Shane, this is gettin' to be a habit."

Five

"Well, I can think of something else I'd like to make a habit, too," Shane murmured.

Rina cocked her head and met his heated gaze. Her bravado melted beneath the heat.

"Ah, what's that?" Her soft, breathy voice tugged at him.

"This," Shane whispered the word as if it were a promise.

He lowered his head until his lips brushed hers. As her lips softened under his kiss, his mouth claimed hers as surely as if he'd spoken.

Rina felt it and knew she should do something, but all her body seemed capable of doing was enjoying the feel of his mouth on hers. A strange weakness coupled with excitement controlled her body.

He kissed her as if he had all the time in the world, savoring the feel of her lips beneath his. His long, smooth fingers threaded through her

73

hair, separating the strands, luxuriating in their silken caress against his knuckles.

Almost as if they were obeying someone else, her arms crept up and wound themselves around Shane's neck. The skin beneath her fingertips was tense and finely muscled. Those muscles rippled and flexed as she drew her fingers across his shoulders.

Rina thought she'd never draw another breath again, it was so very pleasurable. Nothing had ever been like this. She sighed as he moved his lips back and forth across hers. He smelled clean, kinda like the soap Lucas used, but there was another scent, one she'd never noticed before. He smelled all manly to her.

His broad chest covered her, and she could feel her own breasts responding, tingling, aching. The aching continued as his weight pressed down on her.

As if it was the most natural thing in the world to do, she returned his kiss. For surely it seemed purely natural and somehow right.

Shane eased his mouth from hers and trailed feather-light kisses up across her face to her high cheekbone and back down along her jaw.

His touch left the sensation of tiny flames a-lickin' at her skin. Only it didn't really burn; it just left a might fine heat in its wake. Without realizing she did it, she raised her chin, exposing her throat to his ministrations.

Trailing down lower, Shane accepted her invitation and ran his tongue down the column of her neck. At the base of her neck, he paused to suck and lave kisses at the hollow of her throat. She moaned against him, her soft sounds urging him on. Lower.

With his chin, he parted the opening of her shirt, his tongue tracing the edges of the fabric. The deep vee exposed the tops of her breasts, and he couldn't resist their temptation. The soft mounds were a honey-colored tan, just like the skin above her shirt. For a moment he paused to wonder if her skin was that gorgeous uninhibited color all over.

He pressed tiny kisses along the tops of her breasts and heard her gasp beneath him. Her heart raced in time to his own breathing. She caught her fingers in his thick dark hair.

Rina quivered beneath his loving onslaught. Her stomach wasn't just disquieted now; it was a-meltin'. And her heart raced, pounding like she'd been running uphill. Strangely enough, she felt all breathy. Far from being uncomfortable, this new feeling was mighty pleasant.

His tongue was like the wings of a butterfly fluttering against her skin. She arched upward, wanting his touch to continue forever.

He drew back slightly, and his hands replaced the loving touch of his lips. She moaned her disappointment until she felt his thumbs rub across her breasts. The surge of heat that followed nearly took her breath away.

He returned his lips to her wanting ones, and as he closed his mouth over hers, she whimpered in pure pleasure. He deepened the kiss, running his tongue back and forth across her lower lip, searching, asking, begging for entry.

She couldn't deny him anymore than she could willingly deny her own lungs breath. In a movement older than time, she opened her lips to him, surrendering herself to his loving touch.

Her hips were cradled between his strong thighs, and she wiggled her body beneath his, searching for something. Something more, but she didn't comprehend what.

Her action jolted Shane, bringing him to his senses like nothing else could. Rina was an innocent in the truest sense of the word. He had to stop this. It was pure madness.

Rina moved beneath him again, and he groaned aloud. It might be madness, but it was also heaven. The last thing on earth he wanted to do was to stop. But he had to; he couldn't steal her innocence from her. He allowed himself one last kiss before he reluctantly drew away.

Her arms tightened about him, and he gently disentangled her arms from his neck. Damn, he hated stopping. Her soft innocence was like a magic, pulling him closer and closer.

With a sharp groan he drew back. He didn't know which he was fighting harder—her guileless invitation or his own desire.

"Rina," Shane pulled farther back with difficulty.

"Umm?"

"We shouldn't be doing this."

She raised her head, her lips quivering.

"Rina, your pa could come in at any moment."

"Who?"

"Your pa?"

"Pa's up at the clearing," she answered with guileless honesty.

Shane closed his eyes and groaned at her sweet answer. Rina was making it damnedably hard for him to be a gentleman.

With an effort of will, he opened his eyes again, not sure he could withstand the tempting sight of her beneath him.

Rina lay staring up at him, a sweet, innocent invitation in her emerald gaze. Although he felt as if it was killing him to do so, he shook his head, refusing her. With hands whose steadiness surprised him, he reached out and did up the front of her oversized shirt that hid her womanly charms.

Surprise, shock, then hurt followed each other across her expressive face. In a sudden, unexpected movement, she sat up on the bed, throwing her legs over the side, and stood to her feet.

Facing him, she planted her hands on her hips, breasts heaving. She was the picture of outraged dignity, and Shane bit his cheek to keep from smiling.

"Hell's bells, stranger. You gots the oddest ways about you." She ran a hand through her already tousled hair, rumpling it even more.

She shook her head back and forth slowly. A look of puzzlement clouded her beautiful face.

"If'n I can't figure you out. First—you're all hotter than a summer day, then you blow cold as an early frost."

Turning on her heel, she ran from the cabin. The slam of the door echoed behind her.

Rina didn't return to the cabin until dusk. Shane knew the instant she returned. He'd been watching the door for her entrance.

She breezed in, completely ignoring him, and strode across the cabin to the kitchen. Sniffing the biscuit smells in the air appreciatively, she hugged her father and kissed his leathery cheek.

As if nothing had happened between her and Shane, she proceeded to scoop up three plates and set them around the oak table.

"Umm, Pa. That surely smells wonderful."

Ben Taylor smiled at his daughter, seemingly undisturbed by her absence. Shane couldn't understand it. If Rina was his, he would certainly keep a better eye on her than her father had been doing.

The path of his thoughts brought him up short. What in the world was he thinking? Rina wasn't his. And wouldn't be. He needed to marry a lady, one worthy of Belle Rive, and one capable of being the hostess he needed when he had possession of his home once again.

This was just temporary. He was only here to do a job—nothing more. Although he firmly reminded himself of these things, his gaze continued to follow every movement Rina made.

"Gal, you'd best be gettin' ready fer supper, hadn't ya?" Ben Taylor's voice cut through the stillness of the cabin.

Shane found himself almost flinching under the strength behind the man's words.

"It's all right, Pa. I washed up at the trough outside. I—"

Her father's look was more than sufficient to silence her. His impervious glance to her bedroom said more than a week of talking could.

Since Pa had been busy with the whiskey still last evening, he hadn't held Rina to her promise to wear her dress. She'd considered herself lucky. Ben Taylor rarely forgot anything.

She had the feeling that her luck had just about run out. Pa gestured with a thumb toward her bedroom door, and she inwardly cringed at what was coming. *Not that, please Lord.* She hated her one lone dress with a passion.

Rina passed Shane with only the barest of nods. No word of greeting passed her lips. She was still smarting from his rejection of her earlier. And she was shamed by her brazen actions, but refused to admit that to anybody. Much less to him.

It nagged at her, reminding her of her ma. All her life she'd been afeared of being jus' like her ma. Maybe she was more like her ma than she thought. No! Rina pushed the thought away with a vengeance. Someday *she* was gonna be a lady.

Rina pushed the door to her room open, and

her gaze fell on the bed. The pretty coverlet had been her ma's only dowry, and the only thing Rina had left of her. Lily Taylor had left the hand-sewn coverlet behind with as little concern as she had her children and husband. And for what? Her ma had shook off the dust of Possum Hollow for a smooth-talking man, fancy new gowns, and the big city of St. Louis.

Slowly, Rina ran her hand over the flower petals stitched in the coverlet. It made her think of pretty things and fancy ladies.

The latter thought caused Rina to stiffen and snatch her hand away. Her ma had *not* been a lady. But Rina intended to be one someday.

A gaudy splash of color spread across the foot of the bed drew her attention. She turned to it with dread. The yellow dress.

Pa hadn't forgotten at all. The hated dress lay across the bed, the stark white and bright yellow stripes a-shoutin' at her.

Rina wrinkled her nose in distaste. She'd hated the striped thing from the moment she'd laid her eyes on it. Lucas had brung it home, a "present" from Milly he'd called it.

Ha! The only one Milly was a-interested in impressing was Lucas. Milly most definitely visioned herself as the doctor's wife. If'n Lucas didn't watch himself, that's likely what she'd become, too.

Why, yesterday, as soon as Lucas had finished tending the stranger, he couldn't get away fast enough to visit Milly. He'd only stopped by the still fer a short talk—jus' long enough to tell them about the stranger being a riverboat gambler on a buying trip fer whiskey. Then Lucas had high-tailed it to go visiting.

Well, Lucas better watch himself real close if'n he didn't want to be jumping the broom with Milly and her fancy dresses.

Rina looked back at Milly's dress and kicked at the flounced ruffle that trailed onto the floor. Mostest of all she hated the big bright yellow bows that were scattered along the flounce.

Why on this green earth would anybody with a brain want to wear something that looked like a walking yellow-striped outbuilding? Not to mention she felt yellow was the ugliest color the good Lord made. And the dress sure a-shouted it.

A promise was a promise. And a Taylor always kept their word. She crossed to the chest at the foot of the bed, opened the lid, and dug down for her fancy underthings. Wearing a dress was such blasted trouble.

Finally she had everything gathered together and laid across the bed in the order in which it had to go on. Stockings, garters, pantalets, chemise, corset, petticoat. Looking at the pile of items, she wrinkled her nose. Why on earth a body had to put so much on underneath was beyond her.

Quick as a flash, she grabbed up the stiff corset and tossed it back into the trunk. She absolutely refused to wear that thing, no matter what.

Stripping out of her breeches and shirt, she tossed them in a corner. She mighta known Pa would choose tonight of all nights to make her wear a dress. And in front of Shane, too. A spattering of goose flesh crept up her arms in spite of the summery weather.

"Why tonight?" she moaned.

She was uncomfortable enough in a fancy dress, much less when a body added in what had happened today with *him*. Why'd Shane Delaney have to be so powerful appealing?

Pausing to rub her hands up and down her arms to chase away the goose flesh, Rina pulled the chemise over her head, mumbling the whole time.

She flopped down onto the bed, barely missing a beribboned flounce. As she caught up a white stocking, it snagged on her finger.

"Hell's bells."

Why couldn't she have soft, smooth hands like Milly? Instead, hers were roughened from working the still. A frown creased her forehead.

She'd never much cared how her hands looked before the stranger showed up. She didn't want to think on why she cared now.

A memory of Shane's strong hands a-rubbin' over her skin seared her, taking her breath away in a flash. She gulped in a deep draught of air, trying to chase the thoughts away. It didn't do a bit of good; the memory stayed with her. His fingers had been like warm honey against her skin.

She gave in and closed her eyes a moment and

savored the remembered feelings. She'd once heard tell that a real gambler's hands had to be smooth and mighty fast to handle the cards just right. Well, from her experience his were both.

Shaking off the memory of Shane's hands on her bosom, she stuck her foot into the white stocking and drew it up her leg. Then she grabbed up one of the garters and studied it. Why'd they have to be so ruffled? They nearly tickled a body's legs to death a-gettin' them up to the right place. She remembered when she'd been given the pair—her first and onlyest pair of garters.

She'd punched Lucas in the chest and accused him of lying to her and trying to make a fool out of her, but he'd been telling it true. Why, Milly, who'd stood to the side in shock, had promptly showed Rina her own garters, and sure enough, those garters sported even more ruffles and lace than these.

"Rina? Gal, supper's gettin' cold." Pa's voice boomed through the closed door, making her jump nearly out of her skin.

"Be right there," she hollered back.

Scurrying to finish dressing, she yanked on the petticoat and pulled the dress over her head. Wiggling to and fro, she managed to do up the back of the dress. When she'd finished she was breathless and noticed the top felt mighty snug.

She tugged and pulled at the bodice of the dress, trying to loosen it some. Finally she gave up in disgust and smoothed it back into place.

She glanced down, then stared at the top of her breasts spilling over the lace-edged bodice.

"Lordy. It happened. I finally growed some."

Rina turned to the left and to the right, double-checking. Matter of fact, she'd growed enough that the top was so tight she could hardly breathe. Her chest hurt with the effort of trying to draw in air. She sucked in tiny gasps of air until her chest stopped hurting. The dress pinched something awful.

Surely Pa wouldn't expect her to wear the hated dress now. She schooled her grin and crossed to the door. Opening it a crack, she peered out.

"Pa," she tried to make her voice sound disappointed. "The dress, well, it's—"

"None of your excuses, gal. Ya gave yer word, didn't ya?"

"Yes, but—"

"That's all there is to it then," he said with finality.

Rina slammed the door closed. She wasn't about to stick around for a scolding in front of Shane. Besides, there wasn't any sense in trying to change Pa's mind now. He was as determined as a dog a-waitin' outside a gopher hole. Nothing doing but she'd have to go out to the supper table a-wearin' the dress.

She adjusted the top of the dress again, trying to tug it up some. She hoped Pa'd be satisfied, forcing her to wear this awful thing, 'cause she didn't intend to ever wear it again no matter what he might say about it. Planting a forced smile on her face, she kicked her skirts out of her way and walked out of the room.

As soon as she entered the next room, a deep silence fell over the cabin. She sought out Pa and met his look of disbelief with a "are-you-happy-now" smile. His jaw dropped and he sputtered, but she couldn't make out his words.

Shane, on the other hand, had pursed his lips into a silent whistle of surprise. Rina felt her cheeks a-warmin' something fierce under his gaze.

"Pa, I'm ready. Shall we eat?" She had hoped the words would cause a break in the tension that seemed to envelop the small cabin, but they didn't.

She sat down gently into her chair, almost afraid to move in the dress. The petticoats wrapped and tangled themselves around her ankles. Smiling at the startled expressions on her pa and Shane's faces, she unobtrusively kicked the petticoat out of her way.

"Rina," Pa stopped and cleared his throat. "Gal, that dress—

"I don'ts want to talk about it." She met his dismay with a firm look. "I honored my promise. And I'm not about to wear it tomorrow night."

"Definitely." Ben Taylor breathed a silent sigh of relief.

Shane forced himself to concentrate on the food spread out before him, instead of the charms Rina seemed so intent on showing. He swallowed down the desire that seemed to rule his every thought, and tried to spend the meal time looking anywhere but at her.

It almost worked. It might have worked, if not for the damned biscuits on his plate.

They were freshly made, hot and delicious with the spread of rich golden honey across them. However, watching the honey contrasting with the lighter bread made Shane remember the rich honeyed-tan of Rina's skin. He dared a glance at her and wished he hadn't.

The dress barely covered her, and once again he wondered if that delicious tan covered her entire body. The dress was scandalous. And she looked irresistible in it.

With a sheer force of will, Shane returned his attention to the biscuit clutched tightly in his hand. It had been reduced to a crumbled mass. Quickly, he popped the last bite into his mouth, needing something to help distract him from the sight of Rina sitting just across the table from him.

Ben Taylor noticed his guest's intent enjoyment of his homebaked biscuits, and he swelled with pride. If'n anyone in the hills made a better biscuit than he did, he'd be danged if he knew who.

"Shane, care fer another one of my biscuits?" He pointed at the platter beside him with the tines of his fork.

"I'll get them." Rina reached out and scooped up the platter of golden biscuits.

As she twisted to pass it to Shane, she felt a sharp pinch under her arms.

"Ouch." She released her breath in a startled whoosh and stretched her arms up and out to relieve the tight pressure of the gown.

The loud sound of fabric ripping followed. She gulped and dared to look down. Sure enough the dress had split right open.

Across from her she heard Shane cut off a strangled exclamation. He coughed once, twice, and it turned into a coughing fit.

Before she thought, she started to lean across to slap him on the back. Pa's shouted, "Rina!" stopped her instantly.

With a yelp, she dropped the platter back onto the table and grabbed for the gaping front of her dress. She tried her best to tug it closed, but it just wouldn't go.

She watched as Pa's homemade biscuits rolled every which way across the table and then off onto the floor.

"Hell's bells," Rina muttered.

One glance at Shane and any further words she mighta been going to say froze on her lips. She didn't even hear her pa's bellow of shocked reproach. Shane's deeply blue eyes practically devoured her. She could feel her skin heating up beneath his look.

Why'd he have to choose now of all times to give her that look? He'd been ignoring her practically all through supper.

Swallowing, she shoved back her chair, jumped up, and ran out of the room.

Once in her own room, Rina yanked off the

hateful dress. It seemed no matter how hard she tried to be a lady, it didn't work. Now the evening was ruined. And all on account of her pa insisting she wear the yellow dress.

Why, Shane had barely even glanced her way all through supper. She couldn't understand the man for the life of her. When she'd first come into the room, he hadn't been able to do anything but stare at her. She hadn't missed that almost-whistle of his. He'd liked what he saw.

Then why had he up and ignored her after they'd set down to the meal? That man blew hot and cold more'n she'd ever thought it possible for a body to do.

It was 'bout like being tossed betwixt a right hot summer and snow-cold winter. And it was more than she could stand.

And come tomorrow she planned to do something about it.

Six

Rina topped the rise of the hill and stopped to wipe her damp forehead. Below her, nestled in the green-grassed valley, stood Ida's tiny cabin.

Sweat trickled in rivulets down her chest to disappear beneath her shirt. She pulled the sticky material away from her body and blew downward. The air against her sweat-dampened skin felt good.

"Hotter than Hades out here today," she said to no one in particular.

Of course, she'd had to choose the hottest day in August to pay Ida a visit, but she jus' *had* to know. And Ida was the one who could help her.

Rina wiped her forehead again. The tempting thought of one of Ida's sweet ciders and a good talk urged her on and down the last hill.

About fifteen feet from the cabin, Rina let out a whoop of greeting.

"Ida! It's Rina. Hey, are you home?"

She stopped and waited for an answering yell

from the mountain woman. She didn't cotton to meetin' up with Ida on the wrong side of the old woman's shotgun. Besides, Ida's eyesight wasn't what it used to be.

Lifting her hair off the back of her neck to let the faint breeze blow on her skin, Rina stood waiting. The sun beat down, and she blew a strand of hair away from her eyes and raised her hand to shield her face from the fierce sunlight.

"Rina? That you, gal?" an answering shout came from the cabin.

The door swung open, and Ida Connors stepped out onto the wide porch. A print dress hung on her lank frame, and a gaily-patched apron covered her almost to her knees. Tall, lean-boned, ageless with sparkling white hair with the slightest touch of silver threaded through it—that just about described Ida perfectly. Nobody knew her age for sure.

Rina had asked her once, and all Ida would answer was, "Old as these here hills."

She grinned at this memory. Ida was old, wise, and her best friend in the whole world—next to Lucas.

"What's you doing up here, gal? You weren't due to come by until next Tuesday."

Rina crossed the distance separating them and hopped up onto the wide wooden porch. She hugged her friend and received a bone-jarring squeeze in return.

"Can't I jus' come for a visit?"

"Not likely." Ida set her a short distance away and stared hard into Rina's troubled eyes.

Rina was the first to break the contact. She looked away, suddenly unusually nervous around her all-too-knowing friend.

"Well, out with it." Ida propped her hands on her narrow, shapeless hips.

"What?" Rina hedged, wondering how much her expression had given away.

"Get on in here outta the sun and tell me about it." Before Rina could deny anything, Ida added, *"All* about it. And don't you dare leave out one single word."

The coolness of the cabin soothed Rina's flaming cheeks. She hoped they weren't as noticeable in the dimmer lighting of the one-room cabin.

"How have you been feeling?" Rina asked, sitting down in one of the tall straight-backed chairs at the old scarred table.

Ida brushed aside her concern as if it had been a pesky fly. "I'm fine."

As if to prove the fact, she bustled around the room, getting out a container of sweet apple cider and two clean glass jars. Rina watched as she moved about the room, her movements spry and painless.

"Are your joints doing better?"

The woman stopped and flashed Rina a grin. "Sure are. A good dose of your pa's special medicine now and again keeps me going just fine. You be sure and pass on my thanks, you hear?"

Rina smiled. She knew it wasn't Pa's whiskey

that helped; Ida had been swearing on the use of cider vinegar fer her aches and pains fer years. She'd only brought up the subject of Pa's "medicinal" drink 'cause she must be a-runnin' low. This way Rina could offer to bring a new supply without the mountain woman having to stoop down to asking fer it.

"I'll bring you a fresh jug next time I come by."

"Good. Stuff's better fresh. That's what I always say."

Ida poured sweet cider into the jars, set the jug back onto the middle of the table and faced Rina.

"Well, like I said, what're you here for, gal? Something's bothering you. That's for sure."

Sighing, Rina wrapped her hands around the jar and took a deep swallow before she answered.

"I need some advice, Ida. You've been the mountain healer fer as long back as I can remember, and you always know whats the right thing."

"This is different, isn't it, gal?"

Rina nodded, took another swallow of the sweet liquid and let it trickle down her throat. How was she supposed to start? Where was she supposed to start to ask Ida's help with the stranger?

"Ida, a few days back a stranger—"

"Heard all about him."

"How?" Rina chuckled. "No, never mind. Don't know how I coulda fergot the way word travels in these hills. It's a heap better and faster than one of them telegraph wires Lucas is all excited about."

Ida leaned back in her chair and returned the

92

grin. "Well, go on. Heard tell he's as handsome as the devil, folks say." She shrugged off the gossip and waited for Rina to answer that herself.

"That he is. He's tall, too. And dark as Satan's sin—"

"So," Ida dragged the word out, making it last like a tasty taffy. "That's the way of it."

"No." Rina sighed and set her drink onto the table with a thud.

She surged to her feet and paced about the small, clean-kept cabin. Finally, after a few minutes of silence had elapsed with the old mountain woman wisely waiting for her response, Rina returned to the table and sat back down slowly.

"Things are confusing."

"They's supposed to be betwixt a man and a woman at the start."

"No." Rina's cheeks burned under the statement. "I'm not talking about that."

She lifted her hands then dropped them onto her lap. What the blue blazes was wrong with her? She'd never had trouble spitting out any words before.

"He's what's confusing me."

Ida's loud cackle of laughter filled the cabin. "Oh, you gots it bad, gal."

Rina frowned at her. "I don't *got* anything. It's him with the problem. That damned Shane Delaney." She planted her fists on her hips.

Ida's laughter had died, but now it started up again full force.

Rina held her tongue until the cabin fell silent. "Are you finished?"

Ida pulled a lace-edged handkerchief from her apron pocket and dabbed at her eyes. "Land's sakes. Don't know when I've enjoyed a laugh that much."

"Ida, I'm serious."

"Of course you are, gal." She sniffed back her remaining laughter and sat up stiffly in her chair.

However, Rina noticed that Ida's dark eyes continued to twinkle with suppressed mirth.

"What is the problem? Exactly?"

Rina took a deep breath and let the request spill out like water surging over a dam. "I needs to know what's true. One minute he's all hot and full of kisses and sweet words, and the next . . . why, he's cold as a January wind howling down the hills. I need something to tell me true. And I figured one of your potions would likely as not be the answer to it."

Out of breath, Rina stopped and met her friend's intent gaze.

Ida studied her a minute, drained the last of the cider in her jar, then leaned forward to set her drink onto the table.

"Well, then, come with me." Ida stood to her feet and after a couple of stiff steps, she moved with surprising agility across the room and out the door.

Smiling with relief and mounting excitement, Rina followed her to the drying shed. She hadn't realized how nervous she'd been a-waitin' for Ida to give her the answer if'n she would have something to help or not.

The small shed was dry inside and smelled of the strange combination of sweet and pungent herbs and roots. Clusters of over a hundred different herbs and flowers hung on hooks, scattered along each wall.

With unerring movements, Ida moved slowly from wall to wall, searching and checking. She broke off bits of dried herbs, dropping them into the apron held bunched together in one hand.

Rina stood by and watched as Ida removed pieces of herb after herb from small hooks in the walls. Rina knew what each one was, but Ida carefully kept her back turned when she doled out the amounts. This must be one of her more powerful potions, Rina thought. Specially if'n she wasn't willing to share the makings of it.

As far as anyone knew, Rina was the only living soul ever to have been given the ingredients to any of Ida's potions and poultices.

Finally, Ida added a few crumbled flower petals to the mixture in her apron and nodded to herself. Once satisfied, she turned about and without a word, she walked back to the cabin. Rina followed her, eagerly awaiting watching the next steps to the mountain woman's potion mixing.

Inside, Ida carefully dumped the contents of her gaily-patched apron onto the table. Gathering together a bowl, spoon, and odd-shaped jar of green liquid, she set everything onto the middle of the table.

As Rina watched in fascination, Ida dropped pieces of herbs and flower petals into the bowl, then ground the mixture together with the side of the spoon. Little by little she added to it until the pile on the table disappeared.

At last, she finished it up with a generous dollop of the green liquid and held it out to Rina with a lopsided grin.

Rina leaned forward to take the small bowl and gasped. Tears welled up in her eyes, and her throat burned something fierce.

"Whew!"

Ida laughed heartily and brushed off her reaction. "It only smells so bad 'cause it's so fresh. Give it a couple a hours, and you won't hardly be able to smell anything to it at all."

Rina threw her a doubtful look.

"Mix it with something strong tasting so he won't smell it," Ida added as an afterthought.

Rina coughed and wrinkled her nose in distaste. "Most definitely."

She wasn't fer sure jus' how she was going to get the vile concoction down Shane Delaney. But she was going to do it.

"How's it work, Ida?"

"Every time he don't tell you true, his stomach will start a-rolling and a-hurting. Watch for that. And, gal, listen to your heart."

"My heart?"

"It'll tell you the answers better than any potion I can make up for you."

Rina held the potion tightly in her palm and

hugged her friend with her other arm. "Thank you. I—"

"Go on. Off with you. That mixture needs some outside air to breathe and settle itself."

Rina grinned, holding the bowl as far away from her nose as she could. It was going to be a long trip home.

Rina returned home to find Pa and Shane thoroughly engrossed in a game of cards. They sat across from each other at the oak table, a cup of whiskey at Shane's elbow and a tin of whiskey beside her pa.

"Afternoon," she greeted them.

Neither man answered. She'd never seen the likes of their concentration on the cards in their hands.

She needn't have bothered to carefully hide the potion outside. She doubted if either man would have noticed if she'd waved it under their very noses.

"What in blue blazes is going on here?" Rina asked, stepping between them at the table.

"Gambling," Shane answered.

"Bargaining," Pa retorted.

"Hell's bells—"

"Rina, don't swear." Pa leaned closer to the cards in his hand, studying them.

Shane sat back in his chair, an aura of nonchalance about him like a velvet cloak.

Rina knew without looking at the cards which

man held the better hand. It was Shane. She watched as the game played out, wondering how much Pa had wagered. She gnawed on her bottom lip.

"Pa—"

"I'm bargaining, gal. Leave it be."

Bargaining! She'd never heard poker called that in all her life. And Ben Taylor had never played a straight game of poker in all his days.

As she watched in amazement, Shane laid down his cards. His three nines, a jack, and a three beat Pa's two kings, two fours, and a seven. She bit back her grin.

"I believe that's now six extra bottles a month," Shane tallied up the amount.

"Dagnamit, stranger. It's only four."

"Six." Shane's devil-may-care smile silenced his opponent. Pa clamped his mouth shut.

Rina heard him mumble under his breath, "Dagnamit, beaten at my own game to boot."

At her soft slip of laughter, Pa surged up and strode out the door.

"Sore loser?" Shane asked her.

Rina laughed outright. "Pa's not used to losing. He's too good a cheat."

She watched for Shane's reaction to her bald statement of her pa's card playing abilities. He surprised her by flashing her a wry smile.

"Yes, I know," he added softly.

"Ya knew?"

Shane let his smile widen into a grin. "From the start."

At her disbelieving look, he added, "Okay, from the second hand."

"And ya kept on playin' with him anyways?"

"Yes."

"Why?"

He shrugged. "I knew what I was up against. And I was bored."

Rina flushed under his too-meaningful stare. The stranger could say more with a single look at a body than most men did with a mouthful of words. She kept her eyes focused on the opposite wall, not wanting to meet his yet.

"Besides the stakes never got higher than I wanted them to go."

"What were ya playing fer?" she asked, her curiosity getting the better of her.

"How many extra bottles your pa threw in for free a month."

"You mean you all came to terms on selling his whiskey?"

"Not yet. But we're getting closer." Shane chuckled.

He really did have a mighty nice smile, she thought. Not to mention that his face was beginning to get back a real healthy look to it. Added together that made fer a fella it'd be hard to say no to. Rina jerked herself up at her thoughts. What in blue blazes had led her to think like that?

The longer she remained silent, thinking to herself, the more intense Shane's gaze became. She could feel herself warming under his attention. Darn him. He was starting it up again.

She'd find a way to give him Ida's potion if she had to hold him down and pour it down his throat. *Just see if she wouldn't.*

Before he had the chance to turn and go cold on her, Rina made up an excuse and slipped outside. A few minutes later, she returned with Ida's potion hidden in among a few garden vegetables.

The remainder of the day passed all too slowly for Rina, and she even helped Pa with supper, much to Pa's amazement. No matter how hard she searched for a way to slip Ida's potion to Shane, she came up empty-handed. Fate seemed determined to thwart her at every turn.

Nothing at the supper table gave her the option of mixing in the potion—not and make sure that Shane was the only one to eat it.

Afterwards, he turned down her offer of a drink of sweet cider. Minutes later, she suggested a cup of coffee, but he refused. Rina gnawed on her bottom lip in frustration. Pa's coffee woulda been the perfect thing to hide the taste. Nothing on earth tasted as strong as Pa's coffee. Darn Shane for refusing a cup.

Rina was almost at a loss of what to do, when her gaze fell on Pa's whiskey jug. A slow smile crept across her face. Perfect.

She didn't have long to wait before Pa asked her to pour them each "a mite."

She hopped up to obey immediately, then spent some time drawing out two cups and making sure they were clean. She gave the men a short while to deal their cards, knowing that in no time they would be engrossed in the game.

As soon as her pa and Shane checked their cards, she turned her back and slipped the potion into one cup of whiskey, then she handed it to Shane. Careful not to get caught staring, she tried to watch him with as much nonchalance as she could muster.

Shane took a swallow of the famous Taylor whiskey and nearly choked. It seared its way down his throat and burned his stomach. He gasped and blinked against the strength.

"Everything all right there?" Ben Taylor leaned across the table and gave him a hard look.

Shane cleared his throat. "Fine."

"Something wrong with my whiskey?"

Shane could hear the bristle in the man's voice. He knew he had to reassure him quickly before he had the chance to take insult.

"No, not at all." He took another swallow from the cup and smiled.

The second drink did taste better. Either he'd been mistaken about the odd flavor, or his taste had numbed.

"Well, then, drink up," Ben ordered.

Shane complied, swallowing down the remnants in the cup. It tasted fine to him this time, and he held his cup out to Rina for a refill as he saw Ben Taylor doing.

Rina smiled at both men and poured the liquor into their cups. She'd done it—got Ida's potion down the stranger. Well, by tomorrow night she should know the truth.

Shane awoke at dawn, cold, fuzzy-headed and sick. As pain assailed his stomach, he reached for the chamberpot. He retched into it, barely making it in time. Drawing in a shaky breath, he lay back down onto the bed. He didn't know when he'd felt this bad.

Another stomach pain hit him, and he lost the remainder of the contents of his stomach in the chamberpot. Chills racked his body as he lay back. He drew the cover up to his chin.

His movements awakened Rina, and she ran into the room. Pa lay snoring on his pallet. Shane was hunched over on the bed. At the sight of him curled into a ball of pain, she froze her steps. What had she done?

"Shane?" Rina stepped closer. "Shane? Are you all right?"

He shot her a baleful look just before he reached for the chamberpot again.

Rina reached his side in a few quick steps. Guilt assailed her as she gazed at his pale face. This was all her fault. She never should have mixed Ida's potion with Pa's whiskey. The two combined together were jus' too strong fer a body to handle. Even a body as strong and handsome as Shane Delaney.

Shane met Rina's guilt-filled eyes. Suspicions began to form in his mind. What had she conned

102

him into drinking last night? His rolling stomach told him that there had been more in the cup than Taylor whiskey. He should have trusted his own instincts when they told him the drink was foul. Had the whiskey's purpose been to disguise the taste of something else? he wondered.

He shook his head to clear his confused thinking. Lucas's words returned to him abruptly. He'd said that Rina did the doctoring in the hills when nobody else could do it. Surely that meant that she wouldn't purposely make someone sick. The idea was ridiculous, wasn't it?

"Rina." Shane reached for her, intending to force her to tell him what she'd done, if anything.

He never got that far; instead, as he lunged for her, darkness enveloped him, dragging him downward into its velvet, painless warmth.

Rina eased Shane's inert body back onto the mattress. She figured he was better off this way. At least he'd stopped the retching. As guilt threatened to swamp her, she busied herself getting a basin and cool water.

Carrying the basin, she returned to Shane. He lay still and quiet on the feather bed. Gently she sponged his face with the cool water.

Desperate to cool his over-heated skin, she drew the cloth lower across his neck and shoulders. His sweat-dampened chest beckoned to her, begging her, tempting her. She ran the cloth along his broad chest and down the muscles of his lean torso. As his skin cooled beneath her touch, her own skin warmed in response.

"Oh, Lordy," she whispered.

She rinsed the cloth again and drew it back and forth across his chest. The muscles rippled and gleamed with a sheen in the early morning light that slanted through the nearby window.

Shane stirred under her touch, and she stared down at his face as his eyes opened. He smiled up at her, and she felt her own stomach do a somersault in response.

"Hi, angel," he murmured, his low voice stroking her like soft velvet.

"Hardly that."

Guilt swept over her, and she tried to reason with her conscience. She'd had a darned good reason fer using Ida's potion, and she hadn't known it would make him sick. Prickles of guilt still censured her.

"Are you feelin' better?" she asked tentatively.

"Some," he answered.

Rina avoided the questioning look in Shane's eyes and rushed to offer an explanation before he could voice those questions.

"Sometimes Pa's cooking is a mite rich fer a body that ain't growed used to it yet," she stated.

It wasn't a lie, not really. After all, Milly had taken sick once after eating dinner with them one night. And, truthfully, sometimes Pa's cooking was a bit hard to take. However, the half-lie still nagged at her.

"I'm sorry," she added in honesty, biting her lower lip. Her own voice came out much lower than usually. Actually husky-sounding to her own ears.

Shane smiled at the sensual sound. Being ill wasn't so bad if he had his own angel to tend to him. Her hands had skimmed so tantalizingly across his skin, tempting, promising.

He vowed to hold her to the promise her touch had implied. If being sick brought Rina this close and tender, then he'd just have to stay sick for a while. Now wouldn't he?

The opportunity presented too much temptation. He'd use this illness and fake a setback. As he reached out and caught her hand, he ordered his conscience to be quiet. Smiling to himself at the chance of many more days with Rina as his nurse, he closed his eyes and enjoyed the feel of her hands on his skin.

Seven

Best place in town to hear the latest news was always Sheridan's store, Nolan Gant thought to himself. So, as soon as he got into town, he headed straight fer it. Not that he had any intention of buying anything there.

Nolan didn't much care if'n what he heard was the truth or not. What he needed to know was what the townsfolk had to say 'bout his man Shane Delaney. Yep, Possum Hollow was the best place to get wind of what was going on up at the Taylor place.

Stupid fools, he thought. Nolan chuckled under his breath, rolling his cigar around in his mouth. Only ones who knew Delaney was workin' fer him was himself and his boy, Billy. And he knew he could trust Billy not to tell nobody.

At heart, Billy was a good boy. Did what he told him—leastways, most of the time. At least until *she* caught his eye almost five years ago. Rina Taylor was becomin' more of a problem every day she lived.

Fuming angry about Rina and the problem she posed, Nolan crossed the street and headed straight fer Sheridan's place. Within a few feet of the door, he stopped and drew in several quick puffs from his cigar. Much as he hated to, he'd hafta leave it outside here. Bill Sheridan didn't allow no cigar smoking inside.

Reluctantly, Nolan took a last puff from his cigar, then dropped the stub. Carefully he swept a layer of dirt over it to save it until later. Yep, it'd be safe here against the side of the building until he came back out fer it.

With one backwards glance of longing at his cigar, he strode into the store. Leaning against the side of the wall, he eavesdropped without the slightest hint of shame.

Seemed the story of the stranger staying on up at the Taylor cabin was on jus' about everybody's tongue. He clamped his lips together to keep from grinning. Yep, his plan was going along jus' fine.

Sally Sheridan would be better at gettin' folk to loosen their tongues than twenty bottles of whiskey. Nolan sidled a little closer to her so not to miss anything. If'n anybody was gonna be talkin' 'bout Delaney, then they'd be doin' their talkin' to Sally Sheridan.

Why, Bill Sheridan even boasted once that if'n his wife were to spend any time in a cemetery, that the dead would even start talkin' to her. Nolan figured he was likely right.

"Did you hear the Taylors have a visitor?" Sally Sheridan asked Miss Hattie, the town gossip, as soon as the old lady stepped into the store.

Nolan glanced her way. He'd always hated the old crow. She'd carried more tales 'bout him than one could count. But he listened fer her answer jus' the same.

"A man," Miss Hattie said the word with disapproval. "And that Rina Taylor not yet married, too."

Mrs. Sheridan crossed the store's wood flooring to lend Miss Hattie her arm.

"Why, I heard he is almost as handsome as General Lee." Miss Hattie preened and settled her bonnet on her white curls.

Nolan scuffed his foot on the floor. The silly old gossip claimed that General Lee had once danced with her at a fancy ball. Ha, she'd never let anybody in the town ferget it either.

"Humph. Heard he's a Northerner," Mrs. Benson yelled from the back of the store. She spat the last word out as if it left a sour taste in her mouth.

Miss Hattie bristled up, squaring her shoulders as if to do battle.

"No, dear." Mrs. Sheridan patted the old woman's bony arm to calm her. "He's a Southerner," she assured with pride. "From New Orleans."

"He's a friend of Lucas Taylor." Short, plump

Mrs. Benson dropped the bolt of cloth she'd been examining. She crossed to join the two women.

She reminded Nolan of a short, fat little hen rushing to join the others at feeding time.

"That's not true," Mrs. Sheridan corrected. "He's Rina's beau. Why I heard," she looked around the store and lowered her voice, "that she visited Ida Connors for a love potion."

Startled gasps greeted the announcement.

Mrs. Sheridan waited until the other women fell silent again, then continued, "And that he'll propose within the week."

"Could be. You both know that he saved Rina's life when old Ben Taylor's still blew the other day," Miss Hattie put in.

Nolan let the pieces of gossip flow about him. Acting as if'n he cared not a whit, when in fact he didn't miss a single word of the women's conversation.

The temptation to set the folks straight ate at him, but he held his tongue. Let the folks go on believing all wrong. He'd tell 'em straight in the end. But for right now he valued his plan succeeding above all else. Even his pride. So he pretended to play dumb and listen to the half-truths floating around about him.

When he couldn't suppress his desire to laugh any longer, he turned on his heel, grabbed a good-sized handful of candy, and strode out of the store. Sneaking the pilfered candy into his pocket, he turned to his left and stopped.

A careful search of the dirt found the cigar butt

he'd tossed down before going inside Sheridan's store. He picked up the stub, wiped it off on his pants, and put it back between his teeth. He lit the cigar and inhaled. Much better. Sauntering, he continued on his way, rolling the cigar around in his mouth.

After he'd crossed the street and was out of sight, Nolan cackled at being the only one to know the truth from the lies circling about the street. Well, not only himself—Billy, his dear boy, knew it, too. Lately the boy had gotten to be quieter and quieter.

It brought to mind of how unhappy Billy had been when he'd insisted the boy go off to fight fer the Confederacy all those years ago. Not that Nolan had cared at all 'bout the cause; it'd been a ploy to get the boy to stop mooning over Rina Taylor.

Nolan shoved away the memory. He hated those memories. It was Billy's silence and the feeling of distance between them that bothered Nolan and made him remember. To be honest he was afeared of losing his boy. Billy was all he had.

Nolan threw down his cigar and crushed the stub beneath his heel. He'd crush the uppity Rina Taylor before he let her come between him and his boy a second time.

He didn't hold much stock in the rumors of her using a love potion. He didn't figure Delaney was the type to fall fer any kinda love potion, but he'd keep his attention firmly fixed on his man Delaney jus' the same. A body had to be mighty careful where the old woman Ida was concerned. She knew more about herbs and such than anybody else in the hills.

If'n it seemed a potion started to working on Delaney, Nolan would put a stop to it. With a bullet. His eyes glittered with the thought.

He rather liked the idea of putting a bullet into Rina's pretty head, too. Maybe that's how he'd kill her in the end.

Smiling, he hitched up his pants. Weren't no use in standin' around town no more. He'd learned 'bout all he was gonna learn today. Besides, Billy was likely gettin' impatient fer him to return. Nolan fingered the candy in his pocket. Billy had always had a likin' fer candy. It was past time he took the boy a treat.

Nolan set off down the dusty street whistling to himself. He had things to do—planning to get to. Yep, he wanted to plan out jus' how he'd kill Rina Taylor.

Rina sat back against the broad tree trunk and chewed on a piece of grass. Only faint dapples of sunlight invaded the shade from the towering oak. She snuggled back against the rough tree trunk, searching for a more comfortable position.

It'd be another half hour before she'd need to check Pa's bubbling still again. Less than ten feet away, the dented copper pot looked hulking and ugly sitting like it did in the peaceful shady clearing.

111

It'd taken Pa and her less than three days to set up again. This time, though, Pa had moved his site closer to the cabin. He wanted it to be harder for old Nolan Gant to sneak up on them.

Rina grinned at the makeshift still. It had been put together from scraps Pa kept on hand. He remained madder than a rooster in an empty hen-house 'bout losing his favorite still. But, give him a month or two, and he'd be a-swearin' that this one was the best whiskey still he'd ever used in his life.

A bee buzzed past her, and she watched it land on a nearby wildflower. The purty blue bloom reminded her of Shane's eyes. A mental picture of him rose before her, and she closed her eyes to savor it a moment.

The shade, warm day, and exhaustion from caring for Shane most all of yesterday and last night combined to work against her. In spite of her efforts to remain awake, her breathing became slow and steady as she drifted off to sleep.

"Angel?" The word was soft and low against her ear, bringing to mind the buzzing bee she'd been watching.

Rina waved her hand to shoo it away, not willing yet to give up her heavenly dreaming of Shane and open her eyes. Jus' a few more minutes, she promised.

"Angel?"

There it came again. That soft, purring voice tempted her.

The faintest whisper of air caressed her cheek.

Rina smiled. Her dream sure felt good. Once again, that low whisper came, a-ticklin' her ear.

"Umm," she murmured, struggling to keep her eyes closed against the compulsion to open them.

"Umm," a deep voice answered back.

Tender lips brushed her cheek, and Rina's eyes snapped open.

She met Shane Delaney's purty blue eyes a-lookin' down at her. She blinked again, afeared for a moment that she'd conjured him up.

Tentatively, she raised her right hand and laid it against his cheek. Firm skin met her fingertips. Not a conjured spirit, but a flesh-and-blood man, her mind told her.

"Shane?" she whispered, her voice a mere breath of sound.

"Who else were you expecting?"

"Nobody."

Her cheeks turned a becoming shade of pink as the blush stole upwards from her neck. Would she never get over her tendency to speak too quick and too honest?

Shane watched the blush sweep up her skin, wishing it was his fingers stroking her instead. Unable to resist, he traced her cheek with his thumb. The skin was warm and oh-so-soft to his touch.

As he lazily trailed his thumb across her skin, he watched her eyes widen in a blend of surprise and pleasure. She was beautiful like this—freshly awakened from sleep. An instant picture of her waking in his bed filled his mind, the fantasy so real he groaned.

She'd look just like she did now. Her eyes slanted, half-open with a dream-filled look to them. Would her hair be this silvery color spread across the pillow? He smoothed a tendril away with his thumb. The silken strands curled and flexed beside his palm. Awake or asleep, Rina was a sight to behold.

He didn't think she could look more beautiful than now, reclining against a dark tree trunk. The oak's bark set off her fair features to perfection, and for the first time he noticed a dusting of freckles across her nose. Giving in to the temptation, he brushed his thumb back and forth across the tiny speckles, and his body heated in response.

He breathed in a breath of surprise. Even freckles were sexy on her. He'd never thought they could be so, but on Rina they brought out a tenderness, a protectiveness he'd never felt toward a woman before. What was it about this girl-woman that allowed her to hold his very being in the palm of her hand?

Her tousled hair lay in a tempting disarray of silvery curls around her face, and he reached out and gently tucked a strand behind her ear. She stroked his cheek with her hand, then blushed and pulled her hand back.

He drew her hand in his, placing a soft kiss on the center of her palm. Before he released her hand, he kissed it again, suckling the skin.

She stared back at him in wordless wonder.

Shane soaked up the admiration in her gaze. She made him feel special.

He noticed that a tiny streak of dirt ran the length of her cheek, and he lightly stroked her face with a fingertip, removing the streak. A leaf rested in the curls on her shoulder, and he paused to pluck it away before continuing his survey.

The oversized shirt she wore had bunched up behind her, tightening and outlining her breasts, torso, and narrow waist. He forced himself not to linger on what lay beneath the taut fabric.

She'd dressed in men's breeches again, and he realized that he was actually coming to like the sight of her in them. Their snug fit left little to the imagination. He found he liked knowing that it was truly her beneath his gaze, and not a series of ties and corsets.

A glimpse of ankle peeked out at him from the bottom of her pants leg, while her bare feet and toes snuggled into the lush carpet of green grass.

When she laid her hand back against his cheek, he sucked in his breath.

"Ah, Rina." His voice was deep and husky.

"Hum?" she asked, not really caring for an answer.

Nothing in the whole world mattered when he looked at her like he was a-lookin' now.

Shane pulled her into his arms, resting his cheek against her hair. His uneven breathing stirred the loose tendrils of curls.

"What am I going to do with you?" he whispered, his voice tight with an unfamiliar emotion.

Her breath stopped for a moment, and she nestled against his chest.

"What do you want to do with me?" The question slipped out, and she waited impatiently for him to answer.

"This."

At once he took her lips in a demanding kiss, slipping his arms behind her slight body and drawing her up against him.

Rina went willingly, luxuriating in the loving closeness.

"Ah, Rina."

Her heart skipped a beat at the promise his words held. A liquid heat started slowly burning at her thighs and flowed upward.

Sunlight dappled around them, turning the shady spot into a hidden cocoon—a piece of paradise. It seemed like they were locked together in a world of their own, unseen and suspended in time.

Shane eased her shirt open and slipped the fabric down to expose her breasts. He cupped his hands over them, gently circling her nipples, bringing them to life beneath his fingers.

Rina met his eyes and watched a flame spark in their depths.

"Beautiful . . ." Shane ran his fingertips across her breasts, down to her waist, and stopped at her hips, then swept her into his arms, cradling her close.

No one had ever called her beautiful before. Rina stared up into his eyes. Not seeing any sign

116

of pain there from Ida's truth-telling potion, she realized he must be telling her the truth this time. He truly thought her beautiful.

The fresh scent of his skin enveloped her senses, and Rina felt her temperature rise with the motes of sunlight swirling around them.

The sweet quiet of the clearing enveloped them, the only sound their own breathing and the hypnotic call of the whippoorwill. Shane gently kissed her, tasting her mouth, reveling in its sweetness. His hands moved, caressed, cupping first one breast and then the other. Slowly, he lowered his mouth to their ripeness and drew the tip of one between his lips.

Rina jumped at the contact, surging upward toward him, closer. She moaned at his sucking. His tongue swirled around the nipple and traveled lower. Stopping at her navel, he planted tiny kisses across her waist.

Rina writhed beneath him. Her own hands performed a zealous survey of their own as she clasped his shoulders, then felt the strength beneath the skin.

He was making her feel things she'd never felt before, such as the churning in her stomach and heat where it oughta not be.

As she stilled in his arms, Shane drew himself back up to gaze lovingly into her eyes for a moment before he took her lips in a kiss that asked, offered, then demanded. Rina answered, tightening her hold on his shoulders and moaning against his lips. He captured the sound, drawing it to him, making it a part of him.

As her soft mews of pleasure increased, the depth of his kisses did, too. His murmured endearments fell upon her ears, and she returned his kisses, eagerly. Experimentally, she touched her tongue to his lips.

Shane groaned deep in his throat, and she stopped, afeared she'd done something wrong. In answer, he drew her closer, slanting his mouth across hers, assuring her all was well.

Nothing could be more perfect, he thought. Rina was special. Everything about her intrigued him.

"Ah, cherie," he murmured against her ear, whispering love words to her.

"Oh, that's purty," she answered back, her voice a husky whisper. "Say it again." She laughed softly. "I never heard that kinda talk before."

Rina's words jerked him to a halt. Her failure to recognize the few French words was like a splash of cold water to his heated senses. Her naïveté hit him with the force of a blow.

What was he doing? Making love to an innocent mountain girl? Rina was the type who'd expect marriage and a home. Things he could never give her.

Everything about her was wrong for him. He needed a genteel lady to reside over Belle Rive. And Mary Ellen Dupre fit the role perfectly. He reminded himself of his intention to marry a true Southern lady—not some untamed hill country hoyden. No matter how attracted he might be to her.

Shane eased back, but Rina clung to him, planting nibbling kisses on his neck. Drawing in a steadying breath, he unwrapped her arms from around his neck. When she nuzzled closer, he gently pushed her away.

"Rina, no."

Shane sat her back against the tree trunk and drew her shirt closed. He stood to his feet in a quick move. Unable to resist her allure, he turned his back on her.

"This isn't right . . ." he started, then stopped, pausing to run his hand through his hair and around the back of his neck. The muscles beneath his fingers knotted. He took a step away.

Rina shrank back against the tree. She'd never been so shamed in her life. She wished a hole would open up in the ground and swallow her up. What had she been doing, allowing the stranger to touch her and kiss her? She'd never in her whole life acted this way before. He musta bewitched her.

"Rina, I won't be staying in the hills. And I'm . . . I'm to marry someone else."

Rina gasped at his admission. Marry someone else!

"I apologize. I—"

Rina's anger shut out his words. Why that low-down, sneaking polecat!

"Rina? I didn't intend for things to get out of hand the way they did. You were so beautiful, and

I . . ." He clenched his hands into fists. "Please understand, I never meant to hurt you. But I need a lady for the hostess of my home."

The instant he said the words, he knew they'd been a mistake. He'd been so intent on trying not to hurt her that he'd said the wrong thing.

He turned back to Rina just in time to catch her punch full in his stomach. He doubled over in pain.

"Why, you stinking polecat, you. A-kissin' me and then saying . . ." She snapped her mouth closed and kicked him in the shin.

"Rina," Shane gasped out her name. He hobbled on one leg, not sure which hurt worse—his stomach or his bruised shin.

"Don't you 'Rina' me. If'n I wanted to, I could be every bit the lady you'd want."

She glared at him then raised her chin in a show of pride. Tucking her shirt into her breeches, she strode away. She stomped off, muttering to herself.

"Rina." Shane started after her.

"You stay where you are, you hear me? I don't want you within a step of me."

Shane stopped where he was. Maybe it would be wiser to give her time to cool off. Given time, she'd realize he had done the honorable thing.

"If that's right, why do I feel like hell?" he whispered.

Sighing, he watched Rina walk away. The sassy sway of her hips tugged at him.

* * *

"I could be a damn lady if'n I tried to be," Rina grumbled under her breath as she headed for an overgrown trail that led away from the clearing.

Damn that Shane Delaney and his idea of a lady anyways. Jus' how much brains did it take to act helpless and swish your skirts whenever a man came around? Ha! It took more'n that to be a lady.

She could do those kinda things easy—if'n she wanted to. Hell's bells, she could wear dresses, too—if'n she wanted to. She could even make herself all up and look all fancy the way Milly did.

Rina stumbled on the path, and she caught herself with her hands. Rubbing the leaves and dirt on her pants, she stopped and looked down at herself. Dirt streaked the front of her breeches, and she had a small tear at one knee.

The difference between she and Milly became painfully clear. She'd never dressed up fancy the Milly did, or talked all sweet either. Living with Pa and Lucas, she'd never been made to do those sorta things if she didn't want to. But now, maybe she wanted to.

She didn't want to grow up to be like her ma. She *wouldn't* be like her. The whispered remarks heard throughout her childhood returned to taunt her.

Her ma had *not* been a lady. No respectable lady listened to a man's sweet talkin' and left her husband and children to run off with another man. No, Mrs. Lily Taylor had been called many things—none of them a lady. Why, she hadn't even told her children goodbye. She'd jus' up and ran off.

Although Rina had only been barely two years old that night her ma left, she still remembered the hurtin' things about her ma. Tears burned at the back of Rina's throat.

With determination, she pushed the hurtin' memories aside. That was all over and done with years back. It was all Shane Delaney's doing that brought back the past so much nowadays. Him and his talk of a planning on marrying a fancy lady.

"Hell's bells." Rina kicked an exposed tree root.

Why, she could be a lady if'n she set her mind to it, too. Wouldn't that surprise Shane Delaney! It surely would.

Rina smiled a slow, sly smile. She intended to show Shane Delaney a thing or two. Rina Taylor could be as much a lady as anybody. After all, how hard could it be to learn to talk fancy and swish a skirt?

She could compete against any weak, mealy-mouthed fancy lady he'd chosen to marry. Jus' see if she couldn't!

Eight

Rina stood back and surveyed the yellow striped dress. She'd succeeded in sewing up the rips she'd made by removing one of the ruffles and using it for patches.

Although, she had to admit that some of the yellow stripes did go in more than one direction now, and that some of the stitches she'd taken showed up more than she'd hoped they would.

She held the dress in front of her. The color appeared as ugly as ever.

"Rina? Gal?" Pa's voice boomed through the cabin, demanding a response.

"In here," she answered.

He strode into the room and stopped dead still at the sight of Rina and the dress. He stared, then coughed several times.

Unable to stop himself, he burst into a strangled laugh. Turning, he quickly left the room.

Rina stared at the door and then at the dress. Danged if Pa wasn't right. She didn't blame him for laughing. The patched-up dress was a horror. She threw it down on the floor.

"Rina?" Ben Taylor stood at her doorway, a sheepish expression on his weathered face. "I think it's about time that you bought yourself some dresses. New ones."

He crossed to her and shoved a handful of bills into her hand. "Take it. I've had it tucked away for ya. And it's past time."

"Pa." Rina stared at the money clutched in her hands. The rolled-up wad of bills was more than she'd ever seen at one time.

"No arguing. Ya take it." He turned to go and stopped. "I'll take care of the still today. Ya go on into town and see Lucas. He'll know how to help ya spend that right."

"Thank you, Pa." Rina blinked away the sudden tears his generosity and caring brought.

She gripped the money, feeling the crispness of it between her fingers. *Well, fancy Mr. Shane Delaney, you jus' wait until you see me,* she thought, smiling in glee at what the money would buy.

A sudden question made the smile vanish just as fast as it had come. Did it take more than jus' dresses to make a lady?

Rina didn't know the answer for positive. Come to think of it, she didn't even know where to start at to becoming a "lady." With no mother about, and only Pa and Lucas to teach her things, she'd never learned anything about being a lady. Neither Pa or Lucas could be called ladylike in any way. And Ma had been as far from being a lady as she could be.

She gnawed on her bottom lip. As she stared thoughtfully at the floor, she noticed her latest book lying by the bed post. A glimmer of an idea took hold.

Mr. Mossman could be the answer to her problem. The fancy Englishman had plenty of book learning—after all, he taught Lucas and her to read. Surely he could teach her to be a lady. She'd taken to reading right easy; this would be even easier, Rina decided.

Shane stepped back behind the concealment of the broad tree trunk and watched Rina swing astride the tall horse, then ride away. He'd called himself every kind of a fool ever since the moment earlier when she'd looked at him with such hurt in her eyes. Those emerald depths had brimmed with tears before she'd stopped herself. Then the anger had taken over.

She'd most definitely been a sight to behold angry. Her cheeks flushed, her perfect breasts heaving, and her eyes practically shooting sparks at him—he'd been hard put not to take her in his arms again.

No matter how much he wanted her, he knew he had to resist. It wouldn't be right. For all the good his noble actions had accomplished. Rina had raged at him in anger, and he was no closer to getting the Taylor recipe."

The whiskey recipe was his sole reason for being here, Shane reminded himself. Suddenly an unexpected pain shot through his stomach. He gasped, and the pain vanished just as quickly as it came on.

He thought back to what he'd eaten that day, then settled on the breakfast. While Ben Taylor's breakfast of eggs and biscuits and sweet cream gravy had been good, it seemed he was paying for it now, Shane thought. Rubbing a hand across his tender stomach, he dismissed the earlier pain. Just how long did it take to get used to the old man's cooking, he wondered.

The problem he should be worrying about had just ridden off, he reminded himself. Where was Rina going? And what was she up to?

"There ya are, Shane," Ben Taylor's voice boomed out from the cabin porch. "Wanta head up to the still with me for a while? We could likely get in a game or two of cards."

Shane glanced one last time in the direction Rina had taken, then turned back to Ben Taylor.

"Sure." Shane crossed the distance separating them and fell into step beside Rina's father.

Maybe he could learn something about the whiskey recipe by watching him work.

"Where's Rina off to?" Shane tried to make the request sound innocent and unconcerned.

He had the sneaking suspicion he failed, especially when Ben Taylor chuckled.

"That gal? She's headed over to Blueberry Bluff." Ben stopped walking and grinned over at

Shane. "She's gonna buy herself some new dresses."

Shane almost tripped. Rina buying dresses?

Surely she wasn't serious about becoming a lady, was she?

After a quick stop at Lucas's office and a promise to come back before she headed home, Rina headed her horse for Mr. Mossman's house. She knew that's where he'd likely be. Probably reading.

Outside his house she dismounted, brushed her breeches clean, and tied her horse to a nearby post. Taking the steps in an impatient leap, she bounded for the door and knocked loudly.

"Hey, Mr. Mossman? It's Rina," she called out.

Scant minutes later, Mr. Mossman, his white hair combed back from his forehead, opened the door.

"Why, Rina. What a pleasure to see you. Come in."

"Thank you, Mr. Mossman."

Rina crossed the room and gingerly sat down onto the padded sofa. Suddenly unsure of herself, she dug the toe of her shoe into the braided rug.

"It's good to see you again."

"You, too." She kept her head lowered, studying the toe of her shoe.

"Although this is a surprise. Are you wanting to borrow a special book?"

"Ah, no."

Rina studied her old teacher a minute while deciding on the wisdom of asking him for the favor she wanted. Behind his glasses his pale gray eyes looked out at her with an owlish stare. She knew they could brighten and twinkle with laughter sometimes and that offset the stern look he wore like a habit.

He'd never been overly stern with her; instead, he'd indulged her desire to learn to read, teaching her with patience and in the end with pride. Often he loaned her books that he thought specially good for reading.

"Umm, Mr. Mossman?" Rina's voice squeaked, and she cleared her throat and tried again. "Mr. Mossman, I gots a favor to ask of you."

Thankfully Mr. Mossman was 'bout the same age as Pa. Otherwise she'd be too embarrassed to bring him her request. It jus' seemed proper-like to ask someone near her pa's same age for help in this matter.

"What's that, my dear? You know that I will help you if I can."

"I wants you to teach me to be a lady." There, she'd done it. She'd blurted out the words.

Rina gnawed her bottom lip waiting for his answer. She didn't have but a second to wait.

"You what?"

"I said that I wants you to teach me to be one of them ladies."

"Whatever are you thinking? I'm not that kind

128

of a teacher. What you need is to attend one of the schools back east. Why—"

"I don't have time to go back East to a fancy schooling fer ladies. He'll be gone by then." She clamped her hand over her mouth.

"Do you mean Mr. Delaney?"

"It's not what you think. I jus' wants to show him that I can do it. Be a real lady."

"Rina—"

"What I needs is to become a lady. And real quick like too."

She didn't know how long Shane planned to stay in the hills. She didn't really want to think 'bout him leaving. Pushing the unpleasant thought aside, she turned and faced Mr. Mossman squarely.

"I needs your help. And I needs it real bad."

"Rina—"

"Please say you'll do it? Say you'll help me learn to become a fine lady?"

"I don't think this is a good idea—"

"Please?" Rina pleaded, nervously clasping her hands together in her lap.

He sighed. He knew he was weakening, and there didn't seem to be a thing he could do about it. The young girl sitting across from him so hopefully had always been able to wind him around her finger like a skein of yarn. The best he could hope to do would be to hold out a few minutes longer.

"Mr. Mossman? Please don't say no?"

That did it. He caved in to her request, knowing in his heart and mind that he'd regret it.

"Very well," he sighed in resignation.

"Ohh!"

Rina jumped up and threw her arms around him, giving him a firm hug. He coughed at the strength.

"Oh, thank you."

She jumped up and down, then plopped back down onto the sofa.

"Let's get started right away. What do I do first?" she asked, her voice emphasizing her eagerness.

"Wait here."

Mr. Mossman strode out of the room, returning shortly with a bound book. He held it out to her.

"What's that fer?"

"To read. It's a history of manners, and I imagine that's the best place to start."

"All right."

Rina took the blotched and aged volume gingerly, almost afraid it would break in her hands. The book was heavy and much sturdier than it had looked, once she held it in her hands.

She hadn't thought to start her "lady" lessons this way, but she was willing to start anywhere. Besides, she told herself, reading came easy to her. If'n this was the way to start, then learning to become a "lady" was gonna be easier than she'd hoped.

"Oh, Pa gave me some money fer some dresses.

I'm supposed to buy some today. Will you help me?"

"I will deliver you into Mrs. Alberts' capable hands. But first, read."

"All right." She didn't mind putting off getting the dresses a little longer. She'd much rather read a book any day than go get a dress.

"Make yourself comfortable, my dear." He gestured to the room. "I was working in my study. I'll just go back there and let you read for a little while. Then we can talk about what you've read. Then the shopping."

"Umm-huh," Rina mumbled, her nose already buried in the first pages of the book.

She curled her feet up under her on the sofa and turned the next page. Before Mr. Mossman had left the room, she was deeply engrossed in the pages.

Undisturbed by any other sounds in the house, she read page after page. Her brow creased at some of the unusual wording, but she continued reading.

The more Rina read on the book, the more confused she became. If'n she didn't know Mr. Mossman so well, she'd think the teacher was either a dottering old fool or trying to play a joke on her. Shaking her head in disbelief, she finished the last paragraph on the page.

"Hell's bells," she said aloud.

She turned the page and read the next section with avid interest. Her mouth gaped open on the last sentence.

"To lick your greasy fingers or wipe them on your coat is impolite. It is better to use the table-cloth." Her shocked words echoed in the room.

Rina flipped back a page and reread the instructions for ladylike behavior. Nope, she hadn't read it wrong. That's what the words said.

"Well, I never in all my borned days." She snapped the book closed.

Surely Mr. Mossman was pulling a prank on her. He had to be. Everybody knew you didn't use one of Miss Hattie's fancy hand-worked tablecloths for that.

Why, practically nobody in Possum Hollow had tablecloths—except for Miss Hattie. No matter what the book said, Rina couldn't even conjure up a picture of Miss Hattie a-wipin' her fingers on the fancy embroidered tablecloth.

Rina'd had enough of Mr. Mossman's joking. She wouldn't sit quietly and allow him to laugh at her expense. Gripping the book in one hand, she strode down the hall and into his study.

"Jus' what in blue blazes do you think you're a-doin'? This is the sneakiest, dirtiest, damnedest trick you ever pulled in all your borned days!" she shouted at the middle-aged man sitting behind the desk.

"Rina!"

She dropped the book onto the desk and plunked her hands on her hips. Leaning forward until her nose almost touched his, she glared at him.

He pulled back sharply. Behind his glasses, his eyes blinked up at her with an owlish intensity.

"What on earth are you carrying on about, Rina? First lesson is that a lady doesn't shout at—"

"I'll shout at whoever I damned well please." Rina straightened herself up and looked down her nose at him.

"Secondly, a lady doesn't use obscenities," he continued. His voice wavered, showing that he was completely baffled by her outburst.

Rina ignored his remark.

"And I don't like being made fun of the way you're a-doin' to me."

"Rina, I'd never make fun of you."

She picked up the book and shook it at him. "Then what do you call this?"

"That is a history of manners and—"

"Ha!" she shouted.

"Would you kindly explain what you are so upset about," he demanded, raising his voice to match her level.

"The things in this here book." She shook the volume at him again.

"What?"

"Now that bit 'bout not fallin' all greedily on the food, well, any fool knows that. It's some of the other things I don't believe they's telling it true."

"Rina, I assure you that everything in that book is the truth. It is a history of the manners of our civilization."

"I don't care what it is. Some of these things jus' ain't right."

"Aren't," he corrected automatically.

"They still *aren't* right."

"Rina—"

"No, listen to this." She proceeded to lift the book up in front of her and read aloud from it.

"The handkerchief is intended to be hung from the lady's girdle," she paused and sent him an angry glare. "Along with her keys."

As he started to speak, Rina held up her hand to waylay him.

"There's more. Listen to this. 'Among the . . . bourgeoisie,' " she pronounced the word slowly, being sure to sound out each unfamiliar sound, " 'it is accepted practice to use the sleeve.' "

She lowered the book and laughed aloud. "Anybody with a whit of sense knows that's not right. You don't wipe your mouth on your sleeve."

"Rina, that's from sixteenth century history."

His explanation did no good. She quickly raised the book again and flipped to another page.

He reached over and caught the bottom of the book, pulling it away from her.

"Well, maybe I did start out wrong. It appears I went back too far in history."

Rina gave him a look that could have practically stripped the bark off an oak tree.

"I'm sorry, my dear. I had thought to start at

the beginning on manners. Obviously you already know the important items in that book."

Mr. Mossman turned away in embarrassment and searched the shelf behind his desk for a more suitable book. He found an old copy of *Harper's Weekly* from a few years back when his sister had visited.

"Here, try looking through this." He held it out to Rina. "Elizabeth left it here."

She took it with obvious trepidation.

"I'm assured you'll find it more to your liking. Although it's not brand new, it is more up-to-date and should have some lessons for you to learn in it."

"Humm." Rina handled the publication like it was a live snake ready to strike.

"Go on. Go read." He shooed her from the room with a chuckle.

A half hour later, Rina was apt to agree with Mr. Mossman. This had been much more believable; however, some of the new ladies' fashions had left her wide-eyed in wonder. How did a body move about with all those clothes on? Didn't they bind something fierce?

"Are you ready to go shopping?" Mr. Mossman asked from the doorway.

"Shopping?"

"For your new dresses?" he reminded her.

"Oh, those." She laid the publication down with obvious reluctance. "I guess I need dresses to be a lady, don't I?"

"Yes, my dear. Clothing does make the lady. Shall we?"

Mr. Mossman extended his arm, and Rina grabbed his hand and hauled herself to her feet.

"First lesson—a lady places her hand in the crook of the gentleman's arm."

"The what?"

"Like this." He took her hand and placed it on his arm.

On the way to Mrs. Alberts' ladies shop, he instructed Rina on how to walk like a lady. Rina felt funny the way her hand a-rested on Mr. Mossman's arm. She was used to walking without anyone's help or instructions.

"Well, here we are." He released Rina's arm and pointed her toward the storefront.

"Aren't you coming in with me?"

"Absolutely not. That privilege is reserved for your husband and family."

"But—"

"I'll meet you back here in two hours."

"Two hours?"

How could anyone spend that much time on dresses? she wondered.

"You're right, my dear, that's not enough time," Mr. Mossman conceded. "Make it three hours, and I'll pick you and your purchases up in the buggy. Then I'll deliver you to your brother."

"But—" Rina's voice trailed off as Mr. Mossman high-tailed it out of sight.

"Chicken," she called after him, laughing.

Rina watched him until he was nearly out of sight, then she turned to face the shop with the sign "Mrs. Alberts—Dressmaker" hanging prominently above the entrance.

Trepidation swept over her, and she shoved it aside with as much force as she swung open the door. The bell over the door tinkled merrily as she entered, in contrast to the sudden fluttering of her heart.

Before Rina had enough time to catch her breath, Mrs. Alberts descended upon her in a flurry of silken skirts and heady perfume.

"Welcome, my dear. Do come in." She held out her hand and delicately clasped Rina's hand. "I am Mrs. Alberts."

For a scant instant, Rina felt tempted to turn and high-tail herself right outta the shop and back to the safety of Mr. Mossman's house. Instead, she straightened herself up to her full height, took a determined breath, and stepped forward.

"Rina Taylor, ma'am," she introduced herself.

"Ah, yes, you are in need of a dress?" Mrs. Alberts asked in a lilting voice as she attempted to disguise her distaste at her customer's clothing.

"A bunch of 'em."

Rina caught the older woman's brief flash of distaste. Well, money always had the effect of changing a shopkeeper's tune. She reached into her pocket and withdrew the wad of bills from Pa and displayed them for the woman to see.

"I believe this should cover what I'll need." Rina's voice held an unmistakable note of pride.

Mrs. Alberts' eyes widened at the bills in Rina's hand, before she schooled her expression into one of pleased greeting for Rina.

"Why, yes, my dear. I do believe I can help you." She cocked her head and studied Rina a moment, looking her up and down. "I should have a few things in your size, yes, I'm sure I do."

"Good." Rina released a sigh of relief. The first hurdle was passed.

"I think that first we'll have you look through my book of ladies' fashions to place an order. Meanwhile, I'll see what I have made up that can be readied for you today."

Mrs. Alberts turned away and glided across the floor in what Rina noted were real lady-like steps.

"Come along, my dear," she tossed back over her shoulder.

Rina raised her chin and followed in the woman's wake. Once she'd committed herself, curiosity surfaced, fought with her new manners, and curiosity won. From inside the shop a bright mixture of colors greeted her, and Rina turned this way and that, taking in every detail.

Bright bolts of fabrics lined up along one wall, laces and ribbons flowed along another wall, and two fancy chairs were seated behind a dainty, painted table in one corner. It was here that Mrs. Alberts stopped.

"Have a seat, dear." She scooped up a large book and placed it in Rina's hands the moment she sat down. "If you'll look through these, I'll check the dresses."

Before Rina could answer, Mrs. Alberts turned in a swirl of petticoats and silk and hurried across the room. Rina bit back a smile. She hadn't knowed that a lady could move that fast in skirts without tripping. It sure seemed that the sight of Pa's money had put a little extra speed in the woman's walk.

Leaning forward, Rina fixed all her attention on the big book spread open across the table. The pages were plumb full of pictures; it had more pictures of different dresses than she'd ever seen in all her life. The first one was of a lace-trimmed green dress with an embroidered mantilla. She read the words printed beneath the picture. "Carriage dress of taffeta."

She wrinkled her nose. Pa didn't even own a buggy, much less a riding carriage, so what would she be needing a fancy carriage dress fer? She flipped quickly on to the next page. A right purty dress with tiny flowers spread across the bodice and skirt filled the page. A smile replaced her earlier frown. This was more like it.

She turned slowly through the book, eying each and every picture carefully. Day dresses, dressing gowns, riding habits, and evening gowns in a wide assortment of colors fairly took her breath away.

Jus' imagine, a body could have any one of these pictures made up into a real, honest-to-goodness dress fer themselves. And all jus' by asking fer it to be done. Rina nibbled on her bottom lip. The only real dress she'd ever had was Milly's yellow dress. When Ma had left, she'd taken all of her dresses with her.

Rina had never thought much on where Milly's striped dress had actually come from or how it'd come into being. It had never crossed her mind that Milly may have had the dress made up special, in the colors she had wanted. Although, why a body would want yellow and white stripes was beyond her.

Rina flipped past a yellow outdoor dress quickly. As the next page settled, her mouth formed a silent "oh." The blue evening gown a-lyin' before her was the mostest beautiful thing she'd ever seen in all her born days. The deep purty blue was the exact color of Shane Delaney's eyes. She ran a finger down the lace-edged sleeves and flowing skirt and sighed.

"I see you found something you liked?" Mrs. Alberts asked from Rina's side.

"Uh-huh." Rina nodded.

"Well, let's get your measurements then, my dear. We can't make the dress without them."

As Rina continued to sit and stare at the picture, Mrs. Alberts caught her by the elbow and gently propelled her to her feet.

"But—"

"Come along. We have much to do." She sniffed disdainfully at her client's mode of dress, then added, "And not a moment to waste."

She led Rina to a far corner of the shop, then

140

pushed her behind a curtain. "Take those things off, and we'll get started."

The moment Rina slipped out of her breeches and shirt and faced the shopkeeper, the woman took charge. Mumbling to herself, Mrs. Alberts poked and prodded, then nodded to herself.

Then, the "fitting" started. Mrs. Alberts drew a dress the color of soft green grass over Rina's head. Before Rina had the chance to admire the gown, the older woman turned her around and began to fasten the back of the gown.

"No, no, this will not do," she proclaimed in a sudden fit of agitation.

"I think it's jus' fine, ma'am," Rina attempted to reassure her. "And the color—"

"No! No! No!" Mrs. Alberts shook her head and turned away "We absolutely cannot begin to try these on without a corset."

"A corset?" Rina's voice rose on the hated word. It was her turn to say, "No!"

Mrs. Alberts ignored her and returned with a white, lacy corset in her hands. Refusing to listen to Rina's protests, she drew the green gown off over her head and wrapped the corset around her middle.

Before Rina could do more than push her hair out of her eyes, the other woman was lacing away. She caught the woman's hands and stilled them.

"I don'ts want a corset," she stated firmly.

"But you must—"

"No corsets."

Mrs. Alberts pulled her hands from Rina's and

141

stepped back. "I do not sell my dresses without a corset."

"Hell's bells," Rina muttered. She *needed* those dresses.

A sudden thought sprang to her mind. Nothing said that she actually had to wear the hated corset once she got it home, did it?

Smiling smugly, she faced the store tyrant. "One corset," she conceded.

"Very well." Mrs. Alberts returned to lacing the corset, tightening it.

"That's tight enough. I needs to breathe, don'ts I?"

Chuckling, the other woman loosened the strings slightly. "Better?

"Yes."

Next, the green dress was dropped back over her head again. In a flash, Mrs. Alberts fastened the back and turned Rina to face a mirror.

"See, didn't I tell you? The corset makes all the difference in the world."

Rina stared at herself in the mirror. Was that *her* body? She had definitely growed. And it seemed that the corset thing was intent on displaying that fact for the world to see. Her breasts filled the bodice most becomingly, and her waist seemed tiny, even to her own eyes.

"Beautiful," Mrs. Alberts pronounced. "Don't you agree?"

Rina nodded, still awed by her reflection.

"I will make a few adjustments, and then I can send it to you tomorrow."

"What adjustments?"

Mumbling around the pins now held between her lips, Mrs. Alberts turned Rina away from the mirror. She took a small tuck in one shoulder and pinned it in place, then did the same to the other shoulder. Next, she tucked and pinned the waist and sleeves. Rina held her peace as one pin nicked her side. After all, anybody was entitled to one mistake.

In a surprising amount of time Mrs. Alberts declared the dress finished, and swept the gown back over Rina's head. A sharp pin raked Rina's shoulder just before Mrs. Alberts bustled away in a swirl of skirts. She returned shortly with a blue flowered dress.

"Why, that's jus' like the one in the picture," Rina said in awe.

"Yes, a young lady ordered it, then," she shrugged, "changed her mind. Come, raise your arms."

Mrs. Alberts raised the gown over Rina's head, tugged it down and settled it over her hips. Then, she stood back and cocked her head. "With a little letting out, it will fit fine. Yes, the muslin will be just right."

Within moments, Mrs. Alberts set to fitting the dress. She snipped a seam, then set to pinning it back into place.

"Yeow!" Rina yelped as a pin caught her waist.

"I'm sorry," Mrs. Alberts readjusted the loose pin, then took another tuck and placed her next pin.

"Yeow! Hell's bells, what are you a-tryin' to do to me?" Rina rubbed her side where the pin had pricked.

"I am trying to fit your dress. Now, hold still," Mrs. Alberts snapped back.

"If'n you stick me one more time with one of those pins, one of us is a-gonna be sitting on her behind." Rina glared at the other woman, then added, "And it ain't gonna be me."

"Madam!" Outraged indignation turned Mrs. Alberts' face crimson. "I've never been spoken to in such . . ." she sputtered.

"And I ain't never been stuck so many times in all my born days!"

Mrs. Alberts sniffed and carefully picked up another pin between two fingers. As she leaned forward, Rina eyed her with bold challenge. "I'm a-warnin' you."

Mrs. Alberts jutted out her chin and caught a tuck of fabric with her other hand. With utmost care, she slipped the pin in and out of the fabric.

"There. It's finished."

Rina released a sigh of relief. This time Mrs. Alberts removed the dress slowly and cautiously. Not a single pin pricked Rina this time.

The woman returned with two pairs of slippers, one blue, one a deep green.

"Let's have you try these."

Rina slipped her feet into the dainty slippers and wrinkled her nose. "They pinch."

Mrs. Alberts bent down and felt for Rina's toes.

"They are a perfect fit, my dear. Perhaps they will just take a bit of getting used to."

Rina attempted to wiggle her toes in the snug confines of the slipper. They sure would take some "getting used to" as the other woman had said. But they did look purty.

The next hour passed in a whirl of selecting petticoats and stockings. Mrs. Alberts saw to the matching of everything.

Rina watched as her stack of new clothes grew. Another pair of dainty slippers joined the pile before Mrs. Alberts declared them finished for the day.

Rina was plumb worn out. She didn't know when she'd ever been poked and pushed at and prodded so much in her life. If'n Mrs. Alberts had laced her into one more dress or corset, she knew she woulda jus' screamed.

Remembering her manners, Rina thanked the other woman and gathered up her packages.

Precisely three hours after he'd dropped her off, Mr. Mossman drew his buggy to a halt in front of Mrs. Alberts' shop. He eyed Rina and her load of boxes and bags with a wide smile of approval. However, Lucas's attitude was another matter when Mr. Mossman delivered Rina and her packages to his door.

"What on earth?"

"Well, you was mighty busy when I stopped

earlier, so I went to Mr. Mossman. He helped me—"

"He bought this?" Outrage colored Lucas's usually calm voice.

"No, silly. Pa gave me the money. Mr. Mossman jus' gave me a book to read and delivered me to Mrs. Alberts' dress shop fer the dress buying."

"You bought dresses?"

Rina raised her chin in a stubborn gesture her brother recognized. "It's time I started wearing some."

"Hallelujah!" Lucas shouted.

He had a fairly good idea of who had prompted this sudden change, but decided not to say anything more about it. He also carefully avoided any talk about Shane Delaney.

The ride home in Lucas's buggy passed with a lengthy description of his past week, and a glowing account of Milly. Rina feared maybe her brother was a-gettin' serious. A twinge of jealousy sprang up, tightening her chest.

Rina fought the resentful feelings. She wanted Lucas to be happy, didn't she? Of course she did. And she'd make an honest effort to try to like Milly—no matter how hard it might be to do.

After Lucas left to visit Milly, Rina tried on one of her new gowns. This one was a pale blue with tiny flowers. Sprigged muslin, Mrs. Alberts had called it. The dress was almost the same shade of purty blue as Shane's eyes.

However, the special dress she'd ordered to be made had been the exact color of his eyes, but she didn't buy it for that reason, she told herself. She'd bought it because it was purty. Now she could hardly wait for it to be made up—it was her favorite of all.

She shook out the skirt of her new gown. It fit much better'n the ugly yellow dress did, and there wasn't a bow on it. She'd seen to that!

Rina turned this way and that, checking the new dress over in the mirror Pa'd hung on one wall. She looked different in this dress. She felt different, too.

"Rina?" Pa hollered. "Supper's 'bout ready."

She smoothed the skirt down, slipped her feet into the new pair of fancy satin slippers she'd bought, and bit her lip. What would Pa say 'bout the dress? Even more, she wondered what Shane would think of her in it.

Opening the door before she could lose her courage and change back into her comfortable breeches, she stepped into the other room. Both men turned at the sound of the door and froze.

"Gal!" Pa blinked and cleared his throat. "Ya looks mighty purty."

"Beautiful," Shane said.

Rina concentrated hard on remembering all of Mr. Mossman's instructions on how a lady should walk. Mentally she recited them. *Head up. Shoulders back. And glide, don't stomp.*

She took a deep breath and raised her chin. Putting her shoulders back, she slid her right foot out. At the last moment she remembered she was supposed to shorten her strides. She quickly drew her foot back and took a small, lady-like step.

Looking straight ahead like instructed, she couldn't see her feet. How on this green earth was a body to see where they was a-goin' walking all slow and stiff-like this way?

At last she reached the kitchen. It had never seemed so far until today. She scooped up the platter of Pa's deep-golden fried chicken from beside the stove to carry it to the table.

Trying not to think on her Pa and Shane a-sittin' at the table waitin' for her, she took another cautious step. She felt her ankles wobble in her new satin shoes. Fancy things they were, too. But they made a body feel all weak-kneed.

She sneaked a peek down at the floor. The way was clear of obstructions—leastways there didn't seem to be anything between her and the table to run into. Jus' as long as she stopped before she bumped into the oak table, she thought to herself. She gripped the platter.

Raising her chin, she concentrated on taking smooth steps. One, two, three. She counted off each step, remembering to make them small ones. She did feel like she was a-gliding. It was working.

She slid her satin-clad foot out again. A smile of accomplishment teased her lips. This "lady" thing wasn't so hard.

As she brought her weight down on her right foot, she caught the hem of her dress. She felt a hard tug at her bodice and jerked up to straighten it a-fore anything could fall out to be seen that shouldn't.

The next instant everything went wrong. Her feet tangled in her dress hem, and she tripped. The platter of fried chicken flew through the air just as a loud rip sounded from somewhere about her dress. She didn't want to even imagine what split this time.

Chicken pieces hit the floor, bouncing and rolling every which way. Her heel came down on a chicken wing and she lost her balance. Careening wildly to keep from falling flat on her face, she grabbed for anything to catch herself with. What she latched onto was Shane's broad shoulders.

He let out a startled sound seconds before she landed right in his lap.

Nine

"Dagnamit, gal," Pa bellowed. "Get off his lap!"

Rina swatted at the flurry of petticoats tangled around her hips and thighs. She was so embarrassed she thought she coulda died right then and there.

"Rina!" Pa yelled her name.

If'n possible, his voice was even louder than it'd been a minute ago.

She pushed against Shane's rigid thighs with her hand and tried to get to her feet, but only succeeded in settling herself deeper in his lap. A body couldn't hardly move, what with their corset a-diggin' one way and their petticoats determined to tangle up all about.

"Rina!" Pa bellowed. He slammed his fists down onto the table and surged to his feet.

She coulda sworn she felt Shane's chest rumble with laughter. When she sent a sharp look up into his face, he gazed back at her solemnly, no sign of a grin or a smile in sight.

"Hell's bells, Pa." She pushed her hands against Shane's thighs again, trying to get off his lap. "The way you're a-shoutin', a body would think I done this on purpose."

"Did you?" Shane whispered in her ear a second before he caught her about the waist with both of his hands and helped her to stand up.

Rina glared at him, then turned to face her pa. Bright spots of red stained his cheeks, and he was glaring at her something fierce. She guessed that her pa was 'bout as mad as she'd ever seen him. Shane released his hold on her waist.

"It wasn't my fault. It was this damned dress. I tripped," she explained.

She kicked the petticoat with a vicious kick.

"Don't swear."

"Oh," Rina sputtered. "Hell's bells, I'm a-skippin' supper. If'n you want to yell at me anymore, I'll be in my room. Reading," she added.

Grabbing her petticoats and skirt up into one hand, she stomped off. Behind her she coulda swore she heard somebody chuckle. She didn't turn around to see who it might be. If'n she found out it was Shane, she'd likely as not go back and slug him one.

So much for being a fine lady.

The next morning Rina tied her horse outside Mr. Mossman's house. In the wee hours of the morning when she'd had trouble getting to sleep, for the hundredth time since she'd landed in

Shane's lap, she figured what she needed was another "lady" lesson.

Determined to get started early today, she pounded on the door to the house, then smoothed her hands down her blue dress. She glanced down at the hem—it scarcely showed where she'd sewed it up this morning.

"Mr. Mossman?" she called out.

The door stayed silently closed. She pounded again, this time harder.

"Hey, Mr. Mossman."

Rina looked up at the sky. The sun had been up for some time now. Surely Mr. Mossman hadn't taken to sleeping in late.

"Coming," a startled-sounding voice called out from inside.

The door opened to reveal Mr. Mossman fully dressed, his white hair neatly combed. He held his glasses in one hand and a thick book in his other hand. As he recognized her, he blinked and looked again.

"Rina, what's wrong?"

She noted that he seemed surprised as all get out to see her. Well, she hadn't thought she'd be back for another lesson so soon herself.

"Nothing's really wrong. I came fer a lesson," she stated the fact bluntly.

It had been hard to say the words. She'd had to bury her pride to admit to needing more help. And a-needin' it so soon, too.

"What in the world are you doing here this early?"

"I need a lesson *real* bad, Mr. Mossman."

She shook her head and swept past him into the house. Plopping herself on the sofa, she waited for him to join her.

"I left my horse out front. I hope you don't mind none."

"That's fine."

He looked at the crumpled skirt of her blue dress with obvious disapproval.

"But, Rina, a lady doesn't ride astride. Especially in a dress."

"Then how the hell does she get any place?" she asked, interested to see how he'd answer that one.

"She rides in a carriage or a buggy. Secondly, a lady doesn't—"

"I know. A lady don't swear."

"Doesn't," he corrected automatically.

"Huh?"

"I was referring to your grammar. A lady doesn't swear, not a lady don't swear."

He spoke patiently as if talking to a small child. It set Rina's teeth on edge.

"I'll stop a-swearin' if'n you'll stick to working on one thing at a time."

"I beg your pardon?"

"No need fer you to apologize." She brushed off his comment.

"I wasn't apologizing. I was . . . Never mind." He gave up and sat down in the chair opposite Rina.

"I needs another lesson on being a lady. And

153

especially on that gliding-type walking stuff." She released a deep sigh that sounded like it came from the soles of her feet. "I tried. I really did. It don't work worth a damn."

Rina jumped to her feet and paced the length of the room. As she neared the sofa the toe of her slipper caught on the braided rug, and she pitched head first onto the middle of the sofa.

"Hell's bells," she muttered in a muffled voice, her face buried against the cushions.

"Rina."

She raised her head up from the cushions that she felt were about to smother her.

"Don't swear," they said in unison.

Mr. Mossman was the first to start laughing. Rina pushed herself into a sitting position, glared at him, then, unable to resist, joined in the laughter.

After several minutes of laughing, stopping, then starting again, she choked back her giggles.

"That's about the same thing that happened last night. Excepting that there weren't no fancy sofa in the kitchen. I landed in Shane Delaney's arms. Well, to be truthful, it weren't exactly his arms. More like smack dab in the middle of his lap."

Her confession garnered a startled exclamation out of the usually refined Mr. Mossman.

"You shoulda heard Pa."

"I can imagine." He coughed to keep back the laughter that brimmed at the edge of his words.

"Oh, no you can't. Pa was madder than a rooster in an empty hen house. He—"

"Rina, a lady doesn't say things like that."

"But it's true."

"I'm sure it is." Mr. Mossman gave up, letting the laughter burst out.

"Damnation—"

Mr. Mossman stopped laughing and held up his hand.

"I know," Rina recited, "A lady doesn't swear."

"Correct."

"If'n a lady can't use words that come naturally, then what does she say?"

Mr. Mossman stared at her a minute. He opened his mouth and closed it.

"I thought so," Rina snapped. "Don't have an answer fer that one, do you?"

"Rina—"

"What's that book you're a-holdin'?" She pointed to the cloth-bound volume he clasped in one hand.

"It's a series of directions on etiquette for ladies and gentlemen. I have been reading on it to see what items might be of help for you."

"Well, did you find any?"

He smiled broadly. "Yes, my dear. I certainly did find some."

Mr. Mossman opened the book to where a white ribbon marked his place. Resting his glasses firmly on the bridge of his nose, he began to read aloud.

The next half hour passed with what seemed

like to Rina a constant listing of things a lady didn't do. If she heard "a lady doesn't" one more time, Rina knew she'd likely scream in frustration.

"Remember, to be agreeable you must be a good listener." Mr. Mossman pushed his spectacles up with one finger, then turned to the next page.

"Do not argue. Do not contradict. And above all, never offend by—"

"Hell's bells." Rina surged to her feet, almost tripping over her skirts in the movement.

"Rina—"

"Fer the last hour I've heard so many a lady doesn'ts do this and thats—a body couldn't count them all. Jus' tell me one thing. What does a lady do?"

She planted her hands on her hips and proceeded to wait for her answer.

"She behaves like a lady." Mr. Mossman glanced up at her, ignoring her outburst. "Now sit down. We have several more pages to go through this morning."

Rina opened her mouth, but before she could get out a single word, he continued a-readin'.

"A lady never loses her temper."

"I might as well warn you now. I'll never master that one."

A smile twitched Mr. Mossman's lips, but he read on, "Never notices a slight—"

"What's that?"

"Ah, an insult."

"You means to tell me if'n somebody insults me, I'm not supposed to hear it?"

"I guess you could say it that way."

"No. That's where I draws the line. Why—"

"All right. We'll pass on that one," he conceded.

"Well, that's good."

Mr. Mossman returned his attention to the book in his hands. "Let's see, where was I? Ah, yes. Nothing charms more than candor—" He stopped and cleared his throat. "I don't think we need to concern ourselves with that."

"But—"

"Rina, you already have enough 'candor' to fill a book."

Rina snapped her mouth closed, crossed her arms and slumped down in the cushions. Could she help it if'n she'd always been honest with people?

"Never tattle, or repeat in society—"

"Mr. Mossman? Do you think we could lay off the nevers fer a while?"

His lips twitched again.

"Yes, my dear, maybe that would be a good idea."

"Like I asked you before. What does a lady do?"

He flipped past a few pages and then turned the book around to show Rina. "There, one thing a lady does is to wear a bonnet. At all times when she is outdoors."

"Oh, no." Rina sat upright in a flash. "I plumb

fergot 'bout buying one of those yesterday. What with all the poking and prodding that lady did—

"She was measuring you for the garments that she will have sewn and delivered. But don't concern yourself. If I recall correctly, the last time Elizabeth was here she left a few things behind."

"Things like what?"

"Like perhaps a bonnet or two." Rising to his feet, he dropped the book onto the chair. "I won't be but a few moments."

Rina sat still for the first five minutes after his departure, but she couldn't remain so. Jumping to her feet, she grabbed up her skirts to keep them out of her way and strode across to the window.

Outside a clear blue sky and glowing sunlight tempted her. She opened the window sash and leaned out to breathe in the fresh air. A body should be outside on a purty day like this, not cooped up a-tryin' to learn silly things from a book on being a lady.

Rina started to turn away, determined to forget all this nonsense about becoming a lady and instead enjoy the sunny day, when she recalled her vow to herself to become a lady.

"Damn you, Shane Delaney. I can so be a lady," she whispered. "Jus' you wait and see."

Grabbing up her skirts, she spun around and set off in search of Mr. Mossman and his fancy ladies' bonnets.

She found him in a small room, brimming with books and several trunks. He was sitting back on his haunches, several feminine items scattered about him on the floor. She saw a frilly pink para-sol and a lace fan a-layin' at his feet.

"Mr. Mossman?" She stopped at the doorway, waiting for him to tell her if'n she could come in.

"Oh, Rina." He glanced her way. "Sorry I took so long. Come in and see what I've found." He motioned her to join him.

As she entered with obvious curiosity, he stood to his feet and motioned around the cluttered room. "I think I've located a couple of items that will help you learn to walk with ladylike strides. Without tripping."

"What?" she asked with skepticism.

"This."

He picked up what looked to Rina to be a small bundle of lace, feathers and frills. With infinite care, he brushed off a speck of lint.

"I bought this for Elizabeth. She always says that a lady never feels like a true lady without a bonnet on her head."

He held out the tiny green velvet hat with black ribbons and feather trim.

Rina blinked at it twice. The tiny thing was a bonnet? But what a bonnet!

"Why don't you try it on, my dear? There's a mirror behind you there."

She took it gingerly, almost afraid it might break if'n she touched it. It was the purtiest hat she'd ever laid her eyes on. She carefully turned it this way and that way to look at it.

Rina smiled in delight at the sight of the bonnet. It was like nothing she'd ever seen before in her life.

The small bonnet of emerald green velvet came to a small point at the front. From the inside of its brim, a fall of delicate black lace slightly veiled the cap. Two long green ribbons hung down, just waiting to be tied under a lady's chin. The outside of the bonnet also had a trimming of the same delicate black lace that pulled together at the back.

Rina trailed a finger along the lace to meet strings of green velvet ribbons hanging down one side. She rubbed the ribbons between her fingers, then angled the hat to inspect the other side.

Surely. this beautiful creation would only be worn by a real true lady.

"Ohh." Her mouth formed the soft word of awe.

The other side sported three small green and black ostrich feathers. She recognized them from pictures she'd seen in a book.

"Oh, Mr. Mossman. Surely you can't mean fer me to wear this?" Her voice held an undeniable plea for him to say "yes."

She held her breath waiting for his answer.

"Of course, I do. Try it on, my dear. Let's see how it looks."

Not needing any further encouragement, Rina spun around and settled the velvet and lace bonnet on her head. She leaned closer to the mirror and tied the ribbons under her chin.

"Beautiful, my dear."

Rina's eyes met Mr. Mossman's in the mirror, and she smiled back at him. "It is mighty purty, isn't it?"

"Beautiful, Rina," he corrected. "And so are you."

As a blush stole up her cheeks, Mr. Mossman turned away in embarrassment and picked up the frilly parasol. He extended it to her.

"Here you are, my dear. This was my sister's. It will add the final touch. With this you will walk like a regal lady."

"How come?"

Rina studied the pretty pink striped parasol with its fancy trimming of white lace. Granted, the whiteness had dulled and turned to a creamy ivory with age. But it was still purty to her eyes. She couldn't wait to see it fully opened with the fringe a-danglin' all around.

"Because, holding a parasol makes you stand up straighter. And you may concentrate on it instead of your feet."

"But if'n I don't watch my feet, heaven only knows where they'll get off to."

"If you concentrate on something else, your feet will naturally take care of themselves."

Rina threw him a completely skeptical look. "They sure seems to have a mind of their own when I'm in a dress. I don'ts know 'bout—"

"Try it."

"If'n you say so." She grabbed the parasol from him and flicked it open.

"No! No, don't open it inside." Mr. Mossman

161

quickly grabbed for her hands, but missed. "It's bad luck to open one indoors."

His warning came too late. Rina already had the parasol fully opened and was twirling it around, watching the white lace and fringe swirl together.

Once opened, she could see that the parasol wasn't striped at all. The mixture of the original bright and faded shades of pink together made it look striped. But, it was still purty, and the lace hid most of the faded parts, Rina thought.

Mr. Mossman reached across and clasped it from her fingers. Snapping it closed, he handed it back to her.

"Open it outside. And later," he added for emphasis.

"Are we going outside to practice with it?" she asked, her gaze locked on the lacy parasol.

"I think that would be the best. I know I could use some fresh air," he murmured the last under his breath. "Are you ready for a stroll through town, Rina?"

She gripped the parasol tightly. *Was she ready?*

If'n she ever intended to become a lady, then the answer had to be yes. Taking a deep breath, she nodded her head.

"Let's get a-goin'."

Ten minutes later, Rina was inclined to agree with her teacher. She did feel like a lady walking with that parasol. It did seem easier to do that gliding kinda walking when a body held onto a fancy parasol and stopped watching their feet.

162

She smiled over at him, proud of herself that she hadn't tripped once in the last five minutes.

From the corner of her eye she noticed that a man and a woman had stopped and were watching them. Likely as not they were admiring her for being such a lady, she thought. How could a body not be a lady with such a fine bonnet and parasol?

As she reached up to smooth the rim of her bonnet, a man stepped out of the general store and stopped directly in her path. She raised her head and recognized her brother, Lucas. She bit her lip, hoping he wouldn't make one of his usual remarks. Lucas had a habit of finding something funny in anything.

"Rina!" Lucas snickered and tried not to laugh aloud. "You look like a mismatched candy stick. Green, pink and blue? What are you wearing?"

Beside her Mr. Mossman's face blanched, and he stammered. *A mismatched candy stick?* Why, Mr. Mossman had gone to a lot of trouble to help her look like a lady, Rina thought. Damn Lucas.

Rina's temper soared before she could stop it. How dare Lucas insult the teacher for helping her? A lady might not be supposed to hear any insults, but she was sure that didn't mean so when that insult was directed at a friend.

"You take that back, Lucas Taylor." She pointed the parasol at him and took a step forward.

Lucas stared at the parasol with its fringe dangling at him and burst out laughing. Holding his side, he jabbed a finger in her direction and laughed even harder.

Rina snapped the parasol closed and hit him over the head with it.

"Now you take it back," she ordered. "And apologize to me and Mr. Mossman, too."

Instead of obeying her, Lucas just laughed louder. As Rina advanced on him, she heard chuckles from behind her as well. She hit him on the shoulder, and the beautiful parasol snapped in two. Furious, she brandished the broken parasol at him, and Lucas turned tail and took off a-runnin' with both his hands covering his head.

Without a thought, Rina gathered her skirts and petticoats up in one arm and gave chase. Behind her the townsfolk began applauding.

Intent on making her brother pay, she chased him down the street and around the corner into an alley. When she caught up with him, she'd . . .

The alley drew to an end, and she knew she had him cornered. The only way out was over a wooden fence. She'd like to see her brother climb that. Now she had him.

"Rina Taylor!" The shout came from behind her.

She turned and from the corner of her eye she could see Mr. Mossman coming at them in a lopsided run.

"Oh, no." The whispered plea slipped out without her even realizing it.

Rina froze in place, shut her eyes, and inwardly cringed at the unmistakable sound of Mr. Mossman's very displeased voice. She let loose of the bunched-up skirt and petticoats and smoothed them down her legs.

She straightened up and opened her eyes to see Lucas was nowhere around. That figured. It wasn't the first time her brother had spurred her into trouble and then sneaked off to leave her to face the consequences alone.

Mr. Mossman strode up to her and stopped. He paused, huffing and puffing for breath, his face red from the exertion. His usually neatly combed white hair stood out in tufts of wind-blown disorder.

Rina grimaced and fiddled with the broken parasol gripped together in her hands. Mr. Mossman had most certainly been right. Opening the parasol in the house had brought nothing but bad luck.

He reached out and snatched the mangled mess of satin and lace from her.

"Follow me." His sudden order brooked no dissension.

Rina stared at his departing back for only an instant before she caught up her skirts and followed after him. It took all her concentration to keep up with his angry strides and keep the skirts and petticoats out of the way of her feet.

At his house, he strode inside, not bothering with his usual gentlemanly gesture of holding the door open for her. The instant the door closed behind her, he turned about, his hands clasped tightly behind his back. The pink parasol dangled from his fingers.

"Rina—"

"It wasn't my fault. I didn't intent to . . . It's jus' that when Lucas insulted you and then a-started laughing at me, he wouldn't stop. Well, I had to stop him."

"Your behavior today was the epitome of un-ladylike behavior."

"I'm sorry—" she started to apologize.

"Would you look at yourself." His eyes widened at her appearance, and he gestured to the opposite side of the room.

Rina dared a glance at the mirror a-hangin' on the far wall. She gasped at the spectacle the mirror reflected back.

Her beautiful bonnet sat askew on the back of her head. The ostrich feathers had long since disappeared, blown away in the energy of her chase after Lucas. One strip of black lace dangled down one side, and the strings of green velvet ribbon hung bedraggled and tangled together down the other side.

"Oh, dear," she whispered.

It looked like she'd really done it up good this time for sure.

Mr. Mossman dropped the broken parasol on the chair and gave a shudder. He continued to stare at her and shake his head in utter disbelief.

"How could one person, one little person, do so much damage?" he murmured under his breath. "And in such a short amount of time?"

Rina bit her lip at his question. She hadn't meant to cause any trouble or destroy anything. She'd been a-tryin' to be a lady.

"Mr. Mossman, I'm sorry. I didn't . . . ah . . . I'll make up fer it tomorrow—"

"No!"

Rina stared at him, flabbergasted at the strength behind the single word.

"Absolutely not. No more. I'm too old for this." He raised his arms as if to ward her off, then dropped them in a gesture of defeat.

She'd never seen him lose his patience. Not never before. She untied the bonnet and placed it gently on the chair.

"Go home, Rina. Just be yourself. I don't think the town of Blueberry Bluff can withstand you being a lady. And I've just realized that I'm much too old for this much excitement."

"But—"

"My dear, the next time you want a book, come see me. But hear me—a book, my dear. My etiquette teaching days are over!"

"Ah, Mr. Mossman—"

"Absolutely not."

She bit her lip. He seemed awful set in his mind. She didn't think there was anything she could say to persuade him to help her now.

"Please, Rina, don't ask me," he pleaded, his voice weary and strained.

She took a deep breath. "All right," she nodded. "I won't ask you to."

She thought for sure that she heard him sigh in relief.

"But I do thank you fer trying."

In a quick, impulsive gesture, she reached out and hugged him, then fled the house.

Outside, she bunched her skirts up and mounted her horse. Flicking the reins, she knew she had only one place to go.

Ten

There weren't nothing left to do but bury her pride and ask for help again, Rina thought.

Worse than that, it was the *who* she'd have to humble herself before that stuck in her gut. Milly Margaret Bodeen. Lucas's Milly.

The same Milly who'd always had all the menfolks swarming around her like bees to honey, before she'd latched onto Lucas. Rina'd never had much use for Milly's fluttering eyelashes and flattering ways. But it did look like they were gonna be related soon, if'n Lucas married her. For his sake, she guessed they'd better try and be friends.

By the time she reached Milly's parents' house in Possum Hollow, Rina had changed her mind three times. No matter what, she kept coming back to the same conclusion—she was a-runnin' out of people who could help her become a lady for Shane.

Rina sucked in a deep breath and smoothed her rumpled skirt. Much as she hated to ask Milly for help, she didn't have a choice. Without some-body's help, she had about as much a chance of becoming a fine lady as a snowball had in a hot oven.

"Hell's bells," she muttered, then raised her hand and knocked on the door.

A dainty, dark-haired young lady attired in an unwrinkled pink dress opened the door. Milly Margaret Bodeen.

Rina fixed a smile on her face. Seeing Milly face to face always made her feel at a loss.

"Ah, afternoon, Milly."

"Rina?" Milly batted her eyelashes in surprise. "Whatever are you doing here? Is something wrong with Lucas?"

How did Milly always make her feel awkward without seeming to try? Rina swallowed down her nervousness and stiffened her back.

"Lucas is fine." She forced a smile. "Until I catch him," she muttered.

"What?" Milly stared at her.

Might as well get it over with. Rina pulled her shoulders back and faced Milly as if she was fac-ing a gun-toting opponent.

"Lucas is jus' fine. I come 'cause I need your help. I jus' gots to become a fine lady. And I'm running out of time."

There, she'd blurted it all out. Now the only thing to do was wait for Milly's answer.

"You want to become a lady?"

"Yeah, dresses and all," Rina admitted.

"And you want *me* to help you?" Milly asked

in disbelief. A twinge of hope colored the question as well.

"Yes, if'n you will." Rina gripped one hand in a clump of her skirt. "I know we've never been friends, but if'n Lucas is a-gettin' serious 'bout you, then it's time I tried and made us friends."

Milly smiled. "But, Rina, you didn't have to come up with an excuse to come talk to me and pretend to ask for help."

"Oh, but I really needs your help. I gots to become a lady. I gots to show Shane I can be the finest lady he's ever seen."

Realizing what she'd admitted, Rina clasped her hand over her mouth. It was too late to call the hastily spoken words back.

"Rina." Milly caught her hands and dragged her inside. She pushed her into a chair and sat opposite her. "Of course I'll help. A fella, huh?"

Milly's happy smile took any sting out of the words.

"Yes," Rina admitted, as much to herself as to the other woman. "But he's not really *my* fella. The way he blows hot then cold at me, well, he's got me plumb confused. I even went to Ida—"

"Ida? The mountain woman? Whatever for?" Milly's voice held a mixture of awe, respect and fear.

"Fer one of her potions to make him tell me true. Every time he don't, his stomach's supposed to roll some and hurt so's I'll know he's not being true."

Milly's mouth dropped open before she could

171

stop it. "Oh, my. Oh, my." Her eyes widened; nobody in the hills doubted Ida's potions.

"It made him frightful sick the first night, 'cause I mixed it with Pa's whiskey." Rina paused at a gasp from Milly.

"Go on," Milly urged in a hoarse voice.

"Well, that's all I knows so far. Haven't had a chance to test it any yet."

"Oh." Milly nodded. "Well, then, tell me about him instead. What's he like?" She pretended she hadn't heard the town gossip.

"Name's Shane Delaney. He's a real sweet talker. And he's got the comeliest blue eyes and dark hair. Dark as Satan's sin," she added.

"A fella. Oh, but Lucas will be so happy. I can't wait to tell him." Milly clapped her hands in anticipation.

"Oh, yes, you can. And if'n not, then I'm a-leavin' now." Rina stood to her feet and took a step towards the door.

"Wait." Milly caught her arm. "Why ever for?"

" 'Cause that fool would likely laugh himself silly if'n you told him."

"Not Lucas."

"Oh, yes, he would, too."

Rina felt the burning of tears at the back of her eyes and blinked furiously to blink them away. She *never* cried. And she wasn't 'bout to start in here and now.

Realizing the battle Rina was fighting, Milly caught her arm and drew her back to a chair. "Sit down and tell me about it."

"You'll laugh."

"No, I won't. I promise." Milly held her hand up as if she were swearing to keep a vow.

The words tumbled out of Rina like water bubbling over a beaver's dam after a big gully-washer rain. It seemed that once she got started, she couldn't seem to stop the whole story a-comin' out.

Milly sat quiet, almost in awe, as Rina told her about her meeting with Shane and how he up and saved her life when the still blew. Tentatively, she told Milly about the kiss—but only the one up by the clearing. She couldn't bring herself to tell about that second kiss on the bed that had practically burned her, clear from her lips plumb down to her toes.

When Rina got to the part about Mr. Mossman agreeing to help her become a lady, Milly shook her head, and her every feature showed that she knew in advance that nothing good could come from it.

"But he did at least try," Rina explained, attempting to excuse Mr. Mossman's refusal to help her any further in her attempts.

"Rina, he's a man."

"I knowed that."

Milly's lips twitched, and Rina sent her a glaring look of warning.

"Rina," Milly's voice stretched out her name as if making sure she had her full attention before explaining something very complicated. "A *man* can't help you become a lady. Only another woman can do that."

"How come?"

"Why, because . . . because . . ."

Rina waited, tapping one foot.

"Just because he can't, that's why. You'll see why for yourself once we get started. But first, finish what you were telling me. Especially about Lucas." She leaned forward in anticipation.

As Rina relayed the morning's events, Milly sat listening in rapt attention, then began to cough occasionally when she came to the part about the hat and the frilly parasol.

By the time Rina told her about chasing Lucas down the street, to the crowd's applause, Milly was laughing so hard she had to hold her sides to keep from falling out of her chair.

"Stop, Rina. Stop a minute." Milly wiped tears of laughter away from her eyes. "I'm sorry for laughing, but . . ."

Looking over at Rina, Milly started laughing again and couldn't speak for a full minute.

Rina tapped her foot, getting into a fine temper. However, the longer she watched Milly trying to stop her own laughter and failing, the funnier the whole thing began to seem to her.

"Lucas really did look a sight turkey-tailing it down the street, a-holdin' his hands over his head," she admitted.

This brought a fresh gurgle of laughter from Milly before she slid from the cushioned chair and dissolved in a heap on the floor.

174

"Oh, I wish I could have been there. I wish I could have been there to see it." Milly clamped her lips together to stifle her giggles and looked up at Rina.

At the sight of lady-like Milly a-sittin' on the floor holding her sides while her lips a-twitched, fairly aching to laugh again, Rina slid outta her chair and joined her on the floor.

"I don't think you'd have liked it."

"Why, Rina Taylor, I swear to you—I'd have *loved* it. I've never seen Lucas 'turkey-tail' it anywhere."

"Well, he certainly was a-doin' that. And mighty fast, too."

One look at each other and both ladies burst into fresh giggles.

"Rina," Milly coughed, "I think helping you to become a lady is going to be more fun than I've had in my entire life."

"From my experience with Mr. Mossman, I can almost guarantee you it won't be boring fer you."

"Good. It seems except for you and Lucas, my life has been nothing but boring."

At Rina's questioning look, she added, "You may not believe this, but being a lady all the time is anything but fun."

"Oh, I've always knowed that."

"But I've never had the chance to be anything but a lady. I think my momma prayed for me to be born a full-grown lady. She's sure seen that everything I've ever done all my life is to behave exactly like a proper 'lady' should."

Rina frowned. Maybe there was a lot more to Milly than she'd ever thought possible. If'n she could believe her ears, it sounded like Milly was lonesome.

"I never was allowed to play like you did. Momma wouldn't let me play because it might soil my dresses." She looked at Rina, and a smile crept over her lips to become a wide grin. "Maybe you could teach me a thing or two in exchange."

Rina grinned back, truly beginning to like Milly, and stuck out her hand. "Deal."

The two shook on it, then Milly pulled Rina to her feet. Stepping back, she surveyed her carefully, first cocking her head to one side, then to the other.

"What're you a-lookin' at me that way fer?" Rina asked with suspicion.

"What way?" Milly's voice was the epitome of innocent indignation.

However, Rina noticed that a sly look had come over the other woman's usually sedate face. she reminded her of a fox a-lyin' outside a henhouse.

"That way." Unconsciously, Rina crossed her arms over her chest.

"I'm just thinking. Momma and Poppa took the buggy into Blueberry Bluff, and they'll be gone for several more hours yet. We have the house to ourselves." Milly grinned like a co-conspirator.

"What're you a-plannin'?"

"Oh, a lot of things." Milly cocked her head again, then ran a head-to-toe glance over Rina.

176

"Hair, cheeks, hands," she started listing, ticking each item off on her fingers.

"What—"

"I'm figuring up what we need to work on," she explained, continuing to study Rina.

Now Rina knew what a prime hog felt like when it went up fer sale.

"Milly," she began patiently, "I needs to learn to become a real fine lady."

"That's what I'm planning. First we fix the outside."

"But I'm already a-wearin' a dress—"

"That's just the start. We've got a lot more work to do on the outside. That's what a man has eyes for first. Remember that."

Milly bustled around, gathering jars and creams and more items than Rina could figure out what to do with. Before Rina realized what she had agreed to, she'd been bathed and oiled and creamed. Her hair had been washed, then covered with a white greasy cream.

"Hell's bells, there's enough of that smelly stuff to drown me in."

Rina quickly tilted her head to one side to stop a drip from running down her cheek and into her mouth, then swiped her cheek clean.

"Leave it be. It'll make your hair softer and shinier than you ever thought possible," Milly warned her as Rina reached up to wipe away a clump of white from above her forehead.

"I always thought my hair was jus' fine."

"It is. You have the most naturally beautiful

177

hair I've ever seen," Milly admitted, then paused and shook her head adamantly. "But it never hurts to improve some on nature."

Later, while her hair was drying, Milly creamed Rina's roughened hands and bound them in a pair of white cotton gloves.

"Momma will never miss these." She winked.

"Will I really have soft hands?" Rina asked, recalling her earlier wish for soft, smooth hands for touching Shane's skin.

She felt her cheeks heating at the memory. Milly threw her a puzzled glance, but continued her creaming and such without asking any questions.

"Umm, yes. That cream is guaranteed to work. Momma swears by it."

Milly proceeded to smear a different concoction over Rina's face. "Your skin is beautiful. I think we'll skip the bleaching—"

"Bleaching?" Rina started to jump out of the chair, but Milly caught her shoulder and pushed her back down. "Whatever fer?"

"For your freckles. But, never mind, because we aren't going to do it," she assured Rina as she started to stand again.

"I don't have hardly any freckles. And besides, what's wrong with my freckles?"

"Nothing. That's why I'm leaving them alone," Milly explained, stepping back to study Rina's face. "I think they give your face character."

"Character? And here I was a-wantin' beauty."

"You'll have that. Patience."

"I don't have much patience."

"I've noticed," Milly grumbled as she wiped the cream from Rina's face. "But trust me. This will all be worth it. Wait and see."

An hour later when Milly patted the last curl in place and proclaimed them finished, Rina sighed in relief. She hoped Milly was right, and all the things she'd done to her had worked. However, she had her doubts. She didn't *feel* any different. Except maybe for her hair—Milly had curled it and pinned it up fancy.

"Do I really look different?"

"See for yourself." Milly held out a silver-handled mirror to Rina.

"I don'ts know when I've looked in so many mirrors as I have over these past two days."

"Look!" Milly ordered.

Tentatively, Rina took the mirror and, holding it up, peered into the surface.

"Oh, my."

For long minutes Rina just stared at her reflection. Her skin fairly glowed and her hair—why, it jus' shined like a real moonbeam. Tilting her chin, Rina reached up and carefully touched a shimmering curl that was piled atop her head.

"It's really me?"

"Yes, it is." Milly stepped back and surveyed her accomplishment with pride. "And you are beautiful."

"I am, aren't I?" Rina whispered in disbelief. "And I looks like a lady, too. Don't I?"

"Yes, you do," Milly assured her. "Now off with

you. But ride home slow. I don't want your hair windblown on the way."

"I promise."

Impulsively, Rina hugged Milly to her. "Oh, thank you. I think maybe my brother has some brains in his head after all. He found you."

"Oh, Rina." Milly giggled. "Oh, I almost forgot. There's one more thing."

She dashed off, leaving a bewildered Rina waiting and wondering what else.

"Here. The finishing touch." Milly returned with a small bottle cradled in her hands.

"What's that?" Rina asked in suspicion.

"Frangipani," Milly announced, handling the bottle like it was something special. "Wright's Original Frangipani, advertised as the everlasting perfume. It came all the way from Philadelphia. Momma bought if for me for my last birthday. Here, go on, try some."

"But I makes my own scented water to use. I puts in rose petals, and lilac, and a bit of spices—"

Milly caught Rina's hands and dabbed the perfume on both her wrists before she could stop her.

Sniffing appreciatively, Milly announced, "Perfect."

Rina wasn't so sure. She sniffed her wrist and wrinkled her nose. "It seems a little strong-smelling to me."

"It'll fade some. Don't worry. Men love it. Lucas does," she added shyly.

"I'm not a-wearin' it fer Lucas," Rina mumbled.

"Of course not. Trust me. Your Shane will love it, too."

Rina didn't correct her that he wasn't "her Shane." Instead, she said her goodbyes and mounted her horse. Maybe Milly weren't so stuck up after all, Rina thought as she headed her horse for home.

Careful to walk her mount at a slow pace to keep her hair from getting mussed, Rina thought over Milly's parting remarks.

Did she want him to be "her" Shane?

Of course not! Rina shoved the embarrassing thought aside. She was only doing all this to show him that she could so be a lady. She didn't really want him. Did she?

The minute she rode up to the cabin and Shane stepped away from a tree to help her dismount, she knew the answer to her question.

She wanted him all right.

Her eyes met his, and she felt herself a-heatin' from her toes to the top of her head. Shane's hands felt so good around her waist. He held her as if she were a fine piece of fancy porcelain, and he was afraid she might break. The thought made her stomach all disquieted. Or was it the way that he was a-lookin' at her that did it?

She blinked and it seemed to break the spell that had woven itself around them. Shane lowered her to the ground, withdrawing his hands from about her waist.

He forced himself to step back away from her. If he didn't, he knew he'd pull her into his arms and kiss her until the neatly-arranged curls loosened to fall free around her shoulders. Why did a lady insist on wearing her hair bound up when it was so much more beautiful flowing freely around her shoulders?

The thought jolted him. What was he thinking? This was Rina, not a Southern lady. But somehow, looking at her, he couldn't tell the difference between her and the beautiful ladies who'd danced in his arms at the plantation balls all those years ago.

He blinked to wipe away the memories. Seeing Rina looking so pretty and dainty had nearly knocked the breath out of him. She could make him forget the job he had to do, even make him forget to breathe.

"Rina? Gal, is that you?" Pa hurried across from the cabin to where she stood next to Shane.

Pa beamed down at her. "Ain't you purty!"

He looked her up and down, then walked around her like he was checking out a new horse to buy. His scrutiny made her nervous. She half-expected him to ask her to open her mouth so he could check her teeth.

"Where'd ya go to get all purtied up like that? I knowed ya was gonna buy some dresses, but what is all this?"

Rina refused to feel embarrassed. She raised her chin and faced him down. "I visited Milly—"

"Yep, this looks like Milly's doing. Ya two done good."

Suddenly Pa turned to Shane as if he'd just remembered he was there. "Well, outlander, what do ya think of her now? Ain't she something to look at?" Pa's voice was filled with pride.

"Yes, she is," Shane spoke the words in a low voice as if he were saying the words for Rina's ears only.

"Well—" Pa coughed, then sneezed. "Whew!" He backed away from Rina and frowned. "What in blue blazes is that smelly stuff you're wearin', gal?"

He sneezed twice more and stepped farther away from Rina. Bringing out a large handkerchief, he covered his nose and mouth.

"It's Frangipani, a special perfume," Rina explained. "All the way from Philadelphia."

"Dagnamit, gal! Send the damned stuff back. It smells worse'n a bad batch of whiskey gone sour."

"Hell's bells." She planted her hands on her hips and glared at him. "Then I'll jus' go wash it off in the creek."

Rina spun on her heel and strode away, anxious to hide the tears that threatened at the edges of her eyes. She didn't know what was wrong with her—she'd never been one to cry over anything. Now that seemed to be all her eyes a-wanted to do. Darn Pa, why'd he have to go and say those things?

"I'll go on up and check on the still afterwards," she called back over her shoulder, refusing to turn around and face their laughter.

"Leastways that's something I can do right," she murmured under her breath, assuring herself that she was capable at something.

It sure seemed she wasn't any good at trying to be a fancy lady.

"Rina!" Pa hollered at her.

She ignored him, increasing her pace instead. Suddenly she was real eager to get to the creek and wash off the perfume. It wasn't her kind anyways—it belonged to people like Milly with their natural lady-like ways. And to people like Shane's fiancée.

Rina stepped back and surveyed her work in the clearing. She'd banked the fire under the big copper pot, and filled the tinder box with kindling to last them a few days. Absently, she brushed her dirty hands down the skirt of her dress.

"Oh, damn." She rubbed at the streaks of dirt spread across the purty blue flowers of her fine dress. "I can't even be a lady when I'm all by myself."

She'd really tried to stay all ladylike. But it seemed as if everything conspired against her. She tucked a loose tendril of hair behind her ear.

The purty way Milly had piled her hair on the top of her head with ribbons cascading amongst the silver curls looked mighty fine when she'd arrived home. However, after an hour of tending the still, the steam had reduced her fancy hair to a tousled mess of dangling ribbons, bedraggled curls and tangles hanging over her neck and cheeks. She paused to push the edge of a ribbon outta her eyes, and left a smudge of soot across her cheek.

The combined heat from the afternoon sun and the fire burning under the pot was too much for a body to tolerate. Rina felt like she was a-burnin' up. After first looking around and making sure no one was about, she slipped off her two petticoats, rolled them up carefully and tucked them behind a big tree. Next, she rolled down her stockings and garters and added them to the stack.

Feeling free and much cooler, she walked back to the still. She glanced back at the tree trunk, and a single white ruffle of petticoat peered around the edge of the trunk as if looking for escape. Well, let it look, she thought.

Hitching up her now too long skirt, she tied it up to one side. There, now she could move about without a-feelin' like she was about to trip over herself. She bent over the fire, adding a handful of sticks.

Shane froze at the beautiful picture before him. The glowing backdrop of the fire turned Rina's hair to a cloud of silver swirling around her. As she straightened, the fire outlined her every curve, and Shane sucked in a breath. He'd never seen a woman look more tempting and inviting in a dress than at this moment.

He hadn't meant to sneak up on her, but she'd been so lost in thought she hadn't heard his quiet steps. He gave into the urge and watched her for a few silent moments. She moved with a grace that any Southern lady would envy. As a flash of honey-tanned leg caught his eye, his loins tightened in immediate response.

"Hell's bells," he muttered under his breath, copying Rina's phrase.

He stared at the long expanse of leg revealed by her hitched-up skirts. Finally, he tore his gaze away and stepped out from the sheltering shade of the tree and approached her.

"Can you use some help?"

Rina spun around, her heart thumping in her chest at his sudden nearness. She told herself he'd startled her, but she knew the truth. The unsettled feeling a-runnin' through her had been caused by the man Shane Delaney, not by any surprise.

Tossing her beribboned hair over one shoulder, she faced him and ordered her heart to slow its pounding.

"Do you know anything 'bout running a still?" she challenged.

"No, but I can learn." He threw the challenge right back at her.

As he began unbuttoning the cuffs of his fancy, ruffled white shirt and rolling up the sleeves,

Rina coulda sworn that the fire hottened up behind her. What she wouldn't have given for a lady's fan to air herself with.

"Well, ah . . . ah," she paused to run her hand across the bodice of her dress. It was definitely getting warmer. "First, you gotta make sure that the fire hottens up jus' right."

Shane glanced to the banked fire behind her. "And then," he prompted, trying to ignore the heat he could feel building between them.

"Well, right now, all we gots to do is keep the fire burning like it is. No hotter. No cooler. 'Cause too hot will make the steam go through the coils too fast, and that'll make the whiskey too weak."

She glanced back at the still, anywhere to keep from looking at the muscles of his arms revealed by his rolled sleeves. When she turned back to Shane, she'd forgotten what she'd been going to say next.

"Where do you make the mixture?" he asked, aching to wipe the smudge of dirt from her cheek and replace it with a kiss.

It was getting harder and harder to concentrate on asking her questions about the whiskey when all he wanted to do was take her in his arms. Just looking at her with her hair tumbling down around her shoulders, and her skirt pulled up to show the most delectable legs he'd ever seen, set his blood to pounding in his veins.

"Umm, usually here by the still. But most of the fixings are kept down by the cabin." Rina stepped to the side, farther away from the fire, and her skirt revealed another inch of bare thigh.

"What fixings are those?" Shane had to force the words past the sudden constriction in his chest.

"I . . . can't tell you all of it . . . It's . . . ah . . ." The words trailed off as she noticed Shane staring at her hiked-up skirt.

Nervously, she wiped her hands down her dress. "Oh, no. I done it again." She quickly swiped at the dusty streaks along the skirt.

"Here, let me help." Shane closed the distance between them, pulled out a handkerchief, and brushed the streaks from her skirt.

His throat grew tight as he felt her firm thigh beneath his fingers. Straightening in a sudden move, he thrust the handkerchief into her hands.

"I . . . I think you'd better do that."

"What's wrong?" His quick change puzzled her.

"Rina," Shane swallowed painfully. "Where are your petticoats?"

He could have bitten his tongue as soon as the question slipped out.

"Over there." She pointed to the tree trunk with the edge of white fabric peeking out.

At Shane's startled gasp, she wrinkled up her nose. This lady thing was getting worse and worse.

"I'm afeared that I'm never gonna become a real lady," she confessed, gazing up at him, a forlorn look in her eyes.

Rina was right, Shane admitted ruefully. She'd

never be the type of lady that Mary Ellen was, where proper behavior came as naturally to her as breathing. There would always be a part of the hill country gal hidden somewhere beneath the lady's fine dresses and fixings. He knew there would always be that imp of trouble waiting for any opportunity to break free.

Knowing he should resist, but not having the power to do it, Shane lowered his head to hers. He brushed her lips lightly with his, holding back the almost overpowering urge to devour her. Drawing back, he gazed down into her questioning eyes.

"Right now, angel, I think you're perfect," he murmured against her lips.

Rina's smile of happiness was all the encouragement he needed. He caught her up in his arms and drew her close until her breasts pressed against his chest. The blush he saw steal up her cheeks caused his heart to beat even faster. This time he took her lips in a kiss strong enough to steal both their breaths away.

Drawing back to allow her to breathe and tell him "no" if she wanted, he paused. Rina tucked her hands into his hair and pulled his head back to hers. Standing on tiptoe, she placed her lips against his, then experimentally began to move her lips back and forth. As he groaned against her mouth, she increased the pressure of her own lips. The kiss deepened, threatening to sweep her away to a place she knew she'd never been before.

One of her hands slipped from his head to rest

189

on his broad shoulder. She gently touched the muscles beneath her fingers as if testing them, then dug her fingers in and clutched him tightly.

Easing her lips apart, Shane slipped his tongue between her lips. He brushed it back and forth along her lower lip, then her upper lip. She snuggled closer. Taking that for assent, he cupped her chin.

"Open your mouth, sweetheart," he whispered against her lips.

Unable to do anything but obey his request, Rina opened her mouth to his loving onslaught. As he swept his tongue along the roof of her mouth, she gasped. Before she could do more than draw in a tiny breath, he rubbed his tongue over hers.

Rina squeezed her eyes tightly closed and gave herself over to the feelings of pure pleasure that flooded through her. She clutched his shoulders with both her hands, her knees turning weak as he smoothed a hand down her side.

"Rina! Gal!" Ben Taylor bellowed from down the trail. "Are you and Shane gonna come into supper or let it get cold?"

Rina froze at the sound of her pa's voice. *Pa? Here?*

As realization of his approach penetrated her mind, she forced her languid body into action. The last thing she needed in her life was for Pa to find her all caught up in Shane Delaney's arms a-kissin' him.

Eleven

Rina's eyes snapped open, and she met Shane's equally startled gaze.

"Damn," he muttered, releasing her.

"Hell's bells," she said. Sometimes a body jus' had to swear.

"Not now, Pa," she wanted to scream. Supper could freeze for all she cared at the moment.

Instead, she released her hold on Shane's shoulders and scrambled away from him. Refusing to meet his eyes, she began smoothing her dress into place.

"Rina?" Shane whispered her name.

"Rina! Gal!" Pa yelled.

Twigs snapped, brush rustled, and the surrounding squirrels and birds scolded the intrusion as Ben Taylor stomped up the trail. He was making more noise than a mule in a tin barn.

"Over here, Pa," Rina answered.

Grabbing up her skirts, she dashed over to the still. By the time her father stomped into the clearing, she was banking the burned down embers of the fire under the big copper pot.

"Hi there, outlander. She teaching ya 'bout whiskey-making?" Ben Taylor faced Shane and waited for his answer.

Shane now knew what a thief under a spyglass felt like. He tried to avoid looking at Rina, but it seemed the harder he tried, the stronger the urge became. Finally, unable to deny himself, he glanced her way.

She was bent over the fire, poking it with a stick. Shane couldn't resist admiring her profile as well as the rest of her.

"Well?" Pa asked.

Shane turned his attention back to the older man. "Yes, sir. She's teaching me."

Rina's face flamed at the double meaning to Shane's words. She stabbed at the embers with the stick.

"Did she tell ya 'bout how we cooks it up?"

Rina stood by and half-listened as Pa explained the details of whiskey-making to Shane. Relieved that Pa seemed distracted enough by his talking with Shane not to question what they'd been doing, she let her mind wander.

Luckily Pa hadn't been exactly what one would call quiet, and they'd missed being caught. Barely. Goose flesh broke out on her arms in spite of the heat from the fire. She didn't know if it was from excitement or trepidation. If'n her pa had come sooner . . .

Goose flesh spread across her arms again at the

thought. The unspoken code of the hills woulda made Pa require nothing less than a wedding between her and Shane. *Married to Shane.*

Rina toyed with the thought. It wasn't entirely unpleasant. Matter of fact, it was mighty pleasing to think about.

She'd never been one to want to jump the broom with a fella or even much to attract one, until the handsome, smooth-talking Southerner landed in her arms.

Rina straightened and stepped away from the fire. No matter how pleasing the thought might seem, she didn't want any man for a husband who didn't want her. It'd have to be his idea—not forced upon him by her pa.

Nope, when I decides to jump the broom, it'll be in my own time and in my own way—with love. Not with the aid of Pa's shotgun.

Early the next morning, Shane borrowed a horse from Ben Taylor on the pretense of visiting Possum Hollow. Instead, after riding for a couple of miles, he drew the horse to the side of the narrow road and then turned up an overgrown trail.

It was past time to pay a visit to Nolan Gant. Shane had a bad suspicion that if he didn't give his employer a report soon that old Nolan would find a reason to seek him out. And that was the last thing that Shane wanted to happen.

He had enough problems just dealing with

Rina and his increasing desire for her. Over the last couple of days he'd found himself wanting to know more about her than about the secret recipe.

She was a beguiling mix of woman and innocent. It resulted in a potent combination, one he found himself fighting hard to resist. Everything about her was wrong for him, he reminded himself, but the reminder had been doing less and less good lately.

Ever since she'd determined to become a real lady, she'd become almost irresistible. Somehow each of her mishaps succeeded in settling her firmer in his thoughts. One thing to be said for Rina Taylor—she had a love of life that he'd never seen equalled in another woman. The man who made her his would have a lifetime full of excitement.

The thought of that unseen other man bothered Shane. No matter how hard he tried to push aside the picture of Rina held in another man's arms, that picture refused to go away.

By the time he rode within sight of Nolan Gant's one-room cabin, he was in a foul mood. Then, to top it off, a shotgun blast greeted his arrival.

"Damn you, Gant," Shane muttered.

The scruffy little man stepped away from the concealment of a tree and strode forward. He didn't speak until he drew up even with Shane.

"Ya got the recipe?"

"No—"

Nolan tapped the shotgun barrel against Shane's chest. It took all Shane's self-control not to knock the gun away and go after the man holding it.

"Then what the hell are ya doing here? I ain't giving ya no more money till I gets the Taylors' secret."

"I came to give you a report." Shane spoke the words slowly and deliberately. Steel tinged each word as he met the other man's narrowed eyes.

Nolan eased back a step and tightened his grip on the shotgun.

"I don't want no fancy excuses and reports. I wants that there recipe. Ya hear me!" he shouted, his face turning a mottled red with the effort.

Shane held his own anger in check.

"Ya gets me that recipe. And don't ya come back here again until ya do."

"I'll get it," Shane assured him. He needed the other half of his money to purchase his home.

"And you'd better make it quick. I'm runnin' outta patience. I'm thinkin' 'bout doing something 'bout it myself."

"You do that, and our deal is off." Shane's statement carried a definite threat.

"Ya jus' do what ya was hired to do, fella."

Nolan stepped back and turned on his heel. He strode off to the cabin, slamming the door behind him.

After Shane left, Nolan searched the cabin for Billy, then the surrounding outbuildings. However, Billy was nowhere to be found. No matter how loud he called, he couldn't seem to stir up his boy. Finally, he spotted him in the shadows of a cluster of trees. Leaning against a pine tree, he glared at Nolan with sad eyes.

"Billy! What the hell are you doing hiding on me like that?"

Nolan clamped his cigar tight between his teeth. His boy had given him a real scare. He'd been afeared that the boy was gone for good this time.

"No need fer ya to hide, boy. I weren't gonna make ya talk to that gamblerman. I knows ya cain't stand the sight of him."

Billy continued to meet his comments with silence. It made Nolan feel a might uneasy. He could feel the sadness in his boy.

"Now, Billy. I'm sorry 'bout that gamblerman attracting Rina so. But, I always told ya that she's no good fer us. Ya jus' never could see it. Damnation."

Nolan clamped down on what else he'd wanted to say. He didn't want to upset Billy over much, so he kept quiet about his hopes that Rina's interest in the gambler would cause Billy to look elsewhere fer a woman.

"Ah, come on, boy," Nolan wheedled. "Ya knows I ain't mad at ya. And if'n you's mad at me, well, I 'pologize fer it."

His apology seemed to work, for Billy stepped away from the tree and walked towards him.

It was all Nolan could do not to run and grab his boy in his arms, but he knew that it weren't good fer a kid to have too much love showed to 'em. It made them weak. And he had no use fer a weak youngun. So he kept his arms tight at his sides.

Everything he'd done fer Billy had been to make him a strong man. Why, that's the reason he'd insisted that Billy join up with the militia to fight the War Between the States.

Nolan flinched as a pang of conscience hit him. It felt more like he'd been stabbed. All right, he admitted grudgingly, maybe that'd only been a part of the reason. The biggest reason had been to get his boy away from Rina Taylor and her ways. And it'd worked, too.

Nolan looked at Billy and knew he was still thinking on her. Well, he'd put a stop to it.

"Ya think she'd be interested in you?" Nolan burst into harsh laughter. "Why, she's fairly throwing herself at that fancy gamblerman. She's no good fer you."

As Billy turned away, Nolan grabbed for him. "That's what she is."

Billy kept walking away.

"Jus' look at how she's treated ya."

That stopped him. Nolan grinned and waited fer Billy to turn around. Sure enough, he did.

"And I figures it's time we paid her back."

Billy stood, waiting for him to continue.

"Yup, boy, I gots a plan. We'll pay her back fer everything. Our fighting betwixt ourselves, ya going off to that war, and her going after that gamblerman instead of you. Why, she's done nothing her whole life but thumb her nose at us Gants. We'll fix her, boy. You and me together like it's supposed to be."

He seemed to have Billy's interest.

"Come on, Billy," Nolan ordered. "We got something that needs doing."

Rina found herself at a loss with Shane gone for the morning. Furious at herself for mooning over a man, she told Pa she wanted to talk to Milly.

"Ya go on and get outta here then. I'll take care of things 'round here. Ya have a good visit with Milly."

"Thank you, Pa." Impulsively, Rina hugged him tightly.

"Now, go on, gal."

Ben Taylor couldn't have been happier with the changes he'd seen in Rina lately. It sure seemed that Shane Delaney had something to do with it. But he didn't care who had caused it; he was just pleased that his daughter was finally beginning to dress like a female.

Sometimes he got to worrying that her being forsaken by her ma—he refused to say his wife's name—had scarred his daughter. But now, maybe it seemed things were gonna be fine. He smiled at Rina.

Giving her a foot up, he helped her onto her horse's back. Rina smiled back down at him and pulled her skirts into place over her knees.

"I'll likely be a couple of hours or more."

"Take your time, gal. Nothing 'round here that needs your attention today."

He grinned widely, and Rina had no doubts that he was referring to Shane not being there for the day. Refusing to rise to the bait her pa had set out for her, she waved goodbye and rode away.

Rina couldn't help her thoughts returning to Pa's words, and this brought to mind Shane Delaney. It seemed *he* was filling her thoughts more and more lately. It was definitely time for another lady lesson.

Milly met her at the door with a squeal of delight.

"I'm so glad you came. I was going to ride out to your place this afternoon."

"Is something wrong?"

"No. But since Momma was going into Blueberry Bluff yesterday afternoon, I asked her to pick up your new dresses. Come see."

Milly led her into her bedroom where she quickly laid out the packages across the bed.

"Well?"

Rina grinned. It seemed like Milly was 'bout as anxious as her to see what the wrappings held. Without wasting another second, Rina tore open the first package.

The wrappings revealed underthings. Each one in fine fabrics and trimmed with delicate lace or satin ribbons. Lastly, she pulled out an almost sheer chemise trimmed with blue silk.

Rina's eyes grew round with surprise. "I . . . I didn't order these."

"I suspected you'd forgotten the most important things, so I had Momma order them for you. Mrs. Alberts was almost beside herself what with having to do them up in such a rush."

As Rina turned to her with an open mouth, Milly added, "A body *feels* like a lady when she has something special like this next to her skin." She winked at Rina's shocked expression.

Rina ran her hand over the thin chemise. It did feel mighty ladylike. She'd never dreamed of wearing this kinda fine silks for her underthings. She returned Milly's smile.

"I see what you mean." She trailed a finger down a delicate lace ruffle.

"Come on, open another one," Milly ordered. "I swear that I'm dying to see what you ordered."

The next package held a dress the soft green color of fresh grass. Dark green velvet trimmed the bodice and short sleeves. However, it was the last package that took both their breaths away. For the layers of wrapping revealed a lovely gown of blue silk muslin, its low-cut bodice trimmed with an inset of white lace.

Milly caressed the ruffled edges with a hint of envy. "Rina, it's beautiful. Ohh, Mrs. Alberts used real French lace. Just feel it."

Rina smoothed the lace accenting the dress—her favorite one. And her only fancy gown for evening time.

Unable to resist its lure, she pulled the gown

away from the wrappings and held it up in the light. It was even purtier than the picture Mrs. Alberts had shown her in the shop.

The silk muslin fabric caught the light and seemed to reflect it, the deep rich blue almost exactly the color of Shane Delaney's eyes. She held the dress close against her body and stepped in front of Milly's mirror. The white lace trimming the low-cut bodice brought out the honey-golden tan of her skin, seeming to make her skin practically glow.

The short sleeves were puffed and trimmed with the same delicate white lace. The bodice came to a point at the waist, flaring out into a full, swaying skirt. It was a dress fit for a real lady.

"Beautiful," Rina whispered in awe. "I knows I can be a lady in this dress."

Milly hugged her and laughed. "Before we're done with you, Rina, you'll be a lady if all you have on is your drawers."

"Milly!"

"A lady isn't always perfect."

"I gots the not always perfect part down real good."

"Ah, now for your grammar," Milly announced. Rina groaned.

"First, it's *got,* not *gots.* Don't add an 's' when you don't need one."

"How'll I know when I needs one?"

"You'll learn."

Milly spent the next hour correcting and teaching. And more correcting. Rina didn't know when she'd had her words changed so much in her entire life.

"Well, I think that's enough for today," Milly finally declared.

"Thank goodness," Rina collapsed back in the chair.

"Now for your skin—"

"Again?"

"Again. Remember, a man looks at the outside first. So, let's get going."

"I think we'd better skip yer fancy perfume this time. It made Pa sneeze something fierce."

Milly busted out laughing.

Much later, as Rina mounted her horse, she felt that her outside must look mighty good. She'd been rubbed, and cleaned, and near drowned with Milly's and her momma's softening creams. Before leaving she'd changed into her new underthings and the soft green dress.

"Goodbye and good luck." Milly winked and handed the tied packages to her. "The top package has some of that cream for you to use. Don't forget it."

"Thank you, Milly."

Milly waved away her thanks. "I don't know when I've had so much fun as these past few days. Let me know what happens."

Sure to keep a good grip on her precious packages, Rina turned her horse toward home.

* * *

Shane had been watching the trail for Rina long before she rode into sight. He told himself he'd only been eyeing the trail because he was concerned with her being gone so long, and he had to get the secret of the recipe soon.

The last part was true. *His time was running out.* His brief meeting with Nolan Gant proved that the old man's patience was at the edge, and perhaps even his sanity. Shane didn't trust Nolan one bit.

"Good afternoon," Shane greeted Rina and raised his arms to help her dismount.

Rina placed her hands on his bare arms, and her fingertips almost burned at the contact. Once again, he was wearing his shirtsleeves rolled up above his elbows, and the white sleeves, tanned skin, and black pants set him off to where she had trouble breathing all of a sudden.

He held her aloft a moment, then eased her down slowly until her toes touched the ground. Rina felt trapped between the horse and Shane's body. He was much too close. It set her heart to racing away.

"That's a pretty dress, Rina." His voice was low and husky to her ears.

"It's new," she blurted out without thinking, then wanted to bite the words back. Instead, she lowered her gaze to the ground.

"Walk with me?" Shane asked. He placed a finger beneath her chin and tilted her head up to meet his questioning gaze.

"Uum-huh."

Rina couldn't have said "no" even if'n she'd wanted to. He held out his hand to her, and Rina laid hers in his open palm. He closed his fingers tight around her hand as if he'd been afraid she'd been going to remove it.

After a few minutes of walking, Rina asked, "Where are we going? The still's that way."

She pointed over her shoulder and to the right, but Shane kept walking in the direction he'd started.

"We're not going to the still. There's something I want to show you."

Rina frowned at him. Something he wanted to show her? Nobody knew these woods better'n she did. There weren't nothing off this way except trees and grass and more trees.

When they came to a log blocking the path, Shane climbed over it, then reached back for Rina. Before she could move to scramble over the log, he swept her up into his arms and lifted her across the barrier.

Slowly, ever so slowly, he eased her down along his body, lowering her until her feet just touched the ground.

Rina's breath left her in the rush of a whispered, "Oh."

Shane smiled at her. Raising a hand to her cheek, he brushed his knuckles back and forth across her skin in a feathery-light caress. It reminded her of a butterfly landing in the summer—all gently and kinda tickling. Any possible laughter died away as she stared into his gaze.

His eyes had darkened. There was longing and a forbidden wanting in his depths. It drew her with a fierceness that left her wondering.

Her skin tingled under his light touch, and a sigh escaped her now parted lips. Shane's touch was gentle for such a strong man, yet she could feel an undeniable strength held back.

He cupped her chin, drawing her to him. Rina could feel the distance between them dissolving as if it had never been there. With an almost agonizing slowness, he finally leaned closer, his breath fanning her face.

"Tell me no if you want me to stop." His low words were spoken in a ragged voice that tore at her. He pressed her up against the broad tree trunk.

Rina could have easier stopped breathing than to have denied him.

"Yes," she whispered.

Shane slid his other arm around her and pulled her to him. She couldn't have resisted if she wanted, but resisting was the furthest thing from her mind at the moment. She waited.

He leaned forward, and she felt a faint rasp of whisker that teased her chin. Not at all unpleasant. She recalled the feel of his cheek against hers the day he'd saved her life. It had been pleasant then, too.

Slowly he rubbed his chin against her cheek, then along her cheekbone and down to her jaw. Rina almost squirmed against him. Damn, he could be the slowest man when he wanted to be. It 'bout drove her crazy.

Shane turned his head, trapping her lips with his. She surrendered willingly to the warmth of his kiss. He kissed her tenderly, wantingly, thoroughly.

A wonderful sensation like standing close up next to a roaring fire in winter swept over her. She absorbed the heat like a cat seeking the sunshine on a windowsill, and found herself kneading his shoulders with her fingers just like a cat did when it was happy.

The muscles of his back rippled and flexed beneath her fingertips. Following an instinct too strong to deny, she clung tighter. Waiting, holding tightly to the corded strength beneath her hands. Waiting for what she didn't know and didn't care.

She returned his kiss, forgetting to breathe or even so much as think. The power of his embrace thrilled her, aroused her, as she hadn't thought possible for a body to feel.

Without breaking off the kiss, Shane swung her up into his arms and carried her to a nearby field of wildflowers.

"This is what I wanted to show you," he whispered, then raised his head.

Rina tore her gaze away from his. Around them, the blooms of yellow, white, and blue bobbed in the sunlight. He lowered her to the soft cushion of leaves and flowers.

"Ah, Rina."

His velvety whisper caused gooseflesh to break out and run along her arms. Tiny accompanying shivers started deep in her stomach as he dropped to his knees beside her and trailed a finger along her cheek.

Rina caught his hand close, running her own hand up his forearm to where the roll of his shirt-sleeves stopped her. He lowered his body over hers, and Rina gasped at the intimacy, but he swallowed the sound with his next kiss. He ran his hands down her sides, molding her body to his.

Shane supported his weight with his elbows, afraid of crushing her, so strong was his desire. It raged and burned in him, threatening to consume them both. He'd never felt anything so powerful in his life.

In an attempt to regain some sense of self-control, he shifted his weight to the side and splayed his fingers through her hair. The silver strands shimmered to life, the curls springing around his hand, catching along his fingertips, almost caressing him in return.

With a groan, he surrendered. Running his hands down her ribs, he smoothed and caressed the body beneath his fingers. She moved, snuggling beneath him and making him think of warm liquid honey. The green dress set off the golden tan of her shoulders, and once again he wondered if her skin was that same honey-tanned all over. His very blood heated in response to the image it brought to his mind.

He drew in a ragged breath. The thought of

her tan all over reminded him of her innocence. Forcing himself almost beyond the point of endurance, he released her, intending to draw away. But Rina caught his shoulder and drew him back down to her. Raising her head, she nibbled at his lower lip.

It was more than he could stand. Shane groaned and closed his eyes, shuddering.

"Angel, I should stop," he groaned against her cheek, his voice ragged with emotion and desire. "But please don't ask me to."

His request washed aside all hesitation. She could no more have asked him that than she could have stopped the blood from flowing through her own veins or stopped her heart from beating.

Rina drew his head back down to hers, giving, taking, asking for more. She met him kiss for kiss and touch for touch.

Shane drew her up into his arms, lifting her slightly from the carpet of flowers. He cradled her in his embrace, raining kisses along her neck, pausing a second to drag in a shuddering breath as the sweet, familiar scent of her enveloped him, almost taking him beyond the point of no return. He laved kisses along her collarbone and lower to the edge of her low-cut bodice.

His fingers worked at the fastening of her dress until he felt it give way beneath his hands. He drew the top down to reveal her lace-covered breasts. Pausing to brush kisses across the lacy chemise, he drew her petticoats off and tossed them onto the wildflowers. When she didn't deter him, her dress and chemise joined them.

Rina felt as if her body had erupted into flames. Wherever Shane touched, the embers stirred into life. She'd never felt so alive before. As he eased away and began to undress, she watched in fascination.

He stood and stripped the clothing from his body. Seconds later, they joined her petticoats on the carpet of brilliant flowers. Magnificent, she thought.

"Rina, my love," he whispered, gazing down at her.

She swore his very heart could be seen in his eyes. She knew hers could. *This must be what love felt like.*

When he returned to her, he lowered his body over hers, easing his weight onto her gradually. Rina welcomed the weight and firmness of him, pulling him closer. She clenched her hands over his shoulders and reveled in the strength of the corded muscles beneath her touch.

Shane tasted her mouth, his plundering hers, devouring her, stealing her very breath away. At the same time, his hands roamed downward gently along her neck to her shoulders, ever down. He stroked her bare breasts, cupping first one in his palms and then the other. Ending the kiss that had her melting into him, he slowly lowered his mouth to her breasts ripeness and drew the tip of one between his lips.

Rina cried out and arched against him, whimpering her need for more of him. She gave freely of herself, her touch becoming bold in return as she brought her hands around to his stomach and then followed his tight muscles downward. She delighted in the feel of his firm skin beneath her fingertips.

Shane groaned aloud and buried his face in her neck. He drew back, gazed down at her with love, then took her lips in a kiss that stopped time.

He eased his legs between hers and gently, slowly entered her. A sharp pain caused her to cry out, but he kissed away her cry. The kiss deepened, and little by little the pain dissolved in the heat of his loving. As she gasped, his murmured endearments filled her ears and soon mingled with her own sighs of pleasure.

He loved her body thoroughly, passionately and completely. When she thought she'd surely die from the sheer pleasure of the release sweeping them, she arched upward, tightened her arms around his neck and cried out his name.

Shane captured the sound, drawing it to him as she knew he'd drawn her very being to him. She no longer belonged to herself. She was his body and soul.

Shane gathered her close, enveloping her in his embrace. Rina had never felt so loved, and safe, and protected before in her life.

Held close to him, she could feel the pounding of his heart under her palm. She snuggled nearer, and gradually their heartbeats slowed, their rhythms matching in a cadence older than time.

This must be what love felt like, Rina thought drowsily, then let her now heavy eyelids flutter closed.

"Angel."

Shane's whispered endearment stirred the fine hairs beside her ear, tickling. Rina tucked her head sideways, nestling under his chin.

"Angel?"

He drew back from her slowly. It was as if he didn't want the new bond between them to be broken either. She knew jus' how he felt.

Rina reached out for him, but Shane dodged her hands with a low chuckle.

"Why?" she asked, smiling up at him.

" 'Cause, Angel, if you so much as lay a pretty finger on me, we'll be here in this meadow all night long."

Rina cocked her head and looked up at him as if pondering the thought.

Shane's rich laughter stroked her, like a hand sliding down her arm.

He leaned forward and dropped a light kiss on her lips, then stood to his feet, and gathered up their clothing from among the wildflowers. Rina's soft laughter followed his movements until he turned and came to her side. Slowly, tantalizing her, he handed Rina her clothes one piece at a time. First one stocking, then the second stocking, her chemise, petticoats, and lastly her dress. Blushing, she lowered her gaze from the blatant heat in his and slipped into her clothes.

As she reached back to fasten her dress, Shane's

hands were there ahead of her. He fastened her gown, then placed a lingering kiss on the nape of her neck.

Turning her within his arms, he draped an arm across her shoulders and headed reluctantly for the cabin. Rina leaned against him, enjoying the leisurely walk.

The even sway of Rina's hips against his teased Shane almost beyond endurance. He wanted to make her his again with a need that surprised him. Never before had a woman affected him the way Rina did. Overwhelming desire and a strange sense of protectiveness clashed within him. Being so near her was both pleasure and pain combined, and their walk to the cabin ended too soon for Shane.

As the cabin came into view, Shane thought of Ben Taylor, and instinctively he tightened his hold on Rina's shoulder, drawing her more snugly into his protective embrace.

When they entered the cabin, it was empty. Shane glanced around the area in concern. To his way of thinking, Rina was left alone entirely too much.

"Pa must be up at the still," Rina explained her father's absence, then slipped one hand up to hide a yawn.

Staring down at her, Shane caught the action immediately. "Come on, angel, it's time for bed."

Rina blushed at his words, and she stammered, "I'm sorry. I don't know why I'm so tired."

Grinning, Shane dropped a quick kiss on her lips.

"Never mind. Let's put you to bed. Alone," he added, loving the way the blush crept across her face.

Before she could protest, he swept her up into his arms and strode into her bedroom. Her soft giggle of surprise warmed the skin of his neck. He eased her to her feet beside the bed, and turning her back to him, he made short work of unfastening her gown. He knew better than to linger in the room with her a moment longer than necessary, but he couldn't resist the urge to see her safely in her bed.

As the dress fell to a pool at her feet, his throat tightened, and he found it hard to swallow. When she slipped her petticoats down her legs, the constriction in his throat worsened.

Shane cleared his throat and attempted to fix his gaze on the opposite wall. A second later, his eyes returned to Rina. She was a vision of loveliness—an enticing blend of innocent and seductress.

"I, ah, I think that's probably enough," he cleared his throat again, trying to loosen the tightness.

He reached down and pulled back the coverlet. He ached to take her in his arms again, but knew it was too soon for her. And probably way too late for him. Rina Taylor had a hold on him that wasn't likely to loosen anytime soon. He watched her climb into the bed, then he drew the cover

over her, shutting out the tantalizing view of long silken legs, but the temptation remained. And Shane knew that he would be getting little sleep himself that night.

Rina sighed and her eyes drifted closed. She struggled to stay awake, but lost.

"I love you." Rina didn't know if she said the words aloud or not as she snuggled into the mattress and drifted off to sleep.

Shane looked down at Rina, and a feeling of tenderness such as he'd never felt before swept over him. It wrapped itself around him, ensnaring him as surely as a metal trap would do, but this trap was made of gentleness, and warmth, and loving.

For a long moment it even blotted out his compelling need to own Belle Rive once again. The past and the present blurred together into one precious moment of caring.

Shane reached out a hand and brushed aside a wayward silver curl from Rina's silken cheek. Although his touch was feather soft, she stirred beneath the warmth of his hand, turning toward him.

Curled on her side, she sighed in her sleep, and her moist parted lips offered a temptation he could not resist. Bending lower, Shane pressed his lips against hers in a mere breath of a kiss.

Straightening, he trailed his finger down her cheek, before he turned and headed for the next room and his own empty bed.

* * *

The next morning Shane listened for the first sounds of Rina stirring around in her room. Sitting at the kitchen table, he nursed a cup of cooled coffee. He'd spent half the night enthralled with the memory of their lovemaking, and the other half calling himself every kind of cad imaginable. What he'd done couldn't be excused. Or denied.

He'd stolen Rina's innocence and had nothing to give in return. He could not return to New Orleans with her as his bride. Now he had to choose between his long-held dream of owning Belle Rive once again and Rina Taylor.

As much as he hated himself for it, he knew his choice had been made years ago. He'd promised his parents upon their graves that he'd buy back the home. He couldn't do otherwise now.

Rina's entry into the kitchen brought his thoughts to a halt. She saw him, then quickly glanced away. A light blush stained her cheeks.

"Good morning," he called out.

"Mornin'," she said softly.

A sudden attack of conscience hit him, and Shane felt as if he'd been stabbed. Reminding himself that this was the best thing he could do for her, he steeled himself to be reasonable and do what had to be done. For Rina's sake.

"Rina, we need to talk."

Her eyes met his then, startled but with a smile in their depths.

"Rina, I apologize for taking advantage of you yesterday."

His softly spoken statement cut her to the quick. For an instant she crumpled, then stiffened her spine and faced him.

"You're sorry?" she asked in disbelief.

How could he be sorry when it had been the most wonderful moment of her life? She'd felt as if she'd been waiting many years for him. And he was apologizing now?

"Rina, I had no right. I know I can't make it up to you, but I won't touch you again."

"I wasn't a-tryin' to pin you down." Rina raised her chin and wondered if he could feel her anger and if it was burning him the way it was her.

"I've told you I have to buy back my home. And I have someone waiting for me. I . . . augh."

Shane groaned and clutched his stomach, but Rina ignored him.

"You son of a bitch."

She spun on her heel and left him clutching the oak table. For all she cared, he could double over with his pains.

Twelve

"That low-down, sneaking polecat."

Rina hurled a fist-sized rock and watched it hit the center of a pine tree. The rock bounced off into the surrounding brush.

"That low-bellied snake."

She scooped up a stick and threw it with all her might at the same pine tree. As it hit, the stick snapped into two pieces, each flying through the air in opposite directions.

"Damn outlander."

Grabbing up the next thing she saw, which happened to be a pine cone, she flung it as far as she could, drawing satisfaction in seeing it splinter into pieces when it hit a large rock.

"Sweet-talking liar," she yelled.

For every insult she hurled at the absent Shane, she found something else to chuck across the clearing. After nearly five minutes, she'd ran out of ammunition to throw, and had managed to just about use up her last insulting name.

"Hell's bells," she ended her tirade.

She didn't care a hate. She didn't, she told herself repeatedly.

She'd be damned sure Shane Delaney never touched her again!

With the back of her hand, she wiped the unexpected wetness from her cheeks. She hadn't even realized she'd been crying. The anger had drowned out the hurt, but now that her anger was spent, the hurting returned full force with an intensity that surprised her.

Rina hadn't knowed that a body could hurt this bad without having something bleeding. She wrapped her arms around her waist, hugging herself tightly, as if by doing so she could stop the pain. She felt like she was breaking into pieces inside.

The only time in her life she'd come near to hurtin' this bad had been after her ma disappeared. Rina recalled clearly the night a couple of years later when she'd been a-cryin' for her ma, but she didn't come. Instead Pa came into Rina and Lucas's room. She still remembered that he'd looked different somehow. Now she knew it was because the light in his life had gone away—ran away from them.

He'd explained in slow words that his small children could understand that their ma had gone away to visit a friend. And he'd asked Rina and Lucas not to mention Ma again. It wasn't until years later when Rina was old enough to understand the gossip overheard from Miss Hattie and

Mrs. Sally Sheridan that she realized that her ma's "friend" had been another man.

At first, Rina had blamed herself, wondering what she'd done to make her ma so mad that she'd leave them. Later came the wondering why her ma hadn't loved her enough to stay. And now it seemed that Shane didn't love her enough to stay either.

She had no one to lay the blame on but herself. Hadn't she knowed better than to trust a sweet-talking stranger? Hadn't her ma running off with a smooth-talking man, while she was jus' a youngun, taught her anything? It seemed it hadn't.

Shane hadn't forced her. What she'd given, she'd done willingly and with love. She sniffled back her tears, despising the weakness they showed. She wouldn't let him do this to her. She wouldn't let any man reduce her to a simpering mess.

Biting her lip to force the tears away, she remembered the last look she'd had of Shane Delaney. He'd been the one hurting then. Why, he'd been a-clutchin' the edge of the table, his knuckles white. He'd practically doubled over with . . .

With a stomach ache!

Rina's mouth dropped open at the realization. *He'd had a stomach ache.*

Ida's potion was a-workin' on him. He hadn't been telling her true when he'd said he was gonna marry his lady back in New Orleans.

He'd been lying!

A smile tipped the corners of her mouth, and

her tears dried up. Whether the man knew it or not, he wasn't so all-fired set on marrying his southern lady anymore. His stomach ache proved it.

Rina knew the cure for his stomach problems. All he had to do was to start a-tellin' the truth. To himself first of all.

She smiled at her newfound discovery. As soon as Shane Delaney admitted to himself that he cared for her more than jus' a little, his stomach would settle down jus' fine as could be.

Suddenly the day seemed brighter. Matter of fact, it was a beautiful day for a walk.

As she stepped forward, her left stocking slipped down. Without thinking, she hiked up her skirt and pulled her stocking up into place, securing it with the frilly matching white garter.

A girl's shoe comin' untied or her stocking comin' down means her fella is thinking of her.

The old saying of Ida's quickly sprang to mind. A slow smile crept across Rina's face. Ida's sayings were always the truth; everybody in the hills said so. Especially Ida herself.

Rina sure hoped Shane Delaney was a-thinkin' of her right now. If'n she had her way, he'd be a-thinkin' of her a whole heap in the days ahead.

What she needed now was another lady treatment of creams and such that Milly had taught her to use to soften her skin and make her hair shine. It jus' happened that Milly had sent a package of them home with her, along with the new clothes, and they were a-layin' on her bed right now.

Rina smiled to herself. She had a surprise in store for Shane Delaney.

He was running out of time. His meeting with Nolan Gant told him that, Shane thought in disgust. Today his argument and the break with Rina had reinforced that feeling. It was past time for him to return to New Orleans, but first he needed the whiskey recipe to sell to Nolan Gant.

Damn.

Shane prowled the cabin restlessly. The silence in the small cabin was unsettling. After Rina had run off in anger, Ben Taylor had strolled into the cabin, muttering something about women and new dresses. Then, the old man had sauntered off for the clearing to tend the whiskey still.

Shane drew out his watch and checked the time. By his watch, Ben had left about ten minutes ago. He paused to peer out the window, then absently replaced his watch. No one in sight.

Now was as good an opportunity as any to check the cabin over again for the Taylors' special ingredient to their whiskey.

If he ever hoped to regain Belle Rive, he needed that recipe and the money it would bring him. His subtle questioning of Rina and her pa hadn't gotten him any closer to the answer.

Not that Shane had expected either of them to blurt out the secret, but he'd at least anticipated obtaining a clue or two from them. Instead, it seemed he'd been blocked in his quest at every turn. His growing desire for Rina and the ultimate consummation of that desire had only made matters worse.

Now that he'd tasted her sweetness, his desire for her had even increased, threatening to consume him. This morning all he'd wanted to do was to take her in his arms and make love to her again. It had taken every vestige of his self-control to resist her lure, and to quell his desire.

Shane hated himself for the things he'd said to her this morning, but the words had to be said. He could not—would not—allow himself to deceive her about their chance of a future together here. His conscience nagged him, arguing that he'd already deceived her with his presence here in the hills.

All right, he conceded, but he would not deceive her further about their love. He couldn't. His future was in New Orleans. He planned to marry his former fiancée Mary Ellen and buy back Belle Rive.

Unexpectedly, a dull pain creased his stomach, leaving behind a burning sensation. Absently, he rubbed a hand across the now-burning pit in his stomach.

With Nolan getting antsy, Shane was rapidly running out of time. That must be the reason behind the sudden stomach pains, he reasoned, explaining away the unfamiliar feeling in his body. *That had to be it.*

Satisfied, Shane spun on his heel and strode across the cabin with determined steps to Rina's bedroom. This time he'd search her room thoroughly.

As soon as he stepped inside the bedroom, the scent of lilacs assailed him. It seemed as if her very essence mocked him, dared him to deny the hold she was acquiring upon him.

He stared at the bed's white coverlet with its tiny clusters of purple blossoms. Rina's bed. He remembered the feel of her in his arms when he'd put her to bed last night. Remembered how badly he'd wanted to join her in that tempting feather bed. Damn, the little minx was getting a real hold on him.

It recalled their loving yesterday. The memory of her exquisite body surrounded by the wildflowers tormented him. She had been so beautiful. So loving. What they'd shared had been . . .

Had been a mistake, he told himself.

He tried to push aside the picture of Rina with her lips swollen from his kisses by recalling Mary Ellen's face instead, and failed. Remember Belle Rive and Mary Ellen Dupre, he told himself. But instead his former fiancée's face became harder and harder to recall to his mind. It seemed that whenever he closed his eyes, all he could envision was Rina.

Unable to stand the bedroom with its constant reminders of Rina, he turned away and headed for the kitchen. That room was more likely to hold some clues to the whiskey's secret. And less likely to hold memories of Rina, he assured himself.

She didn't exactly have what one could call a natural talent for the cooking and baking usually associated with the kitchen. He should be able to escape her memories there.

Shane learned that he was wrong. The kitchen did indeed hold memories of Rina. They rushed back, hitting him with the force of a flood. The recollection of the evening her too-tight yellow dress had ripped, exposing her womanly charms to his gaze, taunted him.

The room especially brought back the remembrance of the evening she'd tripped and landed right in his lap. A smile curled his lips as he savored that particular tantalizing memory and the pleasant feel of her feminine curves against him.

Realizing where his thoughts were leading, Shane shoved them aside and tried to concentrate on finding the whiskey "fixings" Rina had spoken about.

Twenty minutes later he was no closer to knowing the secret of the Taylor whiskey than when he'd started his search of the kitchen. By smell and very cautious tasting, he had managed to identify the majority of the contents of the jars.

Lemon peel, a fragrant mint, blackberry—he recalled the different jars he'd opened. He didn't remember tasting any of those flavors in the Taylor whiskey. Unless they all mixed together to form a potent blend that was indistinguishable.

While reaching for a dark jar at the back of a

shelf, he thought he heard the soft murmur of movement. Freezing, he held his breath and listened. Nothing stirred around him; everything remained as quiet as before. Shrugging off his nervousness, he stretched out his arm for the jar once again.

"Jus' what in blue blazes do you think you're doing?" Rina's challenge caught him unawares.

Shane snapped his head up and cracked it on the wood shelf above. "Damnation, woman."

He'd been sneaked up on more times since he'd met Rina Taylor than in all the years of his life before that. Until now he'd always prided himself on his alertness. What was happening to him?

"Well?" she demanded.

He eased his head out more carefully this time and, turning around, he looked up at her.

She was the picture of indignation. Arms crossed over her chest, chin lowered in disapproval, and her eyes glaring at him in anger.

"I asked jus' what the hell you think you're a-doin' poking around where you don't have any business?"

Rina uncrossed her arms and planted her fists on her hips. Without giving him a chance to respond, she continued, "The very minute a body goes off and leaves you here by yourself, they comes home and finds you nosing around."

"I wasn't 'nosing around'," Shane denied, shutting his mouth on the lie.

"Then what do you call it?"

"I was looking for something for a stomach ache," he answered back.

As the lie rolled off his tongue with ease, a pain cramped his stomach almost as if his body was trying to assure her that he was telling the truth. Guilt hit him at the same time as a second unexplained pain had him grabbing for his middle.

Try telling the truth, Rina thought, then quickly clamped her mouth closed on the words before they could slip out. It wouldn't do to let on that she had any knowledge of the reasons behind his stomach problems.

Shane rubbed his hand back and forth across his waist.

Biting the corner of her mouth to keep from smiling, Rina tried her best to look sorrowful.

"I'm sorry your stomach is a-hurtin' you," she said to him, blinking her eyes with feigned innocence. "Is there anything I can do to help?"

"Do you have anything in there," Shane paused and pointed toward the shelves, "to ease my stomach? And while you're at it, maybe you could find something for a headache, too? I seem to be developing one."

Rina clamped her lips tightly together to hold back her smile. He looked so pained. And he deserved every second of his misery.

"Here, let me check and see what I've got fer you," she offered.

If'n she'd taken any of Ida's potion, she knew for a fact that her own stomach would be a-hurtin' right now as she pretended to be full of concern instead of laughing at him.

Rina pulled out a chair and gestured for Shane to be seated, then she made a grand showing of looking through the jars. She could feel the heat of his gaze practically boring through her back, and she forced herself to remain calm under his scrutiny.

Weren't nothing going to help his stomach problems but telling the truth. Rina bit the corner of her mouth again to keep from speaking out loud. She sent up a silent, but heartfelt thank you to Ida and her potions.

"Well? Have you found anything yet?" Shane asked.

Rina heard him shoving back the chair and tensed as he drew closer to her. She'd a-knowed that he was nearing without hearing him. It seemed as if her body hummed like the feeling a body got when a lightning storm was drawing too close to where they was standing.

"Nope," she answered quickly.

She knew nothing she gave him would counteract Ida's potion. Besides which, she didn't want to change the effect of the well-working potion. It was doing jus' fine on its own. She dusted off her hands and quickly stood to her feet.

Her sudden action put her directly in Shane's path. He stopped just short of bumping into her and caught her shoulders with his hands. Rina coulda sworn that somewhere nearby lightning had struck out of a clear blue sky, 'cause that's jus' what she felt like had happened to her body where he held her tight. And it seemed as if'n a voice inside her head told her to step into his arms.

Shane's hands were warm and firm on her shoulders. Without thinking of the consequences, Rina gave into the overwhelming temptation a-whisperin' in her brain and leaned closer to him. She met his darkened gaze a moment before he stilled his features and a tortured look came to his eyes, replacing the hot desire she knew she'd seen there just moments before.

The next instant, Shane dropped his hands from Rina's shoulders and stepped back suddenly as if he didn't trust himself this close to her. The thought pleased Rina a whole heap.

"Rina," Shane began, then paused to rub his hand through the thick hair at the nape of his neck. "About what I said this morning—"

"I don't think we should talk 'bout it right now," Rina advised in a low voice.

"But—"

She stopped him with an outstretched hand against his chest. The skin seemed to fairly burn her fingertips. "Talking right now might cause your stomach to start a-hurtin' again."

It took all the restraint she could muster to hold back her smile. She knew for a fact that if'n he started up again 'bout his "fine lady" he was a-gonna marry, his stomach would hurt. 'Cause if'n Ida's potion didn't do the job, why she'd punch him right there in his stomach herself.

"Maybe you should take it easy fer awhile," she suggested.

And maybe she'd best get away from him for awhile too, Rina told herself. Now was a right good time to go fetch Milly's creams. This seemed the perfect time for a lady treatment—away from the cabin and the temptation of Shane Delaney.

While she had control of herself, she stepped away from Shane and headed for her bedroom. Quickly she gathered up Milly's package of creams and returned to the door, but Shane was waiting for her.

"Rina—"

"Not now, outlander. Not now," she warned.

Her fingers still tingled from touching his chest, and she had an overwhelming urge to touch him again. She had to get outta the cabin. And away from him.

"Where are you going?" Shane demanded. This time his voice was firm and brooked no denial.

"If'n it's any of your business, which it isn't," she tossed over her shoulder as she walked through the doorway, "I'm going to the creek for awhile. Alone."

She slammed the door and ran off before he could add anything.

Nolan paced back and forth across the dirty cabin floor. He hadn't trusted that damned Delaney when he first heard of him, but he'd hired him anyways. Now he trusted him even less. He feared the gamblerman was going soft on him. Maybe Delaney'd even become smitten with Rina Taylor himself.

Anger at the thought burned through him, and his footsteps grew into loud stomps of suppressed fury. The woman had no shame. She'd tricked his boy Billy, making him want her so bad that he even fought with his own kin 'bout her. Then she claimed that she'd never encouraged the boy, claimed she'd never even think 'bout marrying him. Well, she wouldn't get away with her lying ways. He'd stop her.

Nolan had seen the way Billy was getting lately. He was quieter, and disappeared more often. Yep, the boy was surely mooning over her again. Something had to be done 'bout it.

The more he paced back and forth across the dirt floor, the more he thought on a new plan to rid himself of his problems. This time fer good.

Once he had it all thought out, Nolan stomped outside and yelled for Billy. It took some doing, but he finally found him sitting under a shady pine tree, plucking at a pine cone. It brought to mind how Billy used to do this same thing before he went off to fight in the war.

"Glad I found ya, boy. Listen to what I got thought out."

Nolan didn't waste any time in sharing his distrust and suspicions about Delaney and Rina with Billy. However, as he outlined the specifics of his new plan to his boy, he could feel Billy's hesitation and disapproval.

When Nolan glanced over at him, he could see Billy's lips turned down in a frown.

"Now, Billy. I jus' aims to scare her a little. Won't any real harm come to her," Nolan lied.

He knew better than to reveal his entire plan to his boy. He shifted back and forward on his heels. As he waited for an answer, he could feel Billy slipping away from him.

"Dammit, boy. You're either with me or again' me. Which will it be?"

Nolan stood tense, waiting for an answer to his ultimatum. If'n he had his way, Rina Taylor wouldn't be comin' betwixt him and his boy again.

"Well?" Nolan demanded, running out of patience.

Silence.

He clamped down on his cigar and strode away. Surely Billy would follow him, wouldn't he?

Straining to hear, Nolan listened for any sound to show that Billy was following him. Behind him, a twig snapped. There it was. Billy had made up his mind; he was coming along.

Relief weakened Nolan's old stiff knees for a moment, and he almost stumbled. He hadn't been sure that Billy would give in and join him, or if'n he'd lost his boy fer sure this time.

For the next half hour, Nolan led the way through the woods without talking. When he stopped, he heard his boy's heavy footsteps behind him. A bevy of quail took off in sudden flight.

"Shh," Nolan hissed. "Quiet, Billy. I never knowed a body could make so much dang noise. Now shush!"

He threw a quick look around, afeared that the clamor had given them away, but nothing else stirred. It seemed that most of the squirrels and birds had taken flight at the first disturbance in the woods. Now, once again, all was silent in the wooded area around them.

Motioning for Billy to follow, he led the way to the beaver dam that had been there for as long as anyone could remember. Nolan quickly set to work. He did all the working while feeling Billy's sullen disapproval. Well, he guessed it was enough to hope fer that the boy had at least accompanied him. He couldn't really expect Billy to knowingly help him kill her.

Thoughts of Shane stayed with Rina most persistently, and she was glad when she reached the creek. The water flowed crystal-clear, thanks mostly to the beaver dam built high above. It managed to filter the water that flowed into the creek, keeping out the debris.

Slipping off her shoes, garters and stockings, Rina tested the water with one toe. Her breath whistled through her teeth. She'd been warmed by the sun and her walk, so that now the creek water seemed almost as cold as it was clear.

She repressed a shiver, refusing to think of the coldness of the water, instead thinking on the way her hair would shine after she used Milly's special rinses on it. A little dip in the cool water would be worth it.

Rina undressed without fear, laying her clothes across a large rock well out of the reach of the water's edge. She had no reason to be afeared. No one ever bothered this area of the creek. It was safely entrenched on Taylor land. For years nobody else ever made use of the clear water but her and her pa. Everybody knowed that trespassers met with the wrong end of a shotgun in these parts.

Leaving on her thin chemise, she caught up her bar of lilac-scented soap and crossed to the creek. Tensing her body for the water's coldness, she waded out into the creek. When the level of the water reached her breasts, she caught up a breath and dove under. Surfacing, she shoved her dripping hair out of her eyes and shrieked with delight. A bath in the creek invigorated a body, leastways that's what Pa always said.

She was inclined to agree with him. The refreshing water, the warmth of the sun overhead, and the thought that Shane might be beginning to care 'bout her made the day near perfect. Laughing, she waded out to the center of the creek.

She ran the soap over her arms and neck, pausing to inhale the scent she loved. The purty soap had been a birthday gift from Lucas last May. Actually, he'd bought her a whole fancy box of the scented soap. She ducked under the water, rinsing herself.

As she surfaced, a roaring sound filled her ears. Rina swept back her thick hair behind her ears and listened, trying to identify the out-of-place sound. Before she could tell what it was, the noise grew louder.

Suddenly a blue jay in a nearby tree flew off with a shrill squawk. Other birds followed, their cries alerting anyone around to danger. Rina jerked, looking around her, and fear pulled at her senses. Something was very wrong.

All about her the water began to move. In seconds the current intensified, tugging at her. She turned around to head to the shore and noticed the water was almost to her chin now, and rising. She dropped the soap, letting it be swept away. One thought controlled her—she had to get to shore. But it was too late.

Before she'd gone more than a few steps, the water around her erupted into fierce movement. The crystal clear water turned muddy as leaves, twigs and tree branches swirled by her. Within seconds, the creek became a churning cauldron with her caught right in the center.

Rina spun around, losing her balance in the force, and a wave of muddied debris-filled water caught her up. It swept her along with it downstream. Behind it, more water surged powerfully along.

God, help me, she prayed. *The dam had given way!*

The swirling mass of water raised higher and higher, making it impossible for her to stand upright. As much as she tried to stand, her toes could no longer touch the bottom. As her toes scraped a rock, another blast of water sent her tumbling head first.

Sputtering, she clawed her way to the surface and struck out for the nearest bank. For every stroke she took, the creek bank seemed to withdraw the same distance away from her. The ever-strengthening force of the surging waters wiped away any chance she had of being able to swim to the bank.

A tree branch crashed past her, banging into her shoulder. She cried out in pain, and the water swept over her head. Surfacing, she struggled to stay afloat in the reeling mass of ever-deepening water around her. The creek bank grew farther and farther away.

She screamed, then went under again. This time it was harder to break to the surface. Water swirled all around her.

As she came up, she coughed and desperately sucked in air for her starved lungs. A log swept by, and she grabbed for it, but the wood whipped past, just out of reach. She screamed again, heedless that anyone would hear her cries for help.

She wouldn't give up, and she wouldn't die without a fight. She kicked out and pushed herself toward the floating log. Reaching her hand toward it, her fingertips grazed the edge of the wood, but it bounced away.

Again, she told herself, try again. As she reached out, a wave of water washed over her.

Rina thought she heard the high-pitched cackle of crazed laughter, then the deep, muddy water closed over her head. She tried to fight against it, but the rushing currents were too strong.

She flailed with her arms, trying to break free of the flood waters. But it was no use; the swirling eddy pulled her down. Down . . .

Thirteen

Shane stood inside the cabin doorway, listening, waiting for what he didn't know. The sure knowledge of an unknown danger taunted him, pulling at him. If only he could place which direction it came from. He stepped outside into the sunlight.

Rina came to mind, and his breath caught rock hard in his chest.

He hadn't been able to drive her from his thoughts since she'd left the cabin much earlier. He glanced around him, suddenly uneasy at how long she'd been gone.

It seemed as if the hills themselves gave off the feeling of holding their breath. Without knowing how he knew, he felt that Rina was in trouble.

Taking off in the direction of the Taylor creek where he'd last known she was headed, he prayed fervently that he was wrong. Or that if he was right, that he'd be in time.

Suddenly, from a distance, a scream for help

ripped through the cloying quiet around him. At the sound of the scream, Shane's blood chilled in his veins. *Rina!*

Bursting into a run, he raced up the trail. *Please, God, let me be in time.*

As he neared the creek, he thought he heard another cry for help, but an unmistakable rushing noise soon covered any further screams he might have heard. He recognized the sound of raging flood waters.

"No!" he cried out.

Let me wrong, please.

He tore through the surrounding brush, frantic to get to Rina. Terror of what he'd find drove him on, pushing him.

Shane rounded the bend and stopped in shock at his first sight of the waters rising over the usually dry, dusty trail. It was worse than he'd feared.

His mouth felt like cotton as he frantically searched the turbulent waters for a sign of Rina. His beloved Rina. No, he wanted to deny, surely she couldn't be in the midst of that.

For an instant, he thought hopefully that perhaps she'd already left the creek or might have changed her mind and gone elsewhere. However, the knot of fear deep in his gut told him he was wrong. It had been her voice he'd heard calling for help. Rina was here in those waters. Somewhere.

A movement of white in the water to his left caught his attention. An arm flailed the flood waters, then disappeared, swept under by the surging waters.

"Rina!" he shouted.

Please let her be alive, he prayed, *let me reach her in time*.

Without waiting or daring to waste another second, Shane waded into the water, never taking his eyes off the spot where he'd last seen Rina. Fully clothed, he pushed forward.

The burgeoning flood waters pulled at him, challenging him to remain standing, not to be swept away. Ignoring the forces clawing at him, Shane pushed on. He had to find Rina. He knew in his heart that it had been her he'd spotted in the raging waters. Rina was out there . . . somewhere.

Shane searched the water surrounding him, hoping for another sign of her, just a glimpse of her. The possibility of her sinking below the surface, drowning, tore the breath from his chest. He dodged as a floating branch surged past him.

Struggling, he kept pushing farther out into the center of the flood waters. The ground gave way beneath his feet and he began to swim, trying to search for Rina at the same time. Every second that ticked past carried his hopes away along with the time.

His fingers brushed something, and an instant later, Rina broke to the surface, thrashing wildly. Shane caught her to him, relief almost swamping him as he held her tightly.

Rina felt the steel-like grip upon her and in-

239

stinctively fought against it. Swinging her arms, she lashed out.

Her fist caught Shane under the chin, and the force of the unexpected blow almost loosened his grip. He grappled to keep hold of her, knowing that if he released her, they might both be swept under by the current which had become a fierce creature he would battle to the death.

He tightened his arms around Rina and dragged her closer, until her back was tucked tight up against his chest.

"Dammit. Quit fighting me!" he yelled in her ear.

The next second he dodged her fist as she flailed her arms back in panic. Water rushed over them, and he swallowed a mouthful of water. He gagged and sputtered. Raising his head as high as he could, he sucked in a deep breath of air for his painful lungs.

"Dammit, Rina. You're going to drown us both!" he shouted at her.

At last his words seemed to sink in, and she sagged weakly against him. Shane didn't know if she'd stopped fighting because she'd heard his commands and recognized his voice, or if she'd exhausted her energy to fight. Whichever it was, he was relieved. He couldn't battle the surging waters and her at the same time.

It took all the strength he possessed to retain his hold on Rina and swim toward the bank. Each second stretched into minutes. Endlessly.

Shane felt as if hours passed while he struggled

against the raging waters. The flood seemed to have taken on a life of its own with its sole purpose being to tear Rina from his arms. He swore he'd get them to shore or die holding onto her.

At last his feet scraped against solid ground. Half-dragging, half-wading, he pulled them both onto dry land. Only when he knew they were out of the reach of the water did he release his fierce hold on Rina.

He laid her down on the thick carpet of grass, and an icy fear gripped him as he gazed down at her. Her skin was the pale translucent color of fine china. He wiped her hair away from her face and called her name.

Rina sputtered and then coughed violently. Struggling to sit up, she clung to him tightly. Shane drew her close, wrapping his arms about her.

Rina dragged air into her tortured lungs and a fit of coughing followed. When it ended, she leaned back against Shane and shuddered. *She was lucky to be alive.*

Why, if Nolan . . .

She struggled to sit upright. She had to warn Shane. She had to.

"Danger . . . no accident . . ." A spasm of coughing racked her, interrupting her words.

"Rina, you're safe now—"

She shook her head no and frantically pushed Shane's hands away. "No. It was Nolan Gant. I'm sure I heard him a-laughing."

He realized from the panic in her eyes that she

was right. The flood hadn't been an accident. No-lan Gant had been behind this attempt on Rina's life.

"He's gone now." Shane put one hand over hers. "You're safe. Rina, darling, you're safe."

She sagged against him, her energy spent, and her eyelashes fluttered closed. *Safe.* It sounded so good. Almost as good as being held close to Shane's body. The warmth from his chest seeped into her, warming and reassuring her.

"Hold me, Shane," she said.

"I am."

"Tighter, please."

He wrapped his arms around her and drew her to him. She snuggled so close it took his breath away.

Rina clung to Shane, savoring the warm dampness of his chest against her cheek. For the second time he'd risked his life to save hers.

His heartbeat sounded strong and reassuring beneath her ear. She'd come very close to never hearing that sound again—to never hearing anything again.

Death—its specter still seemed so close. Too close. She felt that if she reached out her arm, she could touch it. Cold, and wet, and dark like the waters that had pulled her down.

Rina squeezed her eyes tightly closed to shut out the recollection and the fear it brought with it. Instead of helping when she closed her eyes, all she could see was the swirling waters that had surrounded her. The image threatened to engulf her thoughts, her mind, her very being.

She opened her eyes, almost half-afraid she'd see the waters rushing at her again. The fear was foolish; she knew that, but it refused to relinquish the fierce hold it had upon her. She shivered; she'd never been afraid like this in her entire life. It was new to her. And she hated the feeling.

It was as if death was still trying to claim her, refusing to admit that it had lost the battle.

Shivers racked her body, as reaction set in, and she curled her fingers into the damp material of Shane's shirt front.

"Cold?" he asked.

Rina shook her head.

"Rina?" He drew back to look down at her.

"Shane—" Rina met his concerned gaze. "I'm still afeared."

"Everything's okay now," he assured her. "You're safe."

He tenderly brushed a kiss across her forehead, wanting to do so much more.

"Every time I close my eyes, I'm back in the water again. It's all I can see."

"Shh." Shane drew her close, wrapping his arms around her.

She shook her head against his chest. "Death's still a-waitin' for me." She stared across at the water. "I can feel it."

A shiver trailed down her spine like a long bony finger. She swallowed down the sob that suddenly threatened at the back of her throat.

"It'll have a long wait," Shane said in a rough voice. "You're safe, sweetheart. And alive."

"I don'ts feel very alive." She tilted her head back to look up at him.

"Shane." She clutched his shirt front tighter. "Make me feel alive again. Make love to me."

As a moment of silence greeted her request, she whispered, "Please?"

Shane felt his heart lurch at her question. To say "yes" would be so easy. He wanted to hold her tight, to make her his again, to make himself forget that he'd come so fearfully close to losing her. He wanted to make love to her more than anything in the world.

He watched the emotions cross her expressive face.

"Sweetheart—"

"I needs love to wipe away the fear." She pulled away an arm's length from him, then faced him with firm determination. "To take away the awful picture I see when I close my eyes."

First, an overwhelming tenderness, and then desire reached out its tendrils, ensnaring him. He could no more have refused her than refused his next breath. He cupped her chin in his palm.

The poignant mixture of fear and love in her eyes tore at his heart. He'd do anything in his power to take that fear away, to shoulder her burden. He wanted to make her his with a sudden fierceness that shocked him.

"Oh, sweetheart," he murmured.

As he moved, his shirt clung to his back like a

second skin, and he unbuttoned what few buttons remained of the shirt. Stripping the wet fabric from his body, he tossed the shirt onto the grass.

He could feel the heat of Rina's gaze on his naked chest. It practically seared his skin. Suddenly, she raised her gaze to his, and the heat rose between them like the smoke from a campfire. Enveloping them.

As Shane leaned forward and eased first one strap then the other of her chemise off her shoulders, she could feel his breath on her face. Closing the distance, he rained kisses on her cheekbones, her chin, and along the column of her throat. His hot breath bathed her neck, igniting the same white heat as a bolt of lightning.

As she gasped, he returned his mouth to hers, seizing, demanding. Then he took her lips in a kiss that rocked her almost as hard as the explosion at the still when they'd first met.

Rina clung to him, wrapping her arms around his waist. She kneaded his skin like a hungry cat. Running her hands up over his muscled torso, she whimpered, luxuriating in the strength she felt there beneath her fingertips. She needed his strength. And his loving.

At the soft sound from her, Shane slid his hands down her shoulders, pulling the torn chemise from her dampened skin and tossing the lacy garment on the grass. He caressed her silken skin. Lower he went, his knuckles skimming the swell of her firm breasts and hardened nipples, and Rina moaned aloud, beneath his mouth.

Molding her willing body to his, he lowered her to the fragrant, grass-covered ground. Its lush carpet gave beneath their bodies, cushioning the two of them as he covered her chilled body with his.

He laved kisses along the length of her throat, while he stroked first one nipple and then the other with the pad of his thumb. Rina arched upward, the pleasure so great it was almost pain.

At first he tried to be gentle, to go slowly, aware of her bruises. Rina would have none of it. She shoved his clothes away, separating the barrier between them. Skin to skin at last, she opened her mouth, surrendering fully to his kiss.

Shane plundered her mouth, his tongue seeking out hers and performing a ritual as old as time. He withdrew his tongue, then plunged it into her velvet moistness again and again in a dance of passion.

Smothering a cry, Rina caught him close, digging her fingernails into the firm skin of his muscled shoulders and arching her body against his. Shadowed heat enveloped her, warming every part of her body.

She raked her fingernails down his back, crying out his name. She trembled beneath him. With a hoarse cry, Shane slid between her parted legs and entered her in one thrust. Heat consumed her, and she met his thrusts, clutching his shoulders with both her hands.

Their loving was hard and fast, culminating with a fierce intensity that left them both breathless and completely satiated.

Held close to him, she sighed and let her mind wander, as if she could have stopped it. It had all the strength of a newborn colt on wobbly legs right now. Her mind seemed made of lamb's wool at the moment—all fluffy and soft and with a tendency to drift away on a slight whim.

Smiling, she closed her eyes. Colors swirled around her, and she imagined Shane's arms around her, whirling her on the dance floor. Everyone watched them. They moved with perfect rhythm. Shane, so handsome in his fancy clothes, and she the perfect picture of a regal lady in a ball gown of . . .

She shivered as a cool breeze brushed her body, and the picture faded quickly. Opening her eyes, she glanced over to where her ripped chemise lay on the grass.

"My clothes . . ."

At her concern over modesty right now, a smile of thanks tugged at Shane's lips. If she could worry over that after what she'd been through, then she must be feeling back to normal.

He bit back the smile and asked, "Where are they?"

"Over there."

Rina gestured to the area behind Shane and to his right. He glanced around at the wide expanse of water now covering the spot she pointed at.

"Sweetheart, I'm afraid they're long gone."

"But—"

He reached out and caught up his shirt. Tenderly, he wrapped it around Rina and buttoned it closed.

"Better?" he asked.

Even wet, the shirt retained some of Shane's body heat. It enveloped her, and she snuggled down into it.

"Umm," she answered as her eyes drifted closed.

"Rina?" he whispered.

In answer, she cuddled against him and sighed, then slid her arms up to wrap them around his neck.

Reassured she was well, he released a pent-up breath and brushed a tender kiss against her forehead. She was alive and safe from the waters. That was all that mattered to him.

Swinging her up into his arms, he headed for the cabin. He steered clear of the swollen creek banks, keeping a careful eye on the creek waters, not chancing endangering Rina any further.

While Shane was certain that Nolan Gant had fled, he wasn't taking any chances with Rina's safety. That sudden flood hadn't been a force of nature, but rather of one man—Nolan Gant.

As Shane reached the cabin, the door opened and Ben Taylor came out to meet them.

"What happened?" He stopped at the sight of Rina clad only in Shane's shirt and held close in his arms.

"The dam gave way. Rina got swept up in it while she was bathing. But she's safe."

Shane held back his suspicions. This was between him and Nolan Gant now.

Ben rattled off question after question as he led Shane into the cabin and to Rina's bedroom. Throwing back the coverlet, he stepped back.

"Put her down here."

Shane eased her gently onto the soft mattress. As he pulled back from her, she sighed and opened her eyes. She smiled up at him and murmured, "Umm, home." Her eyelashes fluttered closed.

Shane stared down at Rina lying on the bed, and his heart skipped a beat. She was so pale, it scared him. He remembered how close he'd come to losing her. Even now, just the memory of it sent a gut-wrenching fear through him.

"Stay with her, Ben. I'm going to go get Lucas," Shane ordered.

He halted and stared down at Rina a moment longer. If he'd been a little later getting to the creek—

He cut the rest off. He couldn't bear the thought of losing her.

"Take care of her."

Turning, Shane strode across the room, pausing only long enough to grab a white shirt from the stack of clean clothes on his bed. He buttoned the shirt and tucked it in his damp pants, as he strode out of the cabin and crossed to where Ben's horse was tied to a tree.

Swinging up onto the mount, Shane flicked the

reins and rode for Blueberry Bluff like a man possessed.

When he drew the horse to a sharp stop outside of Lucas's office, Shane didn't even bother to tie the reins to the railing, instead leaving them looped around the saddle horn.

He burst into Lucas's office and hauled him away from a patient before Lucas had a chance to even ask what was wrong.

"It's Rina. She almost drowned," Shane relayed the information while he dragged Lucas toward the door. "The dam gave way."

"She—"

"She needs you." Shane gave a sharp tug on the other man's arm, nearly knocking him off his feet.

Lucas planted his feet and caught Shane's hand. "Just let me grab my bag."

"Hurry."

Lucas followed Shane out the door in seconds. "Let's go."

The ride back to the cabin was completed in silence, each man afraid to voice his fears in case they might already be true. It was the longest time Lucas had ever been quiet.

Thankfully, the cabin finally came into view, and both men drew their horses up and dismounted, running for the door at the same time. Shane burst through first with Lucas on his heels.

"She's lookin' better," Ben Taylor greeted them at the door to Rina's room.

Lucas nodded and pushed past his father. Ben caught Shane's arm as he moved to follow Lucas.

"Let him do his doctoring. If'n he needs us in there, he'll tell us. Come on."

Ben walked to the kitchen with slow steps. Sighing deeply, he pulled down two cups and a jug of whiskey. Without asking, he simply poured two doses and handed one cup to Shane.

Shane took it and swallowed the liquid in one gulp. He didn't taste it and didn't even notice the path it burned down his throat. His entire attention centered on the doorway to the bedroom where Rina lay.

The minutes passed with leaden slowness before Lucas finally joined them at the oak table. Ben poured another cup and passed it to his son.

"Well?" he asked.

"She'll be all right," Lucas announced, his voice uncharacteristically shaky.

Ben Taylor released his breath in a loud sigh. "Thank the good Lord."

Shane agreed.

"Right now, she needs to sleep," Lucas pronounced. "I'll need to go back to town, check on my patients, and close up my office." He laughed without humor. "I left it in rather a hurry.

Shane smiled over at him and nodded.

"I reckon you were the one who saved her." Lucas's words were a statement as he faced Shane and extended his hand. "Thank you."

"No thanks needed." Shane's gaze centered on the bedroom door once again.

"She'll likely sleep until morning," Lucas told them. "I'll be back early to check on her then."

Shane walked Lucas to their horses and after watching him ride away, he swung up into the saddle. Turning his mount, he faced the cabin grimly.

"I'll be back soon," he said to Ben Taylor. "Take good care of her."

Shane turned his horse toward Nolan Gant's place. He had a score to settle.

Shane drew his horse to a stop in front of the dingy one-room cabin.

"Gant!" he shouted.

As Nolan sauntered outside, Shane swung down off his horse. He strode toward the man, fury driving his every step.

"What the—"

Shane doubled up his fist and swung. His fist connected solidly with Nolan's protruding jaw. The sound of the impact pleased Shane.

Nolan staggered back and fell, landing hard on the ground at Shane's feet. He stared up at him, his eyes glazed.

"You son of a bitch." Shane clenched his fists, holding himself back, forcing himself not to go after the man at his feet again.

"Make another try at Rina Taylor, and you're dead." Shane's voice dripped chips of ice.

Nolan pushed himself up and swayed to his feet. "Why you—"

"I'm through, Gant. Find yourself another 'sweet talker'. "

"What do you mean through?" Nolan whined.

"That you can tell your secret recipe goodbye. I quit."

"Why, you're no better'n Billy where she's concerned," Nolan spat the words out. "He's always trying to protect her, too. Both of ya not willing fer anything to harm her. No matter what *she* does."

Ignoring him, Shane calmly walked back to his horse and swung into the saddle with ease. He stared back at Nolan's outrage with disgust.

"You'll regret this. You hear me, Delaney?" Nolan rubbed his jaw. "I'll be putting piney-roses on both your graves before winter. You hear me? You and her, both dead."

"Try it, and you'll be the one in a grave."

Shane turned his horse and rode away.

Nolan glared at Shane Delaney's back as the gamblerman rode away. In his younger days, he woulda killed a man outright fer talking to him the way Delaney had jus' done. Much less for daring to punch him.

However, Nolan realized the years had taken their toll on him, and that the rheumatism had slowed his draw more than jus' a mite—in spite of the buckeye he carried in his pocket fer a cure of the rheumatism.

He knew he hadn't a chance against a man like Delaney in a fair draw. And that's why he didn't act now or plan on it being fair when the time came.

"Billy!" Nolan shouted.

The boy had refused to help him pull down the beaver dam above the creek. Billy hadn't been willing to see any harm come to her.

However, this was different. This was a case of honor. Billy had to help him kill that Delaney fella.

It should be easy to enlist Billy's help, Nolan told himself. Why, it was plain the boy had hated the fancy gamblerman from the beginning. He'd help. Nolan knew that fer a fact. All he had to do was explain it the right way to his boy.

"Billy," he called out in a lower voice. "That damned gamblerman jus' attacked me. Fer no reason, too."

He recalled that sometimes the boy had hidden when he took to yelling at him. No use in scaring him off, was there?

"Billy?" Nolan cajoled. "We gots us a debt to settle with that gamblerman. You interested?"

He waited. Sure enough, within jus' a minute or two, Nolan heard Billy's shuffling footsteps coming round the side of the cabin.

"I thought maybe you'd like the sound of that. I was right, wasn't I?"

He was purty sure he saw Billy nod.

"Come on, boy." Nolan grinned and slapped his own thigh with his palm.

He waited for Billy to join him.

"Let's go inside and have us a drink. We got

some planning to do—if'n we're gonna see piney-roses on that gamblerman's grave anytime soon. What do ya think of that?''

Chortling, Nolan slapped his thigh again and led the way into the dingy cabin. Yep, he had his boy back all right. And he intended to see that things stayed that way fer good.

All he had to do was ensure that Rina Taylor died with that gamblerman. Yep, that's all he needed to do.

Fourteen

The next afternoon, Shane sat in a chair in Rina's bedroom and watched her sleep. He knew that if Ben Taylor happened to walk in, he'd be furious, but Shane didn't give a damn.

After the attempt on Rina's life, he wasn't about to leave her alone and unprotected. Not even for a few minutes.

Her stillness as she slept tore at him. Shane had never seen her anything but vibrant from the moment he'd first laid eyes on her. And Nolan Gant had tried to destroy that vibrancy—to kill her.

Shane rubbed his palm over his bruised fist. He didn't regret punching Gant. However, the old man's threats echoed in his mind.

A fissure of fear crept up his spine. He didn't fear for himself; it was Rina he was concerned about. He would not allow Nolan Gant to harm her. But just how was he to stop him?

Shane laid his head back and sighed. He couldn't very well go to Ben and Lucas and tell them that Nolan Gant had threatened Rina. He could not reveal his own part in this. He was trapped by his own lies.

Leaning forward and clasping his hands together, he fixed his gaze on Rina. The danger that she was in tore at him.

I swear I'll keep you safe, Shane vowed silently to himself and to her. *He'd protect Rina until he could ensure her safety.*

He'd find some way to keep Rina in sight at all times—even if it drove him to the edge to do so. Looking at her right now, he didn't doubt that she'd drive him there.

The next two days were hell for Shane. Keeping his vow took all of his ingenuity. Rina had recovered quicker than even Lucas expected, and over the next two days Shane tried his damndest to keep Rina within his sight at all times. But it was taking its toll.

The constant nearness tempted, tantalized, and tried him to the limits. He found that he'd never wanted to make love to a woman so much in his entire life.

The hot, sunny morning of the third day, Shane followed Rina as she headed up the trail to the clearing to tend to the whiskey still. The seductive sway of her hips stole his breath away and sent it back to him with the force of a blow to his stomach.

Damn. It was going to be a long day.

* * *

Roger Chastain gave the dusty main street of Possum Hollow a sneering glance. *Damn hole in the wall place.* He repressed a shudder. He hated small towns.

The people tended to be too friendly for his tastes. Everybody knew everybody else's business. And he preferred to keep his business to himself—especially since he didn't particularly care to attract the attention of any lawman.

He figured that he'd spent more than his share of time in jail cells all up and down the Mississippi. The latest one had been in New Orleans. The only good thing to come out of that time was his knowledge of Shane Delaney's whereabouts. The fool. Delaney had thought he'd been sleeping.

Oh no, he'd heard every word uttered between Delaney and the old man. And he planned to cut himself in on the deal and especially in on the money the old man had offered Delaney.

Why should his enemy, Delaney, be the one to make the money from the deal, he thought, a petulant frown drawing his face. If Delaney hadn't tricked him into that fight during the poker game, he'd have the proceeds from the plantation deed instead of having to scrounge for money like a pauper. And he should have been the one striking the bargain with old man Gant instead of Delaney.

Damn, life wasn't fair.

Chastain reined his horse down a trail to the

left. From the storekeeper's directions, old man Gant's place was only a short ride away.

After five minutes of traveling in the wooded hills, Chastain pulled out his handkerchief and wiped the dust from his forehead. He leaned to the side and glanced down at his boots in disgust. A fine layer of film covered the jet black sheen.

Kicking his horse, he continued down the trail. Old man Gant better pay good. As far as he was concerned, he was already earning his money.

At last, a small cabin came into view. Chastain checked his derringer, replaced it in his brocaded vest, then turned his horse toward the cabin.

At his approach, the door suddenly swung inward, and a long gun barrel appeared. The cabin's shadowed interior hid its owner from view.

"That's far enough, mister!"

Chastain drew his horse to a stop and eyed the shotgun protruding from the doorway. He eased the derringer from his vest, expertly hiding it in his palm.

"Don't cotton to strangers 'round here." Nolan prodded the air with his shotgun barrel for emphasis. "State yer business."

"I'm looking for Nolan Gant."

"What fer?"

"I have some business to discuss with him."

"What kinda business?"

"That depends. I take it you're Nolan Gant? Has Shane Delaney completed the job for you yet?"

"What business is it of yours?" This time curiosity tinged the old man's voice.

Nolan stepped out into the sunshine, keeping the shotgun aimed at Chastain.

"Delaney." Nolan spat the word out.

That and the look of disgust on his face was all the answer Roger Chastain needed. Shane Delaney hadn't completed the job yet. There was still money to be made here. Keeping his gaze firmly fixed on the old man, Chastain kept the derringer tightly in hand and swung out of the saddle with ease.

The aura of nonchalance and defiance told Nolan that this was a man that wasn't afeared of him one little bit. Likely he was a mean one to boot. A thought creased his brow.

Maybe this man was mean enough to get rid of Shane Delaney. And Rina Taylor.

Although, Nolan admitted that he had a particular desire deep in his heart to kill the gal himself. He owed Billy that much. What she'd done to him could never be forgiven, nor forgotten.

Yep, payment time was a-comin'.

Nolan eyed the other man from his fancy broad-brimmed hat clear down to his dust-covered black leather boots. The man's way of dress put Nolan in a mind of Shane Delaney.

Purty dresser. Fancy, too. A lot fancier than Delaney. This man wore a purty silver and black brocaded vest.

As a dim memory nagged at Nolan, he narrowed his gaze on the other man. He'd seen this outlander someplace before.

He couldn't rightly recall where, but the too-faint memory was associated with someplace unpleasant, he knew that much fer sure. He tightened his grip on his shotgun instinctively. Jus' where had he seen this fancy outlander at before?

"How do you know Delaney's a-workin' fer me?" Nolan asked, leery of the man facing him. He frowned, trying his hardest to recall where they mighta met.

A thin smile slowly creased Chastain's face as his icy cold gaze narrowed.

"I shared a cell with him in New Orleans."

"That's where I's seen you!" Nolan announced.

Relief caused his shoulders to slump. This outlander had been a-sleepin' in Delaney's jail cell. No wonder the memory had left him with an uneasy feeling. Jails always did that to him.

"Name's Roger Chastain." He extended his hand.

Nolan Gant chortled and slapped his thigh in glee. "That was you? A-sleepin'?"

The other man's eyes narrowed to thin, angry slits, and he dropped his hand to his side.

"If I'd been sleeping, I wouldn't know what I know, now would I?"

Nolan stopped laughing.

"You hired the wrong man in New Orleans."

"Is that so?" Nolan challenged. He raised his chin in angry defiance.

"Delaney hasn't got you what you want yet, has he?"

"No." Nolan fired the single word out like a rifle shot.

"I'll cost you a hundred more than you offered Delaney. But I'll get the job done," Chastain stated. "And quick, you'll see."

"So you think you can get the Taylors' whiskey recipe from her?"

"I know I can. And I can kill Delaney for you, too."

Nolan grinned and lowered his shotgun.

"Well, let's us get on in outta the sun. And we can talk about it."

He motioned for Chastain to proceed him and followed him to the door of the cabin. Nolan wasn't about to get back shot by anybody.

Once inside the dingy cabin, Nolan sat down opposite Chastain. He watched the man across from him and bit back his grin. *Shane Delaney was as good as dead.*

He didn't question what stroke of good fortune had sent the blond-haired, icy-eyed gambler his way, but he recognized an opportunity when he saw one. And Roger Chastain had the word written all over him.

The two men had one thing in common. They both wanted to see Delaney dead.

"You said you was willing to get rid of Delaney?"

"I'd be happy to. And it won't cost you any extra."

262

Nolan grinned, happy at that. "What 'bout Rina Taylor?"

"What do you want me to do about her?" Chastain asked, leaning back in the chair and slipping the derringer in his pocket.

"I wants you to kill her," Nolan shouted, suddenly agitated, then fell silent.

But, damn it all, he wanted the recipe, too. Jus' maybe, with Roger Chastain's help, he could get all three. The Taylor recipe, Shane Delaney, and Rina Taylor.

The walk to Ben Taylor's whiskey still had never seemed so endless before, Shane thought to himself as he watched the womanly sway of Rina's hips as she navigated the trail.

The view he had from behind her was enough to try any sane man's endurance and self-control. He knew it was sure pulling at his.

Once again, she'd tied her skirt into a knot at one hip, giving her legs free movement. And giving him a painfully tantalizing view of her shapely legs. The skirt yielded with every step she took, providing Shane with long glimpses of sleek calves and even more tempting peeks of thigh.

He breathed in deeply of the mountain air, hoping it would cool his raging ardor. Right now what he needed was a cool drink. A long, cool drink.

Shane knew that was a lie. What he needed was Rina Taylor.

As they entered the clearing, she stopped and

turned around to face him. Almost as if she'd read his mind, her gaze met his. Hers held a question, hope, desire.

Shane released the breath he'd just taken with a silent groan. The overwhelming need he felt for her pushed aside all his good intentions. In two steps, he closed the distance between them.

Rina knew he was going to kiss her. She knew it as sure as she drew breath. And she was going to let him. There was no doubt of that.

She wanted to feel the touch of his lips against hers so bad that it was almost a physical pain a-hurtin' her. She licked her lips, wondering why they had suddenly gone so dry.

Above her, Shane groaned and laid his hand against her cheek. His palm was warm against her skin, and she sighed, parting her lips instinctively, waiting.

As he cupped her chin in his hand, Rina tilted her head back. She waited expectantly for Shane to lower his lips to hers.

When he did, the touch was explosive. Days' worth of wanting and loving had built up between them, just waiting to break free. The kiss rocked Rina from her lips clear down to her toes.

Shane wrapped her in his embrace, crushing her against his body, almost cutting off her breath. When she caught his shirt front with her hands, his lips plundered hers. Desire coiled about them, ensnaring them both.

Rina felt her legs weaken as waves of desire

swept over her. She leaned against him, surrendering herself to his loving.

Shane watched Rina slip on her stockings and then follow them with her lace garters. Suddenly he wished it was his hands sliding up her legs instead of the lace. Even fulfilled by their love-making, he could still want her again. The fact amazed him. He'd never felt this way with any other woman.

Rina brushed her skirt free of leaves and smoothed it into place. Shane bit back a smile; she was turning into a lady much to his amazement.

As if she'd felt his gaze on her, Rina looked back over her shoulder at him. Their gazes locked and held for a moment, before she blushed and turned back away.

Yes, Shane thought to himself, she was becoming quite a lady.

The next instant, she scooped up her skirt, wrapped it into a loop, and knotted it at her hip. Shane stifled the groan that welled up.

He'd known her ladylike aura was too good to last. Rina Taylor would never be a true lady. No matter how hard she tried, the half-hoyden part of her managed to peek through. But, he had to admit that the hoyden part of her tantalized him and tugged at him like nothing else ever had. Somehow Rina had managed to grab onto him and hold him tight to her.

The web of lies tightened around Shane, almost choking him. He couldn't lie to her any longer.

Shane knew that the time had come for him to tell Rina why he was here. He had to tell her the truth—why he'd come to the hills—had to tell her that it hadn't been to buy the whiskey, but to steal it.

As she started to step away, he drew her back against him. Clasping his arms around her, he rested his hands lightly across her midriff.

"Rina? Wait a minute," he asked, his voice low.

"Um-huh."

In response, she snuggled back against him.

Her action took his breath away as a fresh wave of desire overtook him. She tilted her head and glanced up at him. The white column of her neck tempted him, invited him. He couldn't resist its lure. Lowering his head, he nibbled lightly along her neck.

Luxuriating in his embrace and the aftermath of their lovemaking, Rina smiled. It was a piece of pure heaven here within the circle of Shane's arms. As he nuzzled her neck, placing light feathery kisses along her nape, she snuggled tighter against him.

"Shane, I needs to mix a new batch fer Pa," she murmured, tilting her head a little more to the side to give him better access to her neck.

"I really do need to do Pa's work," she insisted halfheartedly.

Instead of moving away, she leaned her head back against Shane's shoulder. It felt so good to be in his arms, she thought. It felt so right, some-how.

Brushing aside her tousled hair, he placed an-other kiss on the side of her neck. "Umm," he murmured against her soft skin. It wouldn't hurt to wait another minute to tell her the truth.

Rina felt a strange lethargy seep through her limbs. If she stayed much longer in his arms, she didn't think she'd be able to stand at all.

"Umm," she answered Shane.

Her body seemed incapable of moving an inch away from his. She sighed in perfect contentment.

A sharp rustle of movement to her left failed to disturb the warm cocoon she was wrapped in. A second rustle drew only the slightest part of her attention. The next instant a pair of bushy-tailed squirrels scampered across the clearing and raced up a tree.

Rina jumped and then yelped, jerked out of her pleasant reverie. She stole a glance up at Shane. His laughing eyes met hers, and she gave in to the impulse to chuckle. It broke the web of seduction that had held them both its prisoners.

Shane knew the moment for truth had passed. He would wait and tell her on the way back to the cabin.

Sighing, Rina stepped back.

"I needs to ready a new batch." Regret tinged her voice.

Shane smiled at the forlorn expression on her face. It was enough for him that he held the knowledge that she'd rather be back in his arms. There was no place he'd rather her be either.

Biting her lower lip, Rina rubbed her hands down her dress and turned away. It was 'bout the hardest thing she'd ever done. If'n she didn't get a new batch starting, Pa would be madder than a rooster in an empty hen house, that was fer sure.

Distracted by Shane's nearness, she almost forgot about the need for secrecy when making up the fixings. The Taylor law was that nobody else was to know the recipe that made up the Taylors' special brand of whiskey.

Rina stared at Shane for a full minute, then made up her mind. She was going to break that law all the way to kingdom come. Ida had told her trust her heart, and that's jus' what she was gonna do.

Carefully and methodically, Rina set to preparing and readying the new batch. From a clump of rocks she withdrew sacks of grains, mixing together amounts from each bag. When she had everything mixed and readied, she withdrew a handkerchief-wrapped packet from her pocket.

"What's that?" Shane asked.

Rina laid the packet on the ground and unwrapped it. The pungent aroma of herbs struck Shane.

"Adding the last ingredients," Rina told him in a soft voice.

She drew out a small vile of liquid and opened it. Shane recognized the smell of blackberry juice immediately. He glanced from the "fixings" to Rina and back again.

Spread out before him lay the ingredients to the Taylor whiskey recipe. He stared at the items with disbelief. Did she have any idea what she'd done? It wasn't like Rina to be so careless.

He glanced at her a second and had his answer. It was there in her emerald gaze.

Shane knew with absolute certainty that Rina was giving him the gift of her trust. The question was—what was he going to do with it?

If he turned the secret over to Nolan Gant, he would be rewarded with enough money to buy back Belle Rive. It had been his dream for so long, and now he had the means to acquire that dream. However, to do so would betray Rina. Shane didn't think he could do that to her.

However, it could possibly save her life, because surely Nolan wouldn't have reason to harm her if he had the recipe he so desperately wanted.

"All finished," Rina announced.

Shane jumped guiltily. If he turned the recipe over to Nolan Gant, the Taylors' whiskey business would be finished. It appeared to be the only means of support they had. He was sure that Lucas didn't earn enough as a doctor to support them all, and besides he knew with certainty that neither Ben Taylor nor his daughter would be willing to move to Blueberry Bluff.

What was he going to do? It all came down to a choice between Rina and Belle Rive.

"Shane?" Rina touched his arm. "You ready to go back to the cabin?"

He nodded, deep in thought. *What was he going to do with the secret he now held?* The question kept repeating itself in his mind. Rina or Belle Rive?

Once Shane had escorted Rina to the cabin and seen her safely in her pa's care, he knew he had to get away for a while alone. The decision he had to make had to be made alone.

When Rina hid a yawn behind her hand, he had his excuse.

"Tired?" he asked.

Ben Taylor turned to her immediately.

"You feeling all right, gal? Maybe you should go and lay down awhile—"

"I'm fine, Pa," she assured him. "I don't need to lay down."

Rina refused to meet Shane's gaze. *He knew why she was tired.* A blush stole across her cheeks at the memory of what had happened between them in the clearing.

Ben Taylor noted the change in her color at once. Reaching out, he laid a hand against her cheeks, then her brow.

"You might be gettin' a mite feverish," he said, frowning at her.

Rina turned redder at his observation. Jus' how was she supposed to explain to her pa that she was only embarrassed?

"Gal, you okay?" he asked, stepping closer. "Maybe we should send for Lucas."

"No, Pa. I don't need Lucas."

"Well—"

"Pa, I'm okay."

He touched her forehead again, and a worried frown creased his leathery face.

"Rina? Gal—"

She slapped his hand away. "Damnation. Can't a body be believed when they say they're fine?"

"Rina, don't swear," Ben Taylor ordered in a firm voice. "Ya must be feelin' better if'n you're swearing," he admitted. "But—"

"All right," she surrendered. "I'll go lay down. Satisfied?" she asked him.

"You go on take a little nap. We'll see how you're feelin' when you get up," he insisted.

Shane held back his sigh of relief over the interchange. With Rina on her way to lay down for a nap, all he had to do now was make his excuses and slip away for a little while.

"Well, boy?" Ben Taylor slapped him on the shoulder. "Care for a game or two?"

"Maybe we'd better wait until she's asleep," Shane suggested in a low voice.

"You're right. If'n she knew we was gambling, she'd likely want to be right in the middle of it."

Ben Taylor clamped his mouth shut in a frown.

"Everything go okay up at the still? Rina feelin' okay then?"

A faint smile touched Shane's lips at how "well" Rina had felt in his arms. He quickly schooled his smile.

"She seemed fine," Shane said.

271

"Didn't overtire herself none, did she?" the older man continued to question him.

"No," Shane told him.

"Didn't let her exert herself none, did ya?"

Shane forced himself not to flicker an eyelid as the memory of Rina's abandonment during their lovemaking swamped him.

"No," he lied, then grimaced at a short pain in his stomach.

"Well, if you say so." Ben Taylor rubbed his jaw. "Did she remember to put the fixins away?"

Shane recognized his opportunity and took it.

"I'll go back up there and make sure everything's in order," he offered.

"Thank ya." Ben Taylor turned back toward the cabin. "I'll jus' go check on Rina."

A twinge of guilt hit Shane as he walked away from the Taylors' cabin. He had to decide between Rina and owning Belle Rive again.

Without Nolan Gant's money, he'd never be able to come up with the needed amount to buy back his home before Mary Ellen married Simon Cooke. Once they were married, the plantation wouldn't come up for sale for a long time.

As Shane walked along the trail, images flooded his mind. Belle Rive as it had been all those years ago—majestic and beautiful. It had always rung with laughter and happiness. Before the war came.

Afterwards, everything had changed. He'd returned home to learn of his parents' death from the fever that had almost wiped out the plantation. He could still see their barren graves in his mind.

Upon his parents' graves, he'd sworn to regain the home that had been passed from father to son for generations. He owed them that much. He'd been unable to prevent their deaths, but he could prevent the death of their dream.

And now?

Now he had the means to fulfill that promise to his parents. He had the opportunity to regain Belle Rive. All he had to do was betray the woman who loved him and trusted him.

Fifteen

Rina paced the floor of her bedroom. Sent to bed like a naughty child—that's how she felt. *Damnation.*

She crossed to the window and peered up at the clear blue sky, estimating the time by the position of the sun. She reckoned that far less than an hour had passed since she'd walked through the door of her bedroom, although it seemed like much more.

She had honestly tried lying down and sleeping, but she wasn't tired. The longer she'd lain in the feather bed, the more restless she'd gotten.

Fact was—she jus' wasn't tired. Far from it. She felt alive and kinda tingly all over from being made love to by Shane. And she wanted to be with him. She wanted to walk with him through the beautiful hills that were alive with the color of the blossoming wildflowers.

The thought of wildflowers recalled the day Shane had taken her to the field of wildflowers, and Rina felt her cheeks heating with the returning memory. He had been so loving, and gentle, and wonderful.

Why, he'd coaxed feelings outta her that she'd never in her bestest dreams imagined possible. Crossing her arms over her chest, she hugged that memory to herself, cherishing it.

He had scarcely left a single spot on her body untouched or unexplored. He'd known how to make her feel truly alive and loved. The feel of his fingertips on her breasts, her stomach, her thighs . . .

The heavy thump of her pa's footsteps jolted her out of her sensual reverie. As she cocked her head to listen, the footsteps came closer.

"Oh, hell and damnation," she muttered under her breath.

It was Pa—coming in to check on her, and by the time he got in the room she'd best be sleeping if'n she didn't want to listen to a lengthy scolding from him. In the past, whenever he'd got worried over her or Lucas, they could always count on him a-checkin' on them jus' to be sure they were safe and sound. This time she'd been too distracted with thoughts of Shane to remember that.

Rina spun around and dashed for the bed as fast as she could go. Reaching it, she flung herself onto the thick feather mattress—shoes and petticoats and all. Quickly, she grabbed up the light summertime cover and pulled it up to her chin.

As the door swung inward with a creak, she snapped her eyes tightly closed and tried her darndest to steady her racing breath so it was all slow and even like she was deeply asleep.

She could feel her pa looking down at her, studying her. Forcing herself to breathe evenly, she gently kicked one foot, mussing the covers, and turned her head away from her pa.

Lucas and she had learned long ago that laying dead still or scrunching up their eyes too tight was a dead giveaway to their too-observant pa that they were playing possum.

After what seemed like endless minutes of scrutiny to her, Pa finally placed a light kiss on her forehead and left the room. The door clicked shut behind him.

Rina's eyes snapped open, and she titled her head, making sure he'd walked away from her door before she dared move.

She tossed back the light cover and bounded out of the bed. Sunshine streamed through the window, leaving patterns of dappled sunlight across the floor. It was too purty a day to stay abed. Especially since she wasn't tired. And she was in too happy a mood to want to argue with Pa about it.

What she wanted was a ride amongst all that beautiful sunshine. And jus' maybe a talk with Milly. Besides, Nolan Gant's flood had swept her lady creams and such away. If she asked her, maybe Milly would help her buy some to replace what she'd lost.

Rina spared a glance for the closed door. Pa would never agree to let her go for a ride. He'd already decided she needed to rest, and when Pa made up his mind, it was nigh to impossible to change it.

She didn't feel much like resting. She felt too alive to try and lay still and quiet under a hot cover. Well, she wasn't about to do it either.

Taking off her shoes, she wrapped them up tightly in her skirt so as not to make any betraying noise to alert her pa. Then, tiptoeing on her stocking-clad feet, she crept to the window, opened it slowly and quietly, flinching when it squeaked.

Freezing stock still with her hands on the window, she listened. No sound came from the other side of the bedroom door. Letting her sigh of relief out silently, she leaned out the window and dropped her shoes to the ground. With a last glance at the closed door, she grabbed her skirt and petticoats in one hand and climbed out the window.

Outside, she paused to slip her shoes on, then holding her skirts up out of her way, she sprinted for the open barn door. Once safely inside, she peered back around the doorway to check on the cabin.

It was quiet all around her. She'd made it without Pa catching her.

Feeling quite proud of herself, she walked into the cool dimness of the barn and headed for her horse. She saddled the mare as fast as she could, keeping half her attention on the cabin, watching for any activity or movement from her pa. Ready at last, she picked up her shotgun from the corner near the door where she usually kept it

Grinning, Rina turned around and led her horse to the open door, then almost walked right into a tall, blond stranger.

She stepped back and gasped, releasing her hold on the horse's reins and tightening her grip on the shotgun. A shiver of apprehension skimmed down her spine. It had almost been unnatural the way the pale man had slipped up on her so quiet-like.

It gave her the all-overs, and she struggled to repress the next shiver that followed. She wasn't about to let this outlander know he'd scared her, or that she was more than a mite skittish around him.

"What do you want, outlander?" she challenged. Her voice held a note of false bravado.

She eyed him, her gaze taking in everything from the top of his blond head down to his dusty black boots. He was dressed much the same way as Shane dressed—only a heap fancier. But that's where any similarities ended. This man's eyes held a bit of ice to them, unlike the warmth that radiated from Shane's wicked blue eyes when he looked at her.

Shane's eyes a-lookin' at her made her feel all warm and womanly; this outlander's gaze made her feel decidedly uneasy.

Pale skin showed he obviously avoided the sun whenever he could, while Shane's tanned skin revealed a love of the outdoors. She honest to goodness didn't understand how anybody couldn't help but enjoy sitting in the pure sunshine. She'd always been suspicious of anyone like that, and studied this stranger extra hard.

Cold narrow eyes warned her of the outlander's character. This man had a mean streak down him jus' as plain to see as the white stripe down a skunk's back. He also reminded her a lot of that particular varmint.

"Ma'am." He bowed his head in a gesture of well-practiced gallantry. "I didn't mean to startle you. I apologize."

It failed to impress Rina, instead bouncing right off her stiff body. She knew better'n to be fooled by a little pleasant talking and fancy manners. This outlander was a skunk through and through. It showed right through his fancy clothes and shiny brocaded vest.

"The name's Roger Chastain." He paused, as if waiting to see if she showed any signs of recognizing the name.

His action plumb puzzled her. Why would he be questioning if'n she had heard of him? She racked her mind for any recollection of him or his name, and found none. He was definitely a stranger to her; she knew that much for sure.

"I'm looking for a gambler by the name of Shane Delaney," he announced with a hint of pleasant sincerity in his voice.

Rina couldn't be sure if it was for real or not. Somehow she doubted it.

"What fer?" she asked.

Nobody in the hills gave out information without first finding out why a stranger wanted it. That was an unspoken rule that everybody jus' followed. Rina had grown up knowing to do this, and she didn't see a single reason to change that now.

A strange new sense of protectiveness toward Shane rose up in her. Roger Chastain wasn't a-gettin' any information outta her until she'd first talked to Shane about it.

She still didn't trust this outlander one little bit. He made her think of Nolan Gant—all sneaky and thieving.

Roger Chastain read the suspicion in the tilt of her head and the way she was standing up straight, gripping that damned shotgun. A burst of anger surged through him. He'd be willing to bet that Delaney hadn't had to face her like this. Why, he'd bet that she was all sweetness and willingness around Delaney.

Jealousy followed the anger. Delaney always had things come so easy to him—like winning too many times at the poker table. It was well past time that somebody put a stop to his good fortune. He owed him for the loss of that deed in the poker game, and Chastain never forgot a debt anyone owed to him.

Chastain tapped down the feelings and forced a smile to his face, knowing it would probably have the desired effect of disarming her suspicions better than anything he could say to her.

He'd always been able to smile and talk his way

out of about anything. This backwoods slip of a girl wasn't going to get the best of him.

He concentrated on his smile, and it paid off. The smile softened his too-lean features, making him look boyish and almost like a friendly puppy to Rina. She barely caught back her gasp of amazement. Maybe she'd been wrong 'bout him.

She tilted her head to study him again. If'n he was a friend of Shane's, then he was likely all right to talk to, she reasoned. However, a nagging suspicion lingered, warning her to be cautious.

"Like I said, ma'am," he lowered his voice to a non-threatening tenor, "I'm Roger Chastain, and you have to be Rina Taylor. I'd recognize you anywhere by Shane's description of you."

"Shane told you 'bout me?"

Confusion warred with disbelief in Rina. What would he have been talking 'bout her for?

"He sure did. But he failed to tell me exactly how beautiful you are."

Chastain smiled a friendly, flattering smile along with the compliment, letting his gaze travel appreciatively over her body. He'd told her part of the truth; he hadn't known to expect a real beauty from the little he'd overheard in the jail cell.

Maybe he'd enjoy getting the secret recipe out of her for old man Gant. Maybe he'd take his time and give her a chance to enjoy it, too.

As he stepped closer, bells of warning sounded in Rina's head. She didn't like the look in Chastain's eyes. While it was similar to the look Shane got jus' before he kissed her, there was definitely something different about it when it came from this outlander. It was almost menacing.

Instinctively, she inched back a step away from him. Her finger curled around the trigger of the shotgun out of habit.

Chastain's jaw clenched as he noted her withdrawal. He'd thought that he just about had her in the palm of his hand. What had gone wrong?

Now she stood stiffly across from him, an even tighter grip on that damned shotgun. He had no aspirations of getting filled with lead trying to seduce her. While she might be a beauty, she wasn't worth it. Or maybe she was. He'd simply have to take care of that gun.

Chastain watched her breasts rise and fall under her bodice as nervousness caused her breathing to change. He had a sudden vision of ripping that material away from her skin. Preferably with his teeth. Oh, she'd scream, but she'd like it before he was finished. The women always did.

Heat coiled in his gut and traveled through his body at the image of Rina kicking and bucking beneath him. He felt his body harden and burn in response.

He'd have her. One way or another, he'd have Rina Taylor.

Maybe he'd save her as his special reward for killing Delaney. He smiled at the thought. Yes, that's exactly what he'd do.

But Delaney came first.

Chastain knew he was going to enjoy what he

was about to do. There was practically nothing more enjoyable than causing trouble between a man and his woman. And when it was through, the women always turned to him for comfort. He could already imagine the feel of Rina in his arms, seeking consolation from him.

He jerked his mind away from the picture. He had some groundwork to lay first. By the time he got through telling Rina about Delaney and Nolan Gant's plans, she'd have a fitting reception for Delaney.

He almost laughed aloud thinking about the fight that would follow. It would be the perfect way to let Delaney know he was here and ready for him.

"Now that I've seen you," Chastain sent an appreciative glance down her, "I've stopped questioning why Shane stayed as long as he has. He always did have an eye for a pretty lady."

Chastain glanced away from her to study the toe of his boot. He stared at his toe as if he had something else to say, but was hesitant to say it.

Sighing, he finally glanced back at her with an embarrassed look. This caught Rina off guard because she hadn't reckoned Chastain as the type to be either hesitant or embarrassed.

"I hate to interfere, you know that, ma'am." He paused and went back to studying his boot.

A sinking feeling hit Rina in the pit of her stomach. Every time a body said how much they hated to interfere, it meant that's exactly what they were going to do.

"But, there's something a sweet, innocent thing like you ought to know." His voice took on an earnest quality to it.

Rina resisted the sudden urge of curiosity to ask him "what."

"Ma'am, although Shane's a friend of mine, I feel it's not fair or gentlemanly of me to not tell you. I couldn't live with my own conscience if I allowed him to lead you on. And use you," he stated.

"Use me?" Rina bristled at his insinuation.

"No insult intended, ma'am," he quickly put in apologetically. "Please forgive me? But the scoundrel has tricked a lot of ladies."

Rina tamped down on the sudden surge of anger, but forced her lips into a small smile for his apology. She'd much rather have slapped him. What the outlander was a-hintin' at was unspeakable.

Shane Delaney loved her, she was sure of it. Wasn't she?

Of course, she was. After all, his stomach aches from Ida's potion proved he was lying to himself about his "lady fiancée" back in New Orleans, and about the true fact that the one he cared for wasn't his fiancée, but her—Rina Taylor.

"Delaney's working for Nolan Gant."

"No!" The denial slipped out before she could catch it back.

"Yes, ma'am. He was bought and paid for by the old man. Gant hired him back in New Orleans. Paid his way out here, too. If you don't believe me, just ask him," he challenged her.

She felt a hint of doubt begin to gnaw at her.

"But watch his face real close, and you'll know I'm telling you the truth."

Rina stared at him, not wanting to believe him.

"Delaney's after the Taylor whiskey secret recipe. And he's being paid mighty good by Gant for it, too."

The statement hit Rina hard, like a fist to the stomach. She knew that Nolan Gant was after Pa's' whiskey recipe. He'd been after it all her life. And if what Chastain said was true . . .

No, Shane wouldn't lie to her about that—not about the whiskey. Would he?

"No, he isn't," she answered Chastain's accusation and raised her chin a notch. "Shane's here to *buy* Pa's whiskey for the riverboats. Him and Pa have been working it all out betwixt them."

A burst of laughter from Chastain greeted her announcement.

"Is that what Delaney told you?" Chastain laughed again. "Honey," he sobered, "Delaney's here to sweet talk that secret recipe out of you. Believe me, I know what I'm talking about." He lowered his voice. "I don't want to see you get hurt."

A twinge of doubt tried to take root in Rina's mind again, but she tamped it down.

"You're a low-down liar," she said. Rina pointed the shotgun barrel squarely at Chastain. "Why, Shane never even *asked* fer the recipe."

So there, she added silently.

"And I don't suppose you up and gave it to him, did you?"

The look that crossed Rina's face before she could hide it was all the answer he needed.

"Honey, Delaney's the liar." He smiled at her in sympathy, then added softly, "Isn't he?"

Maybe he was, a quiet voice in the back of her mind whispered to her.

But Ida's potion was a-workin', Rina argued with herself. It was. Her heart and mind battled over Shane and his trustworthiness. Didn't Ida's potion prove his intentions?

All Ida's potion proved was that he wasn't telling her true about *something*, Rina admitted to herself.

It could be about his feelings for his fiancée. It could, she argued.

But she knew that wasn't all Shane Delaney was lying about. Deep in her heart she knew it, and at last admitted it. Shane Delaney was a sweet-talking liar, and no better'n the man her ma ran off with.

Now she understood in part the pain her pa had felt. He'd never remarried. Rina suspected that it was because he'd always hoped that her ma would come back home someday. He'd loved her something fierce. But that dream had been destroyed years ago. The memory still held a painful grip on Rina. It had been the evening of her tenth birthday when Milly's momma had come for a visit. But instead of bringing a present, she'd brought bad news.

While away on a shopping trip, Mrs. Bodeen had seen Rina's ma on the streets of St. Louis and stopped her. It was the first that anybody had heard anything of Lily Taylor since the night she left. Lily's words had been disjointed, blurred by illness, but she'd asked Mrs. Bodeen to take home her apology for loving the wrong man. Less than a week later, a telegram was delivered notifying them of Lily Taylor's death.

Tears burned behind her eyes, but she refused to give in to them. It was years too late to cry 'bout her ma, and she refused to cry over Shane Delaney either. If'n she was going to cry over that low-down, sneaking polecat—and she wasn't— then she wouldn't be doing it in front of anybody. Much less another outlander up to no good.

She glanced away to blink back the gathering moisture. Fighting to keep her emotions under a firm hand, she drew her shoulders back, and turned to find Chastain had stepped closer to her. Much closer.

Rina started to step back, but with lightning quick action he lunged for her. Catching her arms, he pushed the shotgun hard against her and drew her body up close to his. The gun pinched her fingers, held tight like it was between their bodies.

Before she could stop him, Chastain ducked his head and smothered her mouth with his lips. Grabbing the back of her head with one hand,

287

he held her tight. His other arm wrapped around her waist like a band of iron. He moved his mouth roughly back and forth over hers.

Shock and revulsion hit her, and she tried to push against him. The shotgun hampered her movements, and her struggle only seemed to encourage him.

Chastain tightened his hold on her shoulders, dragging her body even closer to his. Her breasts pressed against his chest, and he parted his legs to pull her thighs between his.

Bile rose in Rina's throat as she pulled back, twisting and turning every way she could. But it didn't do any good, their bodies were too tightly wedged together for her to use her arms. Her thumb caught in the shotgun trigger, and she winced with pain.

Chastain ground his mouth hard on hers, trying to force her lips apart and gain entry to her mouth. She kept her teeth tightly clenched, and continued to fight him the best she could.

Using the shotgun as a wedge, she shoved with all her might. She gained a few inches between them, and quickly before he could move back in, she twisted her arms, ramming the shotgun into his stomach.

Chastain doubled over, swore and backed away from her. Leering, he rubbed his hand back and forth across his midsection.

Rina kept both her eyes firmly fixed on him. With the back of her hand, she wiped the imprint of his kiss from her mouth.

Her action seemed to amuse him, and he straightened and grinned at her.

"That's all right, honey. I like a woman with a little fight in her."

"You'll get more than a little fight from me," Rina swore.

Undaunted, Chastain laughed at her threat and took a step closer. When he reached out for her, she jumped back, well out of his range. Leering at her, he held out his arms.

His narrowed eyes warned her just before he took a large, menacing step toward her. She lowered the shotgun slightly and fired it in front of his feet. Dirt sprayed his boots.

"The next shot will hit more than dirt," she warned.

He stayed still a moment and eyed her.

"Honey, it's only a matter of time," he said. "You don't want to shoot me."

His smooth, assured voice reminded her of the hypnotic rattle of a rattlesnake. Instinctively, she stepped back away from the sound.

"You can't back away from me forever, honey. Come on."

The damn fool, couldn't he get it through his head that she wasn't going to be willing?

"Why don't you just give up and come here?" he invited in a low, almost lilting voice.

"Never."

She stayed put, not allowing herself to get within the man's reach again, no matter what his voice sounded like. She knew better.

A second later, he proved her caution right when he reached for her. She sidestepped him and tightened her grip on the shotgun.

"One step closer, outlander, and I swear I'll shoot," she warned.

Rina pointed the barrel at him, almost wishing he would take a step and give her an excuse.

He did. Grinning widely, he lunged to the side. Rina turned and fired.

Chastain yelled, and she saw the red seeping through his shirt sleeve. She'd hit him in the shoulder. Biting her lip, she stared at the slowly growing stain. The small tear in his shirt and equally small amount of blood showed her that he'd only been grazed.

"You shot me," he whined.

"It didn't do any more than graze you," she told him with disgust.

"Aren't you going to at least help me?"

Rina resisted the instinctive urge to aid any creature who'd been hurt. She knew what helping this critter would get her.

"Rina! Gal!" Ben Taylor burst into the barn and stopped at the sight before him. He leveled another gun at the stranger.

"Everything's all right, Pa. This 'gentleman' was jus' leaving," she assured her father.

"What's he want here? I heard a shot—"

"Something he can't have." Rina met Chastain's icy stare with a determined one of her own. "And wouldn't take no for an answer."

Ben Taylor stiffened to his full height. "If'n my

daughter's saying what I think she is, I'll shoot you myself."

He turned to glance at Rina, taking in her disheveled appearance.

"Gal, did he?"

"He tried and failed." She brushed a strand of hair away from her cheek.

"Aren't either of you going to help me?" Chastain asked them. "I'm hurt."

"You're lucky I don't jus' up and shoot ya where ya stand, outlander. From the looks of your wound, all it needs is to be cleaned and wrapped with a handkerchief. Why, it's nothing more'n a scratch," Ben Taylor said in disgust.

"I—"

"If'n you know what's good fer ya, outlander, ya'll get off Taylor land. Now!" Ben Taylor motioned with his gun barrel.

Chastain looked from the tough old man to Rina. Together they were a formidable team.

"Get off Taylor land." She placed her finger on the trigger for emphasis, then motioned to the doorway with the shotgun.

Chastain took a step toward the door, but halted when Ben Taylor spoke.

"Mister! If you ever try and lay a hand on my daughter again, I'll finish you. Understand?"

Swearing, Chastain turned and strode outside to his horse. Rina followed him at a cautious distance. She watched him ride off, her forehead creased in a thoughtful frown.

What if Chastain had been telling the truth about Shane?

Jus' what was Shane Delaney doing in the hills?

Sixteen

Shane leaned back against the broad tree trunk and closed his eyes. All around him the wildflowers were in bloom. Instinctively, he'd sought out the same field where he'd first made love to Rina.

If he kept his eyes closed, he could imagine her lying beside him, her hair spread out around her like a halo covering the flowers. She was part angel, part hoyden, part lady.

It seemed that she was constantly changing on him. However, one thing that he knew for sure—a man would never be bored with a woman like Rina Taylor.

That thought led him back to his dilemma. He opened his eyes, focusing on a brilliant colored bloom. What was he going to do about the recipe? And his knowledge of what went into it?

The very recipe that Rina had given him out of her trust and love, his conscience taunted him.

Once again, it all came back to a choice between Rina or Belle Rive and his promise on his parents' graves. Sighing, he leaned his head back and closed his eyes, shutting out the sunlight and the memory of the afternoon in this very field of wildflowers.

In his mind, he could call up a picture of Belle Rive the way it had looked so many years ago—beautiful, proud, and majestic. The large, impressive house had been full of laughter and happiness. He so desperately wanted that again.

Now he could have it.

All he had to do was deliver the secret recipe to Nolan Gant, collect his money for it, and return to New Orleans and buy back his home.

It sounded so simple—just give the vicious old man what he wanted and Shane could have his dream. All he had to do was to destroy Rina.

However, if he didn't give Nolan the recipe, would Rina die at the old man's hands? Shane couldn't protect her every second of the day for the rest of her life.

If he turned the recipe over to Nolan Gant and his son, would the old man give up his vendetta against the Taylors? Would he finally leave Rina alone? Give up his vow to see her dead?

"Dammit," Shane muttered, clenching his hands into fists. There was no way to know the answers to those questions with certainty.

He ran a hand through his hair and around to the knotted muscles at the back of his neck. Nothing was worth risking Rina's life.

While he sat there locked in his private dilemma, the peace and beauty of the hills began to do their timeless work on him. He relaxed and felt the tension drain from his body. Closing his eyes, he inhaled the fresh air and sweet aroma of nearby blossoms.

A few minutes later, he opened his eyes, and knew he had his answer.

At the sound of approaching footsteps, Rina snatched up the shotgun again, cradling it in her arms. She wouldn't be caught off guard this time.

She scanned the area around the cabin in all directions, checking for whoever was coming. Tightening her grip on the shotgun, she waited, her heart racing in her chest.

As Shane strode into sight, a sigh of relief swept past her lips, until she remembered the reason she was waiting for his return. Facing him, she raised her chin in firm determination. Shane Delaney had one all-important question to answer for her.

She'd have the answer to that question one way or another.

Watching him walk toward her with his assured, distance-eating strides, she felt her heart begin to race in her chest and felt her stomach begin to flutter. Even though she called herself every kind of a fool, it didn't do much good. Her body jus' wasn't a-listenin' to her. Instead, all her body heard was the man-to-woman call of Shane's body.

Hell's bells, it seemed like the least she could

do was to resist the man. Didn't it? Apparently not, because her body wasn't hearing what her mind told it, not in the least bit. No matter how adamantly she told herself to fight his lure, her body insisted on responding to his approach. Once again she called herself a fool.

After all, she told herself, it wasn't like he loved her in return, was it? No, she definitely feared it wasn't like that at all.

All of a sudden she realized that the opposite was true for her. She was hopelessly in love. In love with Shane Delaney.

Sucking in a breath for the courage to resist the heat and temptation in his deep blue gaze, she planted her feet and leveled her shotgun. It was now or never, she told herself.

"That's far enough, Shane."

"Rina, what's wrong?"

Shane looked from her to the shotgun she had pointed at him. An inkling of suspicion grew in his mind. Had Nolan Gant been here? Had he revealed their terminated arrangement to Rina?

No, he assured himself. Nolan Gant wouldn't have the guts to show up at the Taylor cabin. Besides, the old man had told him how dead set his son, Billy, was against anything happening to Rina.

"I gots one question for you," Rina stated, her voice tight.

Her jaw trembled with the effort it took to hold her emotions in check.

Shane stared at her in puzzlement. What had

happened while he was gone? He'd never seen her like this. Her inner torment showed clearly on her expressive face. Doubt, suspicion, hope all flashed across her face.

"What is it, Rina?"

Rina took a deep breath, swallowed, then fired the question out in one long breath. "Are you a-workin' for Nolan Gant?"

Shane's gut clenched into a knot.

She knew. He didn't know how she'd found out, but he had no doubt that she knew the truth. Or at least the worst of it.

He knew with absolute certainty that he had waited too long to tell her the truth himself. Her determined stance told him far better than mere words could that she wasn't going to be willing to listen to any explaining he might try to do.

It was too late.

While in the peace and beauty of the hills and the memorable field of wildflowers, he'd realized that he'd changed, and that he'd come to love these hills almost as much as Rina did. He understood that he couldn't turn over the recipe to Nolan.

Shane had known that he couldn't destroy Rina's trusting heart, but it seemed that was just what he'd succeeded in doing anyway.

Rina watched him closely. The look of shock and guilt on his face was all the answer she needed. Her heart sank as she stared into his set gaze.

She faced him with the moistness of tears sparkling on her lashes. Swallowing down the lump that was growing larger in her throat with every passing second of silence from Shane, she raised her chin.

"Aren't you even gonna answer me?" she challenged his silence.

No answer was as good as an admission of guilt, she told herself.

A bitterness had crept into her voice, and Shane flinched inside at the unfamiliar sentiment he heard coming from her

"Would it make any difference if I did?" he asked her. "Do you want my answer?"

"Yes, dammit."

"Rina, let me explain—"

"No. I don't want explanations or fancy talking. All I wants is a yes or a no. And don't you bother giving me anymore of your sweet-talking lies. I'm long past believing them anymore."

Rina blinked back the stinging in her eyes. Why, he was no better'n the smooth-talker that her ma ran off with, she told herself. This proved it beyond a doubt. She shoulda known better than to trust this outlander. She shoulda known.

Jus' look at what trusting an outlander had gotten her ma. It had made her up and leave her husband and children. Rina clenched her hands around the shotgun. Why'd she hafta keep thinking 'bout her ma? Especially now? It seemed that being around Shane made her think more and more on her ma and the memories that she'd tried so hard to shut away.

Her bestest memories of her ma were of purty hair the color of the silvery moon, and soft hands that smoothed away her tears after a bad dream, and the sweet smell of lavender.

Rina shook her head, trying to drive the memories back away where she'd kept them locked up. Ever since her ma left, she found she couldn't stand the smell of lavender; that's why she'd chosen to add rose petals to her scented water instead.

Her ma had betrayed her by a-leavin' that way. Why, she'd never even heard from her ma up until jus' before she died. Rina always wondered if they'd have heard from her then if'n Milly's momma hadn't bumped into her. The feeling of betrayal still cut deep. And now, Shane Delaney had betrayed her, too.

"Rina," Shane said her name in a low voice.

She fought the tug she felt on her heart.

"All you were after was the recipe." Accusation came with each word.

No, he admitted to himself. He'd been after Rina from the moment he'd seen the miniature of her in the jail cell.

"And fool that I was, I jus' up and gave it to you. So, you got what you came here for." Her voice broke. "Now jus' go."

"Rina, listen to me."

Shane took a step closer, but stopped when she raised the shotgun. He could see the whiteness of her knuckles as she gripped the gun too tightly.

"Rina, I did come here for Nolan Gant. In the beginning. I needed the money he offered."

Rina snorted at his answer.

"But I quit the day he tried to kill you with the flood up at the creek."

"And I'm supposed to believe you?"

And trust you, she added silently.

"Believe this—Nolan Gant intends to have the recipe. Even if he has to kill you to get it." He tried to make her see the danger.

"Hell's bells." She brushed aside Shane's warning as if it had been little more than a pesky fly.

"Didn't you hear me?"

"Me, and Pa, and Lucas have been fighting Nolan Gant jus' fine by ourselves for years. None of us are afeared of him."

"But—"

"I don't need you sticking around here out of duty as my protector. From—"

She refused to mention his "friend," Roger Chastain, to him. She was too ashamed at what Chastain had almost done to her.

"From anybody," she ended quickly.

"Dammit, Rina."

Shane started toward her, and she lowered the gun to discharge it at his feet. Dirt flew in a cloud around his ankles.

"Now get out." She raised the gun to point it at him. "Go away, Shane. Jus' go away." Weariness shaded her voice.

"All right, have it your way. But I'll be staying at the hotel in Blueberry Bluff. When you're ready to listen, let me know."

"You gots about as much a chance of that as a snowball in a hot oven, outlander."

Shane figured that she was right. There was no way that Rina was going to listen to anything he had to say at this moment. But, after she'd been given time to cool down, he would make her listen. He had to.

"I'll be in town."

He turned away, crossed to the cabin and picked up his belongings. Rina's father stood inside the kitchen, waiting and watching him.

"You leaving?" he asked.

"Yes."

"Damn fools. The both of you," Ben Taylor muttered, and strode toward the door. "Cain't see what's right in front of your noses."

"Ben."

The old man stopped and glanced back at Shane. A glimmer of hope lit his leathery face. "Yeah?"

"Nolan Gant is going to come after her."

Shane stared past him out the doorway at where Rina stood.

"I figured as much. Don't worry, I'll keep her safe from the likes of him."

"I'll be back."

"Give her a day or so, and maybe she'll hear you out then."

"Thanks. Ben? I didn't give him the recipe."

"I knows. Go ahead and take a horse. Bring it back when you come back."

"I will. Thank you."

When Shane stepped out of the cabin, Rina was nowhere in sight. She hadn't reappeared by the time he rode away. He hadn't really expected her to. But he would be back, he vowed. And she'd damned well listen to him.

He'd give her two days. No more. Then, he'd come back and demand that she hear him out.

However, within minutes of reaching Blueberry Bluff, his plans were abruptly changed. The first person he met was Lucas Taylor.

"Shane!" Lucas called out to him. Waving, he ran up as Shane dismounted in front of the hotel.

As soon as he reached him, Lucas clapped him on the back and waved a piece of paper back and forth in front of him.

"Hey, you just saved me a ride out to Pa's place. What are you doing here in town?"

"I—"

"Is everything all right out there? Nobody's hurt, are they?"

"No one's hurt."

"Good." Lucas nodded, then cocked his head and studied Shane. "Everything all right with Rina?"

"Rina's fine," he answered, hating the half-truth.

Shane figured Lucas would hear the news soon enough. Hopefully, he'd hear it from Ben Taylor, and not from Rina. Or not hear it until he'd had a chance to make Rina listen to him.

"Good. I really do need to try and stay close here to town for the next week," Lucas continued.

"Sarah Fergus is due to have her baby any day now. It's her first baby, too."

As Lucas launched into an explanation of Sarah's nervousness over her pregnancy, Shane sighed. Lucas always amazed him. Meeting the young doctor reminded him of being caught in a whirlwind.

"And the reason I was headed out to Pa's was to give you this," Lucas concluded, holding out the piece of paper to Shane.

Shane blinked at the abrupt change of subject, then took the paper from Lucas.

"It's a telegram. It came for you this morning. I hope nothing's wrong?"

Lucas stared at him, waiting expectantly for him to open it.

Shane opened the telegram and scanned the words, then reread them more slowly.

Belle Rive up for sale. Simon Cooke tiring of the South and Miss Dupre. If you want Belle Rive, be here by Friday.

It was signed "Brad Weston."

Shane stared at the words before him. Maybe there was still a chance to buy back Belle Rive. Maybe . . . if he got there in time.

"Lucas," he caught the other man's arm. "I have to get to New Orleans."

"A riverboat's leaving today."

At Shane's look of surprise, he added, "I expected if what was in there was important," he nodded to the telegram, "then you'd need to leave right away. So I did some checking around for you."

"Thanks. But Rina—"

"I'll get word to her and Pa. You will be coming back, won't you?"

"I'll be back," Shane promised.

"Glad to hear it." Lucas smiled, waved and headed for his horse.

Lucas wasted no time in riding out to the cabin and relaying the news to Rina and Pa.

"He's leaving on the riverboat for New Orleans. Today," he informed her, sitting down at the big kitchen table.

"Well, then, good riddance." Rina forced herself to say the words. "He was a-workin' for Nolan Gant the whole time."

"Rina, gal—"

"Pa, it's true."

Ben Taylor rubbed his hand across his chin, then dropped his hand to the oak table.

"Rina, gal, you're a fool."

He slapped his hand down hard on the table for emphasis.

"I knows that, Pa. I never shoulda trusted him."

"Hell, no, you're a damned fool fer ever letting him leave."

Rina blinked at her pa's emphatic tone. She didn't think he'd ever called her a "damned fool" in all her borned days.

"But he—"

"Dagnamit, gal. That man loves you something

fierce. You're a fool if'n you don't see that, and do something about it!"

"But he's going to marry his lady fiancée in New Orleans—"

"Dagnamit, gal. Didn't you hear a word I said? It's you he loves. He ain't gonna marry anybody else, lessen you run him off and then let him get plumb away."

"But—"

"Gal, I don't want you making the same mistake your ma did."

He reached out and drew Rina down into a chair. "Sit."

Puzzled, she went willingly. Her pa hadn't spoken 'bout her ma in years. Why now?

"Gal, there's something you needs to know. Our marrying wasn't your ma's idea. Our families, they set it all up years before. Lily . . ." he paused over her name.

It was the first time Rina had heard him say her ma's name since the night she ran off. Rina caught her pa's hand in hers in an attempt to offer comfort.

He cleared his throat, then continued, speaking in a low voice. "Lily never loved me."

He raised a hand to stop Rina's instant protest.

"No, it's all right. I always knew it. I jus' believed that I loved her enough for the both of us."

He stopped and drew in a deep breath. When he released it, his voice was louder, stronger, more determined to get his message across to Rina. "But it weren't right. She jus' couldn't live

305

her entire life with a man she didn't love. I'm telling you this 'cause I don't want to see you making her mistake all over again. I don't want you passing up your chance at love and later settling on a man you don't truly love."

"Pa—"

"Think hard and deep, gal. Do you love this here Shane Delaney?"

Rina met her pa's questioning gaze and answered truthfully, "More than life."

"Well, hell's bells, gal. Go tell him that."

As she worried her bottom lip, he reached out and tilted her head up until she looked him square in the eyes.

"Don't you start to worrying 'bout that man's feelings. They's clear as new glass. He loves ya, gal. Don't let him git away. Now, ya git."

"But what about the recipe?" she asked. It had always been every Taylor's job to safeguard it, for as many years back as she could remember. "I've spent my life—"

"Exactly!" Her pa slammed his palm down on the table again. "Why, you've spent so much of your time on our whiskey that you haven't gotten yerself a husband. And that's a hell of a lot more important to me than the whiskey."

"Pa . . ."

"Well, it's the truth. Besides, Nolan Gant ain't got the sense of a flea. He couldn't make good whiskey even with the recipe."

Rina couldn't resist joining in Pa and Lucas's laughter at this.

"Well, gal, what's it gonna be? You gonna fight or jus' give up?"

Pa was right. She wasn't a quitter or likely to jus' lie down and give up like a wounded gopher. Oh no, she'd always fought for what she wanted. And damn it all, she wanted Shane Delaney.

"I'm going after him."

Rina hugged her pa tightly.

"Good," her pa pronounced.

As Rina turned toward the cabin door, he laid a hand on her arm and stopped her.

"You'd best go purty yourself up first. Then go after him."

Rina smiled. He was right. And she knew exactly what dress she'd choose to "purty herself up with," too.

She dashed to her bedroom and pulled out her special dress—her favorite one. It was the one that was the same color as Shane's eyes.

Throwing open her trunk, she tossed out her new lacy underthings and petticoats. As she picked up a sheer chemise, she recalled Milly's remark about how a body *feels* like a lady when she has something special like this next to her skin.

Rina felt her cheeks heating with a blush as she ran her finger over a tiny blue satin bow. She wondered what Shane would think if he could see her in this.

With her mind on Shane and their upcoming confrontation, she dressed in record time. As she turned to look at herself in the mirror, her breath caught in her throat.

She looked like a real lady. Honest to goodness.

The deep blue silk muslin seemed to shimmer in the light with her every move. She ran her fingers lovingly over the ruffled edges of French lace, trimming the low-cut bodice. My, but there was plenty of her to see—it seemed that the white lace emphasized the wide expanse of golden tanned skin, seeming to make her glow.

She trailed her hands down her cinched waist where the gown flared out into a long, full skirt. Everything about the dress was perfect.

Snapping out of her reverie, she quickly brushed her hair, grabbed up a bag and tossed two dresses and the fixings for them into it. She was ready. She'd show Shane Delaney that she could so be a perfect lady when she set her mind to it. She turned away and headed out into the other room.

Pa met her at the door with a whistle. "Gal, you looks mighty purty."

He caught her close and wrapped her in a bear-like hug.

"Good-bye, Pa."

"Don't let him get away, gal." He released her. "I want that boy fer a son-in-law."

Her pa's parting instructions stayed with her on the ride to Blueberry Bluff. For once in his life, her brother Lucas was quiet, concentrating on getting them into town as fast as he possibly could.

The riverboat's shrill whistle sounded as they rode up. Grabbing her bag, Rina jumped down from her horse and ran for the boat.

She was the last one to race up the gangway, but she'd made it in time. That was all that mattered.

Breathless, she leaned against the white railing and paused to catch her breath and ready her courage for her meeting with Shane.

In too much of hurry before, she took a moment now to survey the fancy riverboat. Painted white, it was multi-decked, and seemed to stretch out forever to her. She stared up at the two, tall fluted smokestacks in awe. It was purely a sight to behold.

Puffs of smoke rose from the smokestacks to float off into the sky above. Taking in her fill of the beautiful boat, she turned back to watch the shoreline of Blueberry Bluff as it became smaller and smaller. Under the beginning rays of sunset, the river turned the color of unripe peaches.

The same view drew Shane to the railing. He stared longingly across the water at the town. From the corner of his eye, he noticed a blonde beauty avidly watching the shore. *Something* about her stance drew him.

Unable to resist, he turned for a closer look, and his throat closed on his next breath. *Rina.*

It couldn't be. But it was.

"Rina?" Her name was a mere whisper of sound on his lips.

She turned at the sound and her gaze met his, holding him fast. Swallowing down her nervousness and a tinge of fear, she forced herself not to look away.

Shane stared in disbelief. She was a vision. Breathtaking. Enough to steal a man's heart away.

She stood with her back to the white railing, one hand on the rail. The same crisp white was repeated with the lace trim at her bodice, calling his gaze to the golden skin laid bare. Her blue gown shimmered with the rays of sunset.

Under the deep blue silk, her body called to him. She looked like an angel, set in blue against the backdrop of white rail and pink and gold setting sun. An angel and a temptress.

As he continued to stare at her, Rina knew what she felt in her heart must surely show in her eyes. Without shame, she met his gaze.

He was dressed like the first time she'd seen him. Dark pants, white ruffled shirt—every inch the riverboat gambler. A lock of dark hair dipped over his forehead, and she ached to lovingly brush it back.

Dark as Satan's sin. The thought came back to her.

"Hi, outlander," she said softly.

It was all the invitation he needed. Shane strode toward her and swept her into his arms. His mouth descended on hers with breath-stealing quickness.

His lips claimed hers, demanding, possessing her very soul. She returned his kisses, breath for breath, wrapping her arms around his neck.

He splayed his hands around her tiny waist, loving the feel of her beneath his touch. Her breasts pressed against his chest, inflaming the passion she'd set loose with the sound of her soft voice.

He continued kissing her until they both were forced to draw back for a breath. However, he kept both of his arms linked about her, refusing to chance her escaping his embrace.

"I can't believe you're here."

"You didn't think you'd get away that easy, did you?" she teased.

"Rina, I wasn't leaving you." His voice deepened with earnestness, as he tried to make her understand. "I was coming back."

"I know. Lucas told me."

"Today, I was half-afraid I'd lost you." The admission was torn out of him.

He caught her close again, raining kisses over her upturned face.

"Never," she whispered against his lips.

"Rina, sweetheart, I love you."

She pulled back suddenly.

"You . . . love me?" The question was a hesitant whisper.

"Yes, I do."

Her heart soared, and she was sure it had taken wings and flown to the heavens. He loved her!

"Rina, I need to explain—"

She laid her fingertips against his lips. "Later. For now, jus' love me."

Catching her up into his arms, he carried her to his cabin and proceeded to do just that, loving every inch of her. Thoroughly and completely.

Seventeen

"So, are you gonna buy it back?" Rina asked Shane.

She paused and leaned against the white railing of the deck of the riverboat. They were taking a stroll around the dock, following a successful evening of gambling.

Shane stopped and joined her at the railing. Staring down at the muddy water churned up by the riverboat, he thought before answering.

"I'm going to try. Tomorrow's Thursday, so we'll make it to New Orleans in time."

"You won a lot tonight, didn't you?" She grinned at him, wanting to wipe away the frown that had marred his brow at the mention of his upcoming attempt.

Shane joined her happy laughter. The night had been very profitable, and personally he felt a large part of it was because Rina had been at his side, cheering him on.

"Did you enjoy yourself?" he asked her.

"Um-huh. I haven't even seen Pa play cards for that long a time at a stretch."

"I certainly hope you don't think of me the same way," he said indignantly.

"Oh, no. You're my sweet-talking gambler."

"Then I guess that makes you a gambler's lady," he teased.

"Oh, Shane, am I really a lady?" she asked earnestly.

"Yes, sweetheart. You're a lady."

Shane caught her up in his arms, pulling her close. Their bodies molded together from chest to thighs.

Rina's happy laughter flowed like warm honey. She snuggled closer against him. The trip had been like a dream come true. Except for the time at the gaming tables tonight, they had spent the days in a world of their own.

Since the evening she'd joined him on the riverboat, they had shared so much together. Loving, and laughter, and more loving, of course.

Shane had told her of his home and his desire to repurchase it. He'd admitted how he'd originally planned to get the needed funds, and how, in the end, he couldn't turn the recipe over to Nolan.

But best of all, Rina noted, Shane's stomach hadn't hurt him once in the past days.

Rina smiled at the thought. Ida's potion sure seemed to be telling her that Shane had been speaking the truth these last days. Especially about how he loved her.

Slipping her arm through his, she snuggled against him. Instantly, he stepped away from the rail and pulled her close.

"Let's skip the rest of our walk tonight, shall we?" he bent down and whispered in her ear. "I find I'd rather spend our last night on board in our room. Together."

His reminder of the passing time caused Rina's smile to fade. For the dozenth time that day she wondered what New Orleans would bring them.

A vague uneasiness settled over her. How was she to fit in with his fancy home? What would the big city of New Orleans and his friends be like?

The big city life of St. Louis hadn't been kind to her ma—it had killed her in the end. An uneasy sense of foreboding settled over Rina. Would the big city destroy her, too?

"Ready?" Shane wrapped his arms around her.

Rina forced a smile for him, keeping her inner fears and uneasiness to herself. She had tonight to savor, and she intended to fully savor each kiss, each touch, each moment of loving. She'd face tomorrow when it came, and not a moment before.

The loud, clear whistle of the riverboat heralded their arrival in New Orleans. All around them, the docks jumped to life. Carts, wagons, and people clustered around to greet the departing passengers.

Rina felt lost in the hustle and bustle surrounding her, while Shane chuckled and strode through the throng of activity without batting an eye. Looking first one way and then the other, Rina tried not to miss a single thing.

Shane hailed a carriage, assisted Rina inside, and ordered the driver to take them to a hotel. Rina leaned back against the seat, relieved to be up out of the crowd's reach for a few minutes. All the activity combined to overwhelm her.

Shortly the docks with their clutter of crates, barrels, and trunks gave way to the warehouses. As they drew away from the docks, the scenery changed to wrought-iron gates guarding courtyards and two-storied homes.

Rina stared open-mouthed at the houses. She'd never knowed anybody who lived in houses this big. Why, she bet Miss Hattie's whole house could be put in the parlor of one of these city houses.

Ladies in fancy dresses walked along the streets and peered into shop windows. Rina stared at the ladies' parasols and ruffled dresses.

She glanced down at her plain green dress that she'd thought so purty when she'd put it on that morning. Suddenly, her dress didn't feel so right—here in the big city. A strange, unknown sense of being out of place assailed her, and she drew quiet.

Shane checked them into the hotel and led Rina to their room. Going to the balcony, he stepped out and watched the activity below. He seemed to thrive on it, Rina thought.

She stepped back into the room and crossed to the pitcher of water. Running her finger along the edge, she tried to put her mind at peace.

"Rina? Sweetheart, is anything wrong?"

She jumped when Shane brushed her shoulder with his hand. What could she tell him? That she was afeared of a feeling she couldn't even explain?

"I'm jus' tired," she lied.

She waited, almost expecting for her own stomach to hurt at her lie. She'd have felt silly a-tryin' to explain her unknown fear to him. Why, she wasn't even used to the feeling of being afeared, much less of explaining to somebody when she didn't even know what it was that she feared.

The uneasiness increased. Along with it came a strange sense of impending doom. If only she knew where the danger was coming from, then she'd know how to fight it. Maybe it was jus' the unknown that was making her nervous, she tried to assure herself.

"If you'd like to rest, I think I'll ride out to Belle Rive and talk to Simon Cooke."

Hope tinged his voice, and she didn't have the heart to deny him.

"Yes, that sounds fine," she forced the lie out.

She could see that he was anxious to go, and her stomach knotted in response. What she wanted to do was to ask him to catch the next boat home with her. But she didn't. Instead, she kissed him goodbye.

"Wish me luck?" he asked softly.

"Always."

Shane left the hotel with a smile. Everything was looking much better now than when he'd headed out on this trip from Arkansas. This time he was sure to be in time before Belle Rive was sold to someone else.

Thanks to luck and skill, he had enough money to meet the likely purchase price. And most important of all—he had Rina's love.

The ride to Belle Rive took much more time than Shane had anticipated. His eagerness to see his home again made him impatient. Finally, the house came into sight.

Shane reined his horse in and gazed at his former home. It stood tall and proud in the sunlight, surrounded by lush grass. It seemed every bit as large as he'd remembered, but now it also seemed a little cold and imposing to him.

Flicking the reins, he nudged his horse forward. A servant he'd never seen before met him before he dismounted.

"Is Mr. Cooke at home?" Shane asked, feeling a strange sense of not belonging anymore.

"Yes, sir. He's in the study."

"Please tell him that Shane Delaney would like to speak with him."

Shane dismounted and looked around him, slowly taking in the changes. He guessed that he shouldn't have expected it to remain exactly the same.

His mother's rocker no longer sat peacefully on the veranda, and he could no longer feel his parents' presence or their laughter. The house stood before him, freshly painted, cool, a stranger.

"Mr. Delaney? Welcome to Belle Rive." Simon Cooke greeted him.

As the Northerner stepped forward, his hand outstretched, Shane studied him. The man was balding, and shorter than Shane had expected. Much older, too. Probably nearing his fifties.

"Glad to meet you." Shane shook the older man's hand. "I hope I'm not imposing, but I used to live here. Years ago. I was in town for a visit and wondered if I could see the place again." He made up the story as he went along, not exactly sure what to say now that he was here, and everything around him had changed so much.

The sudden roll of his stomach caught him off guard. It must be the trip, he thought absently.

"Of course," Simon Cooke answered. "William here will be happy to show you around." He gestured to the tall, slim servant standing nearby. "As I'm sure you've heard, I am putting Belle Rive up for sale. My fiancée and I are leaving for Philadelphia next week, and there are a lot of arrangements to see to. If you'll excuse me, I have some things to attend to, but feel free to look as long as you like."

"Thank you," Shane answered.

Shane followed the servant into the entry of his former home. At the sight of the highly-polished, curved stair railing, he stopped. It captured his full attention as a long-forgotten memory brought a smile to his face.

His mother had kept the railing polished, too. How he'd loved to slide down that gleaming railing as a child. Somehow it seemed that his mother would always be waiting for him as he reached the bottom. Arms crossed over her chest, she would pretend to be angry, but he always detected the twitching of her lips as she tried unsuccessfully to hold back her laughter.

"Sir?"

The servant's voice drew Shane out of his reverie, and he turned and followed the man through the wide doors to the ballroom. The room was as spacious and magnificent as he remembered. It had hosted many a ball before the war; Belle Rive had always been renowned for its parties. His boots clicked smartly on the flooring as he crossed the room to look out the sparkling windows to the grounds beyond.

"Mr. Cooke has seen to the restoring of the grounds," William informed him.

Lush greenness spread as far as Shane could see. To his right stood a proud oak tree. As he stared at the spreading branches, his throat tightened. The massive oak marked the beginning of the family graveyard. Generations of Delaneys rested there.

It had been there, upon his parents' graves, that he'd made his vow to them to regain the plantation. Shane blinked away the tightness in his throat. Belle Rive had been passed from father to son for generations—a legacy of love, his father had called it. And now? Now Shane had the funds to finally fulfill that vow.

Strange, but that realization failed to send a thrill through him like he had expected it to do. In fact, standing within the walls of Belle Rive, looking out over the lands, he felt nothing except a fading connection with the past. Rina was his future—he knew that without a single doubt.

At that moment, he could almost swear he heard his mother's voice, so real was the memory. It had been here, in this very room, hours before their annual Belle Rive ball that his mother had drawn him aside. Neither of them knew it would be the last gala hall they'd hold at the beautiful plantation before the war swept everything away.

Or perhaps she had known, Shane thought.

"Find love, son," his mother had told him in a firm voice. She'd caught his hands in hers and held them to her cheek.

"Find it and treasure it," she'd insisted.

Love.

More than anything else, he remembered love when he looked around the large, now opulent room. Love, and laughter, and happiness.

His parents' marriage had been so filled with love that the happiness spilled over into the lives they touched. Much the same way that Rina's vibrancy and love of life reached out to touch those she encountered.

The thought drew him up. He'd seen enough. His path was suddenly clear. Although Belle Rive was as beautiful as ever, it no longer held him fast. All the plantation held was memories and the past.

His future wasn't here. It was with Rina. Shane knew without a doubt that Rina would be smothered in the lavish plantation and its social customs—much the same way that he would be now. He turned back to the wide window and the graves under the large tree.

"I found love, Mother," he whispered.

It was as if he could feel his parents releasing him from his vow. He knew they would want his happiness above all else. And he knew that happiness lay only with Rina.

Smiling, suddenly feeling freer than he'd felt in years, Shane turned from the window and the past to face his future.

"William, I believe I've seen enough. Thank you for your patience."

Mere minutes later, he was back in front of the house. As William went to tell Simon Cooke that they had finished, Shane looked out over the grounds. While the plantation was as majestic as ever, it was no longer the all-consuming need to him that it once was. As he studied the change in himself, he realized he no longer needed Belle Rive to feel complete. Rina had completed him, healed him. The past was truly over.

A smile brightened his face, and he turned away from the view to face Simon Cooke.

"Thank you for letting me visit Belle Rive

again." Shane extended his hand. "Best of luck to you."

"You're not interested in purchasing it?"

"No, I'm sorry, Simon, but I'm no longer interested in buying Belle Rive."

A weight lifted from Shane's shoulders. He could hardly wait to get back to Rina and tell her the news. Suddenly he understood her earlier quiet and withdrawal; she had feared living here. She had known deep inside what he'd yet to realize—Belle Rive was not "home."

Shane had scarcely left the grounds of Belle Rive when a lone rider cantered up to him. He recognized the dark, glossy hair, and fine horsemanship of Mary Ellen Dupre. He waited for the familiar response inside, but felt nothing.

"Shane, darling," she stretched the endearment out as she drew alongside him. "How wonderful to see you. I'm sorry I wasn't home for you."

Her tone of voice and the look in her eyes implied much more. Shane felt absolutely no reaction to her invitation. Instead of her voice sounding shy as he'd always thought in the past, he now recognized its blatantness.

"I stopped by to visit Belle Rive."

"Then it's true? You're going to own it again. You don't know how happy that makes me."

She laid a hand on his arm and leaned toward him, allowing him an unhampered view of the tops of her breasts revealed by her riding habit's low-cut bodice. He looked away.

"Oh, Shane. It has been so horrible. A Yankee never should have been allowed to own Belle Rive. Much less a man like Simon." She sniffed. "Belle Rive always belonged to you. And now it will again."

Shane raised his brows at her disparaging remark about her fiancé. Lover's quarrel? he wondered.

"No, Mary Ellen," he corrected her. "Belle Rive no longer belongs to me. And it won't."

"But surely you have enough money to purchase it. I'm sure Simon could be persuaded to sell for less. He can't wait to get back to Philadelphia."

Shane shook his head. "I'm no longer interested. In fact, I don't plan to stay on in New Orleans."

"What?" Mary Ellen blanched, straightening on her mount.

"Within a few days, I'll be returning to Arkansas with my fiancée." *Fiancée.* He tasted the word on his tongue, liking the sound of it. Granted, he hadn't actually asked Rina to marry him yet, but he knew what her answer would be.

"Oh, Shane, that's wonderful." Mary Ellen twisted in her saddle to glance back at the house. "Ah . . . would you mind if I rode into town with you?"

As Shane hesitated, she added quickly, "I need to talk to you. To somebody." A hint of desperation entered her usually cultured, calm voice.

"Mary Ellen—"

"Please, Shane A favor for old times? I'm . . . I'm in terrible trouble. I'm not safe here. Please," she pleaded, tears welling up in her dark, expressive eyes.

Shane found he couldn't refuse her earnest plea for help.

"Of course," he answered. "Let's go."

"Oh, yes."

Mary Ellen cast a fearful glance over her shoulder that didn't go unnoticed by Shane. This was completely out of character for Mary Ellen. She usually sparkled and bubbled with flirtatious laughter, never afraid and nervous like she was now. She must be in serious trouble.

"Mary Ellen?"

She jumped at the sound of her name, then shuddered.

"Please, let's just get away from here. I can't talk here."

Her bottom lip quivered, and she tightened her hold, on the reins. Kicking her horse, she sent the mare into a gallop well ahead of Shane.

He caught up with her, and seeing the tears streaking her face, handed her his handkerchief. She dabbed at her eyes daintily, and suddenly he was reminded of the differences between her and Rina. Compared to Rina, Mary Ellen's ladylike actions now appeared stilted and contrived to him.

He chastised himself for his thoughts. Mary Ellen needed his help, not his criticism and comparisons.

Mary Ellen sent him a weak smile. Carefully,

she turned her head, hiding her face from his scrutiny. It wouldn't do for him to look too closely at her tears. She feared that maybe she was over-acting. But she was desperate. Belle Rive was about to slip through her fingers, and she'd do anything to keep hold of it. Anything.

Being mistress of Belle Rive had been her goal since the day she'd turned thirteen, and she didn't intend to fail in achieving that goal. She'd only maneuvered Simon into an engagement for that purpose. And now the fool wanted to leave it all and move North. *North!* Never.

She wasn't about to blithely go off to Philadelphia with a Yankee and leave Belle Rive behind. She could have tolerated marriage to Simon if Belle Rive had been part of the bargain. The wealthy Northerner had only two things going for him—the plantation and his money. However, since he'd cut off her credit last week, his money had paled in her eyes. Why, the man had actually been stingy to her.

Oh no, she wanted someone generously rich and virile. Like Shane Delaney. If she played her hand right, she knew she could have him, too.

"SS-Shane," she stammered over his name. "It's been so horrible. I need help from someone, and you're the only person I can turn to. I know I can trust you not to fail me."

"What about Simon?"

"Oh, please, don't even mention his name to me." Her voice broke, and she gave a delicate shudder of revulsion. "I never wanted to marry him. He forced me into this engagement."

"Mary Ellen—"

"Do you think that I would willingly marry a Yankee?"

"Perhaps, if it got you Belle Rive," he said.

"Shane, how can you think so little of me?" Her voice caught on a sob. "If that's how you feel, I'll go to someone else for help."

She whirled her horse around. Shane felt like a cad. It wasn't Mary Ellen's fault that he now found her theatrics tiring and a bit much. He had grown used to Rina's naturalness and honesty, and found he liked those traits much better. He couldn't blame Mary Ellen for simply being herself. The fact was, he wished it was Rina at his side right now.

"Wait," he called after her.

She pulled her horse up and quickly joined him. "You'll help me?" Her face brightened.

"That depends. What do you need?"

"Some place to hide until Simon leaves for Philadelphia. If he finds me, he'll force me to accompany him."

She clasped her hands together, wringing the handkerchief tightly between them.

"You don't know him like I do." She lowered her voice to a whisper. "He's cruel and heartless."

"Don't you have any place you could go?"

"Not where he wouldn't find me." She fell silent, then sent her horse into a canter.

As the city of New Orleans came into sight,

Mary Ellen slowed and grabbed the reins of Shane's horse. Fear and desperation clouded her face when she looked at him.

"Please, Shane, hide me from him? It will only be for a few days. You could get me a room down the hall from yours, then I'd feel safe," she implored.

Reluctantly, Shane agreed. He couldn't turn away an old friend. He owed Mary Ellen—the woman he'd intended to marry, his conscience chided him. For an instant, she almost made him feel guilt at the happiness he'd found with Rina, while Mary Ellen was so unhappy and afraid.

It took only minutes to rent a second room under his name. However, he did gather a few curious stares. Shane knew he'd need to explain it to Rina before she heard any idle gossip.

Eager to be with Rina again, he handed the key to the new room to Mary Ellen.

"Please, come up with me," she beseeched him, then rushed to add, "only until I get settled and stop feeling so weak and faint." She glanced around nervously.

The gentleman in him wouldn't allow him to refuse her. Unfortunately, his reunion with Rina would have to wait a few more minutes.

Once inside the room, Mary Ellen leaned on his arm. He helped her to a chair, and she sank onto it, wringing his handkerchief between her hands.

"Oh, I'm so ashamed for being so weak. Oh,

Shane, would you please pour me a sherry? To help steady me?"

Nodding, he crossed to a side table and poured a glass of the liquid. Returning, he extended it to her. She accepted it gratefully. With the glass halfway to her lips, she stopped, lowering it to look up at him.

"Where are my manners? Won't you please join me?" Standing to her feet, she crossed to the side table and set her glass down.

"No, thank you. I need to get back to Rina."

"Oh, please." She turned around to face him. "Just one? We can toast to happier days. And to *your* happiness." She sniffed delicately.

As he hesitated, she added, her bottom lip quivering, "For old times?"

"For old times," he agreed.

Mary Ellen turned away and poured a second glass of sherry. Careful to keep her back to Shane, she eased a small packet out of her pocket. Quickly she emptied the powdery contents into one of the glasses, swirling the liquid around with her fingertip to mix it in.

Smiling to herself, Mary Ellen acknowledged that her plan was progressing beautifully. She had to separate him from his new fiancée, and this little plan she'd devised would do it quite aptly.

Come morning, she would be his newest fiancée. Then everything else would work itself out. He'd come around for her—within the week, he'd be buying Belle Rive for her as a wedding present.

Assured that the powder was well mixed in, she

328

turned around and extended the glass to Shane. As he took it from her, she raised her own glass in a toast.

"To better times," she said.

To my success, she added silently.

Mary Ellen sipped her sherry, watching Shane's every move. Soon. Very soon. She raised her glass and took another sip, her action subtly encouraging him to drink from his glass.

Trying not to appear eager to be gone, Shane rolled the glass between his palms, the liquid swirling in the glass, and thought of Rina waiting just a few doors down the hall. He took a deep swallow from the glass, then a second, draining the contents. The sweet sherry burned its way down his throat.

Shane set the empty glass back down on the table and cleared his throat. Now to extricate himself as quickly as possible from Mary Ellen Dupre. He'd forgotten how persistent and demanding she could be. Or perhaps he'd never really looked closely before.

He yawned, hiding it behind his palm as a sudden sleepiness surged over him. Blinking his eyes against the growing drowsiness, Shane stepped forward. A strange lethargy engulfed him, and his vision blurred. He blinked his eyes again, shaking his head to clear it.

The sherry? He focused his eyes on the glass. It seemed so far away.

He reached for the glass, but it seemed to move away from his outstretched hand. Mary Ellen's face moved closer, and she seemed to smile at him. He yawned again.

What was happening? A sharp pain shot through his head, muddling his thoughts, and he swayed unsteadily. Sleep, he wanted to sleep.

In the next instant, the room around him darkened, and he pitched forward.

Mary Ellen caught Shane as he fell and eased him into the chair. Both sherry glasses crashed to the floor.

Swearing, she stepped away from the broken glass, then hurried to clean it up. Returning to Shane, she stared down at him. He was sound asleep.

"So, you thought you could leave me, did you?" She laughed, not concerned about anyone hearing her.

He was out cold. And he'd remain that way until morning. She'd given him enough of the sleeping powder to see to that. Nothing would mar her plan.

Grabbing him under his arms, she half-dragged, half-carried him to the bed and dropped him onto the thick mattress. She drew his feet up and stretched his unconscious form out on the sheet.

Sighing, she sat down on the bed and caught her breath. A few minutes later, she stood and looked down at Shane. Her face creased in a wide grin of triumph.

His eyes were closed, his dark lashes resting against his contrasting pale skin. He really was quite a handsome man. Marriage to him wouldn't be bad; besides, she'd have her little diversions to keep her satisfied, too.

Bending over him, she tugged off his boots, first, then followed it with his clothing. When he lay naked on the sheet, she stepped back and surveyed his body, mentally comparing him to Simon Cooke. Yes, marriage to Shane Delaney would be fine.

Shrugging, she turned away and undressed, then slipped into the bed beside him. Artfully she arranged the covers to reveal what she wanted to have shown to anyone looking in. The stage was set for her little play. Morning couldn't come soon enough for her.

Rina paced the width of the hotel room again. She figured that she'd practically worn a pathway betwixt the window and the door by now.

Where was Shane?

He hadn't returned yesterday afternoon, or evening. She crossed to the window again to stare out the glass. To the east the sky was growing lighter; at last the darkness of night was beginning to lift. As she watched, the faint streaks of dawn colored the sky.

Morning.

She hugged her arms about her waist. Trying to keep the fear and worry at bay, she concentrated on watching the sunrise.

Suddenly, a woman's shriek cut through the

331

early dawn's silence that blanketed the hotel. Doors opened and slammed up and down the hall. Rina turned away from the window and dashed to the door.

One thought held her tight, cutting off her breathing. Shane. Something had happened to him.

Throwing open the door, she rushed out into the hall. The commotion was coming from a room a few doors down where a hotel maid stood with her hands over her mouth.

Curious, Rina joined the small cluster of people outside the open doorway. What she saw inside hit her with the force of a powerful blow to her chest. Her breath rushed out in a cry of denial, and she covered her mouth with her hands.

Before her, in the large bed lay a man and woman, naked and entwined. *Shane. And another woman.*

From the scene, they had obviously been making love before the commotion of the maid interrupted them. Unable to stop herself, Rina stared at the embracing couple sprawled across the bed.

Shane had both his arms wrapped around the woman's waist. His head turned sideways and snuggled on her large breasts. The dark-haired woman had her hands clasped in the curls at the nape of Shane's neck.

"Shane?"

Rina didn't realize she'd spoken aloud until Shane's bed partner looked up at the door and screamed.

With a loud shriek, Mary Ellen grabbed up a cover, wrapping it around herself. Scooting up, she buried her head in her hands and broke into sobs.

"I'm ruined."

She looked over at where he lay beside her.

"Shane Delaney, you've ruined me!"

Horrified, Rina backed away from the scene.

Shane murmured something she couldn't make out and snuggled closer to the other woman. Rina thought surely she felt her heart break clean in two. Pain racked her, almost buckling her knees with its intensity.

"No," she whispered.

"I agree, miss," a middle-aged woman dressed in a nightgown and wrapper spoke. "The scoundrel will have to marry that poor woman. That's the only decent thing he could do."

A murmur of agreement went up along the hall from the spectators.

Another woman gasped. "Why that's Mary Ellen Dupre in there."

"I shouldn't wonder. They were engaged before the war, you know," a third voice put in.

Engaged. Shane's fancy "lady" fiancée. That's who lay in the bed with him, Rina thought to herself.

He'd never loved her at all. He'd planned all along to marry his fancy "lady." Well, let him!

Rina spun around and blindly ran for her room. Slamming the door behind her, she locked it and leaned against it.

Her eyes burned, but they were as dry as a bone. This time the pain went too deep for tears.

She'd lost everything. Her love, the recipe, and her self-respect.

"Damn you, Shane Delaney," she whispered.

Eighteen

At the sound of the door slamming, Shane sat up, then caught his head in his hands with a groan. Ribbons of pain cut through his head.

Blinking, he caught sight of Mary Ellen curled up against the head of the bed, and he jerked away from her. What was going on? Where was he?

He tried to think back to the night before, but it was all a blur. He remembered getting a distraught Mary Ellen a room, having a drink with her, and then nothing.

"What in the hell have you done?" he accused Mary Ellen.

"Me?" she shrieked, the picture of outraged indignity.

Doubt clouded his mind for a moment, and Shane questioned his own actions. He had no memory beyond drinking with Mary Ellen. Just how much had he drunk? It was a blur.

"Oh, Shane."

Mary Ellen made a show of drying her eyes with the edge of the sheet, then scooted closer to him. "Maybe you shouldn't have drunk so much last night."

"What?"

She pointed to an empty bottle beside the bed and shrugged.

"Not that it hampered your . . ." She paused delicately and colored. "Performance."

"What?"

She gestured with an airy wave of her hand to the two of them in the bed.

"But, darling. As you well know, now I truly am ruined." She sniffed delicately.

Shane stared at her.

"The maid," she replied. "The woman came in while we were sleeping. Why, her loud shriek woke up half the hallway.

Mary Ellen wrapped the sheet more tightly around her nude body in a display of sudden modesty.

"The silly fool left our door wide open. Do you know how many people saw me? Like this?" She dropped the sheet abruptly for emphasis.

Her action brought him fully awake. If what she said was true, then word would spread through the hotel like a raging brush fire.

Rina. His mind flashed to her. He had to get to her before she heard about this.

Grabbing up the crumpled spread, he wrapped it around himself and surged out of the bed. He spotted his clothing spread across the floor and caught it up. Dressing as fast as he could, he shut out the sound of Mary Ellen's ongoing chatter.

He had to go after Rina.

Dressed, he dashed for the door, forgetting all about the woman in the bed.

"Shane?" Mary Ellen's petulant voice stopped him as he reached for the door knob. "Where are you going? Are you just leaving me like this?"

He ran a hand distractedly through his hair. "I'll be back. Don't worry. I'll straighten everything out."

But he'd be damned if he knew how he was going to do it.

Striding down the hall, he rapped on the door to his and Rina's room, hoping against hope that she was still asleep; that she had missed the maid's commotion. Somehow he feared this wasn't so.

"Rina. Sweetheart," he called out softly.

"Go away!" she yelled from the other side.

Damn, she'd obviously heard the news.

He tried the door and found it locked.

"Rina!" Shane pounded on the closed door.

Silence greeted him this time. He rattled the doorknob to no avail. Slamming his fist onto the wood, he knocked louder.

"Rina. Open the door."

"Go away, outlander."

Whenever she called him that, he knew she was mad and unwilling to listen to anything he might have to say. But he had to try.

He continued knocking. He wouldn't leave until he talked to her; he had to explain what she'd witnessed, or thought she'd seen.

As the door remained tightly closed, his anger and frustration grew. Stepping back, he slammed his shoulder into the door. The wooden panel shuddered under his weight, but held.

Once, twice, three times he hit the door with his shoulder before the wood holding the lock splintered, and the door swung open to slam against the wall.

"Get out," Rina ordered him, backing away to the center of the room.

"Dammit, Rina."

Shane stepped toward her, and she retreated to the dressing table. The sparks of fury in her eyes warned him a second too late.

A hairbrush sailed past over his head to hit the hallway wall behind him. A second later, a lady's shoe skimmed the top of his shoulder.

"If you think you're gonna come in here sweet-talking me after spending the night with another woman, then you're a worse fool than you look, outlander."

"Rina . . . Listen to me."

"No!" she shouted.

As Shane took another step toward her, she reached back and caught up the water pitcher.

"Stay away." She brandished the pitcher.

"Put it down, Rina."

He held out his hand to grab the pitcher from her, and she threw it at him. Water sprayed in a wide arch. The pitcher slammed into his shoulder, bounced to the floor, and shattered.

Looking at the shards of broken pottery on the floor, Rina felt like it was her heart a-lyin' there all broken to pieces.

Murmured voices came from the hallway, and Rina looked up to see a small crowd of people watching her through the open doorway. She could see the open disdain and curiosity in their eyes, hear it in their snide remarks. The people in the fancy town looked at her like she was something dirty they didn't want around.

She felt shamed and struggled to hang onto her pride.

Shane glanced back at the hallway, saw the people staring at them, then slammed the door shut. The sound echoed in the room.

"There's nothing you could say that I want to hear."

Once again, shame rushed over Rina. She was nothing to Shane.

She wanted to scream at him, but her voice had been calm when she spoke. It sounded lifeless, even to her own ears. That's jus' how she felt—as if all the life had been drained out of her.

"What if I said I love you?"

"Go tell it to her, outlander. I'm sure it'll mean a whole heap more to her than it does to me now."

He'd told her he loved her before, on the riverboat, and she'd been fool enough to believe him. But not again.

She'd believed him. And he'd betrayed her.

Pain cut through her with the sharpness of the shards on the floor. Oh, it hurt so bad. Worse than anything had ever hurt in her entire life.

She raised her chin in defiance; she wouldn't crumple before him. No, she refused to let him see how badly and deeply he'd hurt her.

He likely hadn't even wanted her along on the riverboat trip. It hadn't been his idea for her to travel with him, had it? She'd been the one to follow him after he'd left, and pushed her way in.

A sudden thought struck her like a lightning bolt. It left behind the same feeling of the hairs on her arms standing on end. *Shane had been coming to New Orleans when she caught up with him on the riverboat. Had he been coming to meet his "lady fiancée?"* Well, he'd certainly done that, hadn't he?

"Dammit, Rina, I love you."

She ignored Shane's proclamation. Instead, she watched him carefully to see if he clutched his stomach from a sudden stomach ache. She hadn't asked Ida how long the potion would last. Was it even still working?

"Why are you looking at me that way?" Shane stared back at Rina.

"I was a-waitin' for your stomach to start hurting you like before," she told him with characteristic honesty.

"My stomach . . ."

Realization dawned for Shane, as he remembered the odd times in the past when he'd been overcome with sudden, unexplained stomach pains. Somehow Rina was that explanation.

340

"Rina?"

She faced him with a glint in her eye. "Care to know why you've been having stomach problems?"

"Yes," he answered curtly.

"It was one of Ida's potions."

"Who is Ida?"

"The mountain healer. I went to her for a potion to let me know when you was telling me true or not."

"What?" Shane's voice boomed through the room.

"Well, you was blowing hot, then cold. I had to have some way of knowing."

"You could have asked me."

"Hell's bells, outlander. I couldn't trust what you was saying. Why would I up and ask you?"

"Exactly how did this potion work?"

She shrugged. "Every time you was lying, your stomach was supposed to start roiling and hurting."

At his look of astonishment, she added, "It worked, didn't it?"

"A potion was the explanation for my stomach?" he roared at her. "And not your pa's cooking?"

Rina snapped her head in a defiant nod of assent. "Yup."

"And just how long was this supposed to last?"

Rina shrugged again, indifference written on her movement. "I never bothered to ask her. And,

341

it doesn't matter to me anymore. Because I don't rightly care if'n you tell the truth or not, now."

Shane clenched his hands into fists and took a step forward. He didn't know which he'd rather do—shake her or kiss her.

Rina put up a hand to stop him. "No, outlander. You aren't touching me again. If'n you come near me, I swear I'll blacken your eye like I did Billy Gant's."

Shane stopped. He knew she was serious. "Rina?"

"No." She crossed her arms defensively and stiffened her spine. "Jus' go!"

Her voice raised a note. "Jus' get out. Now. You got your 'fancy lady' after all. That's what you wanted, wasn't it'?"

Shane knew she wouldn't believe him if he told her "yes, in the beginning," but that he had changed his mind. He didn't want a "fancy lady"—he wanted Rina Taylor. How could she believe him when he didn't even know when the change had taken place? He didn't know exactly when he'd stopped wanting a proper hostess for Belle Rive. It had happened at some point up in the hills. Now all he wanted was Rina beside him forever.

"Rina—"

"No!" she cried out. "I mean it, Shane. I don't wants you. Go away."

He could see the struggle she was having trying to keep control of her emotions. It made him ache to take her in his arms, but he knew that now was not the time. He was honor bound to another woman.

Reluctantly, he turned away from her and walked out the door. He felt as if he were leaving a part of himself behind.

The second the door closed behind him, Rina dashed to it and turned the lock. Covering her mouth with her hand, she fought back the tears.

She wouldn't cry. She wouldn't.

Scalding tears streamed down her cheeks, wetting the hand she held over her mouth. She bit her knuckles to force down the tears, but it didn't do any good. They jus' kept coming and coming. She sank to the floor and buried her face in both hands. The pain gripping her was so great that she couldn't move, could scarcely even breathe.

She didn't belong here.

It was almost as if the words had been spoken aloud to her. She raised her head and wiped away her tears. She could feel the hills calling to her. The hills had never failed to heal all her hurts before. Ida always swore it was the best place for healing a body.

She was going home.

Brad Weston caught up with Shane at a small saloon, after trying three other saloons first.

"I thought I'd find you here." He dropped into the chair opposite Shane.

"Why's that?"

"I heard about your *engagement* to Mary Ellen

Dupre. Are you a fool or have you completely taken leave of your senses?"

Shane didn't meet his friend's curious gaze. He'd had his fill of curiosity and whispered comments behind his back. He poured himself another drink from the nearly full bottle on the table. He swished it around in his mouth, then swallowed. It lacked the smoothness of the Taylor whiskey. He set the glass back onto the table with a thud.

It seemed everything he thought about brought him back to Rina. Lowering his head into his hands, he groaned.

"Both, I suspect." He finally answered his friend's question.

"Why, Shane? Why in the hell did you do it?" Brad shook his head in obvious disbelief. "I saw you and Rina Taylor together. Why would you give up someone that sweet and beautiful for the likes of Miss Dupre?"

"It wasn't my choice."

Shane tossed back the rest of the glass of whiskey, slamming the glass back onto the table top.

"Mary Ellen needed help—"

Brad's snort of incredulity interrupted him.

"I got her a room," he continued, ignoring his friend's skeptical look. "Had a drink or two for old time's sakes—"

"And ended up in her bed?"

"It doesn't matter now."

Shane stared at the amber liquid in the whiskey

bottle. Since he'd lost Rina, nothing much truly mattered to him anymore.

"It looks to me like it matters one hell of a lot, my friend."

"It doesn't matter now," Shane repeated. "It's already done. Mary Ellen's already been compromised. I'm doing what I have to do."

"Shane, old buddy, that woman was compromised long ago."

Shane opened his mouth to defend her, but Brad's next words silenced him.

"Hell, man, half your friends spent time with her down by the river before the war."

"How would you know that?"

"I was one of them," Brad admitted.

"You?"

"It was only once. Like you, I was tricked. Our dear Mary Ellen Dupre is much more clever and underhanded than anyone gives her credit for. Believe me, I've been witness to it first hand."

Shane met his friend's gaze and was surprised at the bitterness revealed there.

"She destroyed any chance I might have had with the woman I really loved," Brad confessed.

Shane recalled a long-forgotten memory of his friend's brief engagement to a store owner's daughter. Shortly after the engagement was abruptly broken off, the young lady had gone East to school and never returned. It all made sense now.

"You know the worst of it?" Brad asked. "Our dear Mary Ellen did it all for spite, because I wouldn't fall at her feet. Don't let her do the same thing to you, friend. Be very careful before you willingly give up love to rescue Miss Dupre."

Shane nodded, as he recalled the events of the day before.

"Beware, Shane. Mary Ellen needs rescuing about as much as a rattlesnake."

Shane passed the bottle of whiskey across the table to his friend. "Here, help yourself. I think it's about time I had a long talk with our Miss Dupre."

"By the way, Shane. I heard a piece of interesting news. It seems that Simon Cooke just happened to cut off Miss Dupre's line of credit last week."

Shane returned his smile. "Yes, now that is interesting."

Brad Weston's shout of laughter followed him out of the saloon.

Shane strode down the street and in through the hotel's front door, oblivious to the curious stares or whispered gossip surrounding his movements. He had one thought in mind—getting to the bottom of this mess, then settling things with Mary Ellen Dupre.

He didn't stop until he reached the door to her hotel room. A shiver of revulsion for last night and this morning's events swept over him. Shaking it off, he pounded on the wood door.

When Mary Ellen opened the door, she blinked at him in surprise.

"Oh, Shane." She glanced around at the stack

of boxes and wrapping strewn over the table. "I wasn't expecting you back so soon."

"You've been shopping." It was a statement, not a question.

Mary Ellen colored slightly at his comment. "Why, yes, I have."

She gestured down to her obviously new gown of rose taffeta, then pulled her embroidered mantilla close about her shoulders, and performed a pirouette.

"Do you like it? I purchased it this morning so I could look especially pretty for you."

"Purchased? Or charged it to my name?"

She yawned prettily into her hand, stopping what he'd been about to say.

"I'm afraid I didn't get much sleep last night—" she broke off and giggled.

Shane pushed the door open and strode into the room. "That's what I'm here to talk to you about."

"Oh, yes, we must start making plans for the wedding. Don't you think it would be wonderful to have it at Belle Rive? We could invite everyone we know."

She slipped her hand through his arm and smiled up at him.

"Although, I don't suppose there will be time to have the place fixed up very much before the wedding."

A petulant frown replaced her smile. "I had at least wanted the master suite redone."

Shane raised a brow at her comment.

347

"And what would you know of the master suite?" he asked in a voice laced with sarcasm.

"Why, Simon showed it to me." She lowered her lashes. "He did make me live there for the last month or so."

"Mary Ellen," Shane paused to disentangle himself from her. "I've told you that I have no plans to purchase Belle Rive. I've let go of the past."

"But surely that's all changed now."

"No, I haven't changed my mind."

"But, are you telling me that we won't be living at Belle Rive?" Her voice rose with the question, and she stepped away from him.

"That's correct."

"But I had planned—"

"Exactly what did you plan, Mary Ellen?"

Shane faced her, and the sudden coldness in his face took her by surprise.

"What are you getting at, Shane?"

"The truth. That is, if you even happen to remember what that is."

"Shane!"

She was the picture of indignation. And he wasn't believing it one little bit.

"You know, I've done a lot of thinking about last night—"

"I have, too." She giggled and covered her mouth with her hand.

"And," Shane continued as if she hadn't spoken, "I only remember having one drink—the one *you* poured me and handed to me."

"I don't like what you're implying—" She broke off and sniffed delicately.

"Neither do I."

Shane met her suddenly teary gaze with an ice cold one of his own.

"And since I am not in the habit of getting so drunk that I forget the evening's events, I can reach only one conclusion. You drugged me."

"What?" she shrieked.

"You drugged me," he repeated. "It's the only explanation. You see, Mary Ellen, I had no desire to make love to you. And I know that I didn't."

"How?"

"Because there is only one woman that I've had any desire for these last weeks. And you may have cost me her love."

"But, Shane—"

"I was willing to help you for old times' sake. But I won't give up my life for you. And Rina happens to be my life."

"You're not marrying me?" A tremor of disbelief tinged her cultured voice.

"No."

"You can't break our engagement. I won't let you."

"There's nothing you can do to stop me."

"But what am I going to do?" she wailed. "I'm ruined."

"I suggest if you want to salvage what's left of your reputation, then you'd better marry Simon Cooke before he leaves for Philadelphia."

Mary Ellen gasped and looked at the door.

Shane watched the play of emotions across her face. Seconds later, she caught up her hatbox and dashed out the door.

Shane chuckled softly under his breath. It appeared she had taken his advice to heart.

He was free of her. The realization brought a heartfelt smile to his lips. Now he could go to Rina.

Turning, he strode down the hall to her room. However, there was no answer to his knock. No sound from inside the room. A vague sense of uneasiness clawed at him.

A stop at the front desk confirmed his fear—Rina had checked out of the hotel and asked directions to the docks where a riverboat, the *River Glory*, was due to depart New Orleans for points north.

Shane whirled away from the desk and headed for the docks, hoping against hope that he'd catch up with her before she boarded the boat. Who knew what kind of trouble she could bring down on herself, if he wasn't there to protect her?

Reaching the docks, his heart sank when he noticed the empty space where the *River Glory* had been. He was too late. The riverboat had left hours ago, carrying Rina away from him.

He booked passage on the next departing boat, but as luck had it, the boat was older and slower than the *River Glory*. It would take him an extra two days to reach Rina.

* * *

Rina gripped the railing until the wood cut into her palms. *She was going home.*

She watched the muddy water churn in the riverboat's wake, feeling like she was churning inside along with it. The pain of Shane's betrayal still went so deep that it felt like she'd taken a mighty beating.

Releasing her grip on the railing, she rubbed one hand back and forth across the wood. The *River Glory* wasn't as fancy as the riverboat she and Shane had taken to New Orleans. Pain shot through her at the memory, and she bit her lip to keep from crying out.

That low-down, sneaking polecat had lied to her. He'd deceived her and betrayed her. All along he'd been a-wantin' a fancy "lady." Well, he got what he wanted.

And she hoped he was jus' plumb miserable!

Why shouldn't he be? She was.

Hell's bells, jus' thinking 'bout it hurt. Somehow, she'd thought that the awful hurtin' would lessen with time. She reckoned now that was wrong. The hurtin' hadn't let up a bit; it was as powerful strong as when Shane had first destroyed her dreams. Even the thought of his name in her mind caused a pain to cut through her. And she didn't think it would ever stop hurting.

It felt as if somebody was a-squeezing her chest as hard as they could. Only it hurt from the inside. On the outside she reckoned she looked the same—excepting for her eyes. The first day of the river trip they'd been all red from cryin', but even-

351

tually she ran outta tears. They jus' seemed to have all dried up.

Now it hurt too bad for cryin'. The pain went too deep fer tears to be of any good to a body. Leastwise that's what she figured. She felt about as mixed up inside as the water beneath the boat 'cause damned if'n she still didn't love him.

Rina forced her gaze away from the turbulent water behind the riverboat; instead she followed the trail the boat left in the churning muddy waters. She let her gaze trail it back to where the river became jus' a ribbon betwixt the riverbanks.

The waterway stretched out plumb to New Orleans. *New Orleans and Shane Delaney.* Was he even now strolling the streets of the fancy town with his "lady" fiancée? Or were they entwined in bed together like when she'd seen them in the hotel room?

Pain racked her at the memory, almost doubling her over with its intensity. She didn't how a body could hurt this bad and keep on a-drawin' breath. Had her pa hurt this bad when her ma ran off?

Pa's words of warning 'bout not making the same mistake as her ma returned to haunt her. They seemed to rise up before her. Well, she'd gone off after the man she loved jus' like her ma had done—'cepting Shane Delaney hadn't wanted her. The back of her throat burned with unshed tears, and she thought of her ma.

Her ma musta loved the man she'd run off with something fierce, Rina realized. She'd never thought much on that part of it before, but now she did. It seemed all she had was time for thinking. Maybe, jus' maybe, she was beginning to understand what had happened all those years ago.

"Ma . . ." Rina bit her lower lip. "Mama," she looked off across the muddy water to a distant point where the water and sky seemed to meet.

"Mama, I thinks I understand why ya left. If'n ya loved him this much," she paused and wrapped her arms around her middle in an attempt to lessen the pain that stole her breath away. "If'n it hurt this much to be without him, I knows why ya left to be with him."

Rina blinked away the tears that suddenly insisted on gathering behind her eyelids. "And I forgives ya," she whispered.

She turned away from the railing, unable to watch the water that was taking her farther and farther from Shane with every mile the riverboat traveled. If'n only it would take the pain along with it. But she knew it wouldn't be doing that. This hurtin' was gonna be with her fer a long time. Maybe forever.

She wouldn't be a-runnin' off to be with the man she loved, like her ma had, but at least she was going home.

Home. The word tugged at her, offering a small measure of solace. The only one she had.

Soon she'd be home. And then she'd have to start learning to face the future without Shane Delaney.

Roger Chastain stepped back out of sight, behind a stack of crates. His gray coat and pants blending in with the dust-covered crates, he watched the small group of passengers disembark from the old riverboat. *There he was. Shane Delaney.*

The waiting had paid off. He'd been watching for Delaney for two days—waiting and watching—ever since he'd seen Rina Taylor arrive alone on a riverboat. While checking the boats' arrivals, he'd been lucky enough to spot her coming off the gangway. Alone.

Chastain knew it wouldn't be long before Delaney'd arrive, too. He figured, and rightly so, that Delaney wouldn't be far behind the tempting Rina Taylor. All he'd had to do was wait, and eventually Delaney would track her back to the hills. He smiled, more than ready for Delaney this time.

Chastain caressed the gleaming gun in his holster, trailing his fingers back and forth across the polished handle. He preferred his derringer, but he had no intention of getting too close to his prey.

He watched Delaney walk away from the riverboat. Soon, he promised himself, very soon now. The long days of waiting had been worth it.

Delaney was his now. It wouldn't be long before he had him in his gun sights, and he anticipated how good it would feel when he'd pull the trigger. Delaney would die for sure today.

Nineteen

Shane bounded off the gangway of the boat. It felt good to be on solid ground and close to Rina. This time the river trip had seemed endless to him.

Without stopping for anything else, not even to drop in at Lucas's office, he strode straight to the livery and rented a horse. Swinging into the saddle, he headed for the Taylor cabin.

Intent on reaching Rina as quickly as possible, Shane failed to notice the lone rider, dressed in gray, following him out of town at a safe distance.

The surrounding hills seemed even more colorful than when he'd left. He felt as if he'd been gone for months instead of days.

How would Rina greet his sudden arrival? He'd decided against sending her a message. Instead, he wanted to catch her off guard. It might give him a better chance to make her hear him out.

A smile touched his lips as he recalled her temper. She was never more full of life than when she was angry, and Rina Taylor in a full fit of anger was a beautiful sight to behold. All he had to do was get to that shotgun before she did.

Not that it would do her any good anyway. She might run him off, but he'd keep coming back. Again and again—until she listened. And believed him.

The thought of the truth made him touch his stomach with a tentative hand. The little minx—she'd actually sneaked him a potion. He smiled.

Well, two could play at that particular game. If Rina refused to hear him out, he'd go to the old mountain woman, Ida, himself. He knew once he assured the woman of his love for Rina, he could convince her to give him a potion to make Rina see reason—if there was such a thing.

He sobered. Rina had to see that he loved her. She had to. He didn't even want to think about the bleakness of his life without her.

The sharp snap of a branch underfoot cut through his thoughts, then there followed a menacing stillness. The hair at the back of his neck began to prickle, and he knew there was trouble.

Carefully, Shane eased his pistol free. He whirled around, gun in hand, but his opponent was ready for him. Roger Chastain stood facing him, gun cocked and aimed at Shane.

They took each other's measure in a taut, charged silence.

"Chastain," Shane greeted him in a low tone.

"Hello, Delaney." Chastain gave him a thin-lipped smile. "Good day to die, isn't it?"

The next instant, Chastain pulled the trigger, and the roar of the pistol shattered the silence around them.

Pain exploded in Shane's head. He grabbed for the saddle, but missed and pitched off his mount to the hard ground.

He heard harsh laughter and wondered if it was death laughing at him, then blackness closed in.

Keeping his gun trained on the fallen man, Chastain swung down out of the saddle. He approached Delaney and surveyed him coldly.

Blood covered the side of Shane's head, oozing from a wound about his temple. Chastain stared down at him, smiling at the sight before him.

"Now we're even, Delaney. It's a pity you can't hear me."

Spinning on his heel, Chastain laughed and crossed back to his horse. Mounting, he flicked the reins and kicked his heels hard. He couldn't wait to tell old man Gant the good news. And get his money.

He set off for Gant's place, whistling a jaunty tune.

"Hey, Gant! You in there?" Roger Chastain called out from the edge of the trees.

He'd met up with the old man and his shotgun once before, and was warned of him now. He wanted the foolish old man to know it was him.

Eager for the money he was owed, Chastain became careless. Riding his horse closer to the cabin, he didn't stop until he was in the center of the clearing in front of the small cabin.

"Gant! Get out here."

As the cabin remained quiet, anger urged him on. Chastain pulled out his derringer.

"You know what I've come after. Now get out here," Chastain ordered.

Nolan pulled back a weathered curtain from the window and looked out at his visitor. The bright sunlight created a haze over the clearing, blurring his vision.

He squinted and shielded his eyes with one hand. His eyesight wasn't what it used to be. Leaning forward, he blinked and made out a rider dressed in gray.

Gray! His heart thudded, then raced with fear. It was the gray of the Confederate soldiers. Suddenly, past and present blurred together in his mind.

As he rechecked, taking in the gray coat and pants the man wore, a cry of rage was torn from his throat.

"Billy, it's that Confederate captain come back again fer ya. He's gonna take ya back to the war."

"Gant!"

"No!" Nolan screamed and whirled away from the window and the threat he saw in the man outside. The soldiers had come once before and taken his Billy back to fight. Not again—he wouldn't let them take his boy this time.

It wasn't that his boy was a coward—he was jus'

tired and sick of fighting. This time they'd take Billy away over Nolan's dead body. But he intended to take many a soldier along with him.

"Billy," Nolan hissed, frantically searching the cabin's single room for his slim son, "hurry, go hide, boy."

Picking up his shotgun, he spared his Billy a fleeting glance.

"Now, get, boy. Soldiers are a-comin'. But, don't you worry none."

He shouldered the shotgun and poked it out through a window. Glass shattered, falling to the ground with a clatter.

Pulling the trigger, he released a booming shot. It fell short of the man on the horse.

"I won't let 'em take ya back, boy."

Nolan shoved the shotgun back through the open window. He fired again, and this time the rider fell from his horse into a crumpled heap on the ground.

Screaming his glee, Nolan pulled his shotgun back inside.

"We got 'em, Billy."

Nolan threw the door open and ran out into the clearing. Approaching the stranger, he stopped and looked him over.

Now that was funny. He'd never yet seen an officer without a fancy uniform hat. He nudged the man with his booted foot, rolling him over.

The gray jacket was awash in red blood. Seeing it, Nolan jumped up and down, cackling in glee.

He'd got the man dead center of his fancy uniform jacket.

This soldier wouldn't be taking his boy anywhere.

Nolan kicked the officer, then spit on the gray jacket. In his mind, he saw the decorated ribbons of a Confederate officer gleaming in the sunlight.

Turning away, Nolan left the dead man where he lay and swaggered back to the cabin. Triumph gave him a new spring in his steps.

He hadn't felt this good in years. Why, his rheumatism didn't bother him at all.

Matter of fact, he felt good enough to take care of the last threat to his boy, Billy. *Rina Taylor.* And he knew jus' how to do it, and get ahold of that Taylor recipe while he was at it.

Cackling to himself, he entered the cabin, and walked straight to the table. He laid the shotgun across the table's scarred surface, then hunted around the cabin until he'd found a piece of paper and an old quill pen. He hadn't written anything down in so long that he'd about forgotten where he kept them.

Carefully, he wrote out each word of his message. It took him three tries before he got the wording like he wanted it to sound. Then he signed it, making sure to smear the ink jus' a little over the name.

He waved it back and forth, drying the ink real good. Squinting, he held the page out at arm's length and reread the wording, checking it over real close to be sure it was right.

Rina,

I must see you. Please meet me at your pa's whiskey still. Urgent!!

Love,
Shane

Yep, it'd work jus' fine. Nolan looked at the paper with pride.

Folding it carefully, he put it in his shirt pocket. He'd have Rina Taylor within his grasp before sunset. Laughter bubbled up in him.

"I'm gonna go to town fer a while," he shouted for Billy's benefit, then left the cabin.

Outside, he squinted at the bright sunlight, then spotted the dead soldier's horse. Riding would save him a heap of time. Without the least remorse, he sauntered toward the mount.

Yep, once he got into town, he knew a boy who'd deliver his message and keep quiet about who'd given it to him. All it'd cost Nolan was a handful of coins. Money well spent, he figured.

Stepping over the dead man's body, Nolan pulled himself up into the saddle, and steered the horse toward the trail to Possum Hollow.

Rina unfolded and read the message Pa handed her. Her heart leaped for her throat and lodged there. *Shane was back.*

And a-wanting to see her.

She curled her fingers around the edges of the paper and stared down at the words.

"Well? Ya gonna go or not?" Pa asked her, from his vantage point looking over her shoulder.

"Pa!"

"I has a right to know, don't I?"

As she hesitated, nibbling thoughtfully on her bottom lip, he added, "So, are ya gonna let him defeat ya? Or are ya gonna show him what a Taylor's made of?"

When Rina stiffened her spine in indignant pride, he bit the corner of his cheek to keep from grinning. She was his daughter all right. And she was gonna do jus' as he figured she'd do. Somebody would have a mighty hard time keeping her from seeing Delaney now.

Not that he intended to be that somebody to stop her. All he wanted to see done was for her and Delaney to meet some place off alone. And then nature would take care of the rest.

Unless he missed his bet, there'd be a wedding coming before the month was out. A smile slipped past his defenses before he could stop it.

"What are you grinning at?" Rina asked him, her eyes narrowing on his pleased expression.

"I was thinking that ya might jus' want to purty yourself up some. Show him you's a real fine lady now. Humm?"

The idea caught Rina's attention. Wasn't that what she'd set out to do in the beginning, she asked herself? Well, she was gonna succeed.

"You're right, Pa." She reached up on tiptoe and placed a kiss on his leathery cheek.

Whirling around, she headed for her bedroom

with a smile. She wasn't happy to be seeing Shane, she denied silently. No, she surely wasn't.

In her room, she opened the chest, and memories swamped over her. It was so much like the last time she'd "purtied" herself up for Shane. Pain cut through her at the thought. This time it was different, though. This time she was going to be seeing him for the last. She was seeing him to say goodbye.

With determined movements, she laid out her gown and what fancy underthings she had left, spreading them out over the bed. Her supply of purty clothes was dwindling away. This lady business sure sent a body going through clothes and such awful fast, didn't it?

Stripping out of her old pair of breeches and the oversized shirt she'd donned that morning, she slipped into the last fancy lace-trimmed chemise that she owned.

This time she was a-wearin' it purely for herself. Shane Delaney would never see what she had on under her lady's dress this time.

Another shaft of pain hit her, sucking the breath clean out of her. She sat down heavily on the edge of the bed and blinked back the sudden moistness that had gathered in her eyes. It must be the weather, she told herself; she wasn't a-startin' to cry over him.

Scooping up her stockings, she eased one on, pulling it up to her thigh, then did the same with the mate. She followed them with a pair of blue and white lace-edged garters.

Standing, she stepped into the layers of petticoats and tied them snugly. She had to search the room twice before she found her pair of blue satin slippers under the feather bed.

She turned around and sucked in a deep breath of courage. She needed it to face the memories of the dress laying across the bed.

Carefully, she shook out the shimmering blue gown. Memories rose over her in crashing waves, threatening to batter her. An image of Shane looking down at her at the riverboat railing rose up before her like a specter. He'd told he loved her then. That time on the riverboat deck had been her most cherished memory of all.

In an attempt to shove the painful recollections aside, she quickly lifted the dress and pulled it down over her head. Concentrating on arranging it over the layers of petticoats, she told herself that she didn't care a hate. No, she didn't, did she?

She'd only chosen this blue gown she'd worn for Shane on the riverboat because it was her best one. It was her purtiest dress, and the one that made her look the mostest like a real lady. She wanted Shane to see what he was losing.

Her hands shook as she brushed and pinned her hair up atop her head. *She'd show him that she was every bit the lady his fancy fiancée was. She'd show him—jus' see if'n she didn't.*

Readied at last, Rina clenched her hands into her skirt and walked out of her bedroom. Her pa was waiting for her, jus' like she'd expected.

His slow whistle filled the air.

"Gal, you'll surely take that man's breath away. Jus' see if'n I'm not right. Why, I'd bet—"

He cut off what he'd been about to say and caught her cold hands together in his, rubbing them briskly for a moment.

"Well, I'd best be going;" she told him.

"You show him, gal."

She raised her chin and smiled up at him. "I will, Pa."

It only took her a few minutes to walk most of the way to the clearing. She spent those minutes gathering up her anger and pain around her like a woolen cloak to shield her from Shane's charm.

She swore he could charm the blue jays right outta the trees if'n he tried. But it wasn't going to work on her this time.

Stopping on the trail, she brushed down her skirts and tucked back a loose tendril of hair. She guessed she was about as ready as she'd ever be.

The woods around her failed to calm her as they usually did, and she pressed on. Within a few more minutes, she entered the clearing.

"Shane?" she called out, but no one answered.

Well, if'n that didn't beat all—he wasn't even here yet. She crossed her arms over her chest in frustration and kicked at a pine cone with the toe of her slipper.

All around her was silent. She cocked her head, checking. It was too quiet. Once again, it felt as if the hills around her were holding their breath. It wasn't a good feeling.

A smattering of goose flesh broke out on her arms in spite of the warm day. She didn't like it one bit. Her neck prickled with uneasiness.

Turning, she decided to head back to the cabin as fast as possible. She'd taken two steps before a voice stopped her.

"Well, well, lookee who's here."

Rina spun around at the sound of shrill laughter. *Nolan Gant.*

She swallowed down the sudden lump of fear that wedged in her mouth.

"I sees you gots my message, missy."

Rina's eyes widened in growing uneasiness.

"Your message." Nolan, not Shane, had sent the note.

"I didn't figure you'd be too willing to come up here all alone to see me. So, I put the gamblerman's name down instead."

Nolan looked her up and down, grinning.

"Worked jus' fine, didn't it? And ya even dressed up real fine fer me."

"What do you want, Nolan?"

"Why, the recipe, of course. Then, I wants to see you die, Rina Taylor." He spit her name out with unveiled hatred.

Rina forced herself to stand still under his baleful glare. She shook her head at him. "It won't work. I won't give it to you."

The silly old fool thought all he had to do was *ask* her, and she'd hand over the secret. Ha! He had a lot to learn.

"Yes, you will!" he shouted at her.

Shaking her head, Rina laughed out loud at his orders. "Not hardly."

"Oh, yes, you will," he repeated. "If'n you don't want to die before you take your next breath." He curled his palm around the shotgun barrel. "I've already killed me a Confederate officer today."

"A Confederate officer?" she whispered, growing suddenly afeared at the strange glint of madness she saw in the old man's eyes.

"Yep. Shot him dead. Silly yellow-haired fool came after my Billy."

A sudden remembrance of Roger Chastain's blond looks sprang to mind. He was jus' the sort to be working for a man like Nolan.

She covered her mouth with her hand, holding back her cry of alarm as she realized it had been Chastain that Nolan had shot in his fit of madness.

Nolan jerked his head, pulling his attention back to the job at hand. "Now, missy. It's your turn, lessen you give me that recipe now."

She couldn't do that. If'n she did, she knew he'd surely kill her right away. Trying not to let her growing fear of him show, she scanned the clearing, but found nothing of any help.

Oh, if only Shane had sent that message to her. Where are you, Shane? she implored. Please help me.

Shane blinked his eyes against the sunlight streaming down on him. As he attempted to sit up, a wave of dizziness washed over him, followed by a sharp pain at the side of his head.

He guessed if he could feel pain, then he was still alive. The good Lord had certainly spared his life. He had no other answer for why he'd turned his head at the exact instant that Roger Chastain had fired his pistol. That action had saved his life.

Shane raised his hand and tentatively felt the streak of caked blood above his temple. It hurt like hell, but luckily it was just a graze.

He stood to his feet, and the world around him wavered, then steadied itself. Luckily, Chastain had left him for dead and high-tailed it out of here instead of sticking around to be sure he had killed him.

Likely as not, the bushwacker was long gone. Shane scanned the surrounding area just to be certain of that fact.

From the corner of his eye, he spotted his horse grazing a short distance away. Murmuring softly to him, Shane walked up and caught hold of the reins.

He eased himself into the saddle and waited a moment, satisfied when the dizziness didn't return. He glanced down at his dirt-stained clothes. He definitely looked worse than when he'd started out, but nothing else was keeping him from Rina.

He turned the horse back onto the trail and headed for the Taylor cabin at an easy canter. Eagerness tugged at him, urging him to hurry.

At the Taylor cabin, he swung out of the saddle and strode to the door. His knock was answered almost immediately by Ben Taylor.

"Shane! What in blue blazes are you doing here?" Ben's voice boomed at him.

"I've come to see Rina."

Shane braced himself for her father's anger. He was unprepared for the sudden aging in the other man's face and the fear he saw in his eyes.

"She isn't with you?" Ben fired out the question. "Don't ya know better than to leave her up at the whiskey still alone after what Nolan Gant tried to do?" he practically barked out the words.

"I—"

"Dagnamit, Shane. It's downright dangerous for her to be there alone in the clearing without anybody else at all around!"

"What the hell is she doing up at the clearing? How could you let her go up there by herself?" Shane advanced a step, as anger at her father's carelessness surged through him.

Ben Taylor seemed to crumple before him, grabbing hold of the door frame with both of his hands.

"You didn't send her that note, did you?" His voice was bleak.

Fear caught at Shane's heart, squeezing it hard. "What note?"

"The one that sent her scurrying up to the clearing alone."

They looked at each other, and Shane spoke first, "Nolan Gant."

Ben Taylor charged forward, but Shane caught his arm, pulling him to a stop.

"You go to Gant's cabin and get Billy. First, make sure Nolan didn't take her there. Bring Billy back, he might be willing to help us."

"Shane?" Ben spun around to face him. "Billy Gant died in the war—"

"What?"

"A fever took him shortly after he was dragged back fer deserting."

Horror filled Shane's heart. "He's dead?"

Ben nodded his answer. "The only place that boy's alive is in old Nolan's mind. Talks to him as if'n he were still around—"

Shane grabbed Ben's shoulder. "Nolan thinks there's something between Billy and Rina."

"If'n that's true, he'll kill her fer sure."

Shane jerked away and raced for his horse. Swinging up into the saddle, he turned the horse for the narrow trail to the clearing. He could hear Ben Taylor running after him.

Urging the horse into a gallop, Shane raced for the clearing. Fear that he wouldn't be in time clawed at him. The realization that if anything happened to her, his life wouldn't be worth living coursed through his veins. *She* was his very life.

Just short of the clearing, he jerked the horse to a stop and vaulted down. He tied the reins to a slim tree, not wanting to chance the horse bolting and alerting Nolan to his presence.

Shane pulled out his pistol and kept low, running for the clearing ahead. *Please, let Rina be there. Let her be alive,* he prayed.

He wanted to yell out her name, but forced himself to be as quiet as possible. Everything depended on him sneaking up on Nolan.

"That's far enough, Delaney," Nolan screamed out at him, stepping out from beside a pine tree. He dragged Rina alongside him.

Shane froze in his tracks, his pistol pointed unwaveringly at Nolan.

"Drop the gun, Delaney. Or I'll shoot her right where she stands," Nolan threatened, pushing Rina toward Shane.

She stumbled and caught herself.

At Shane's reluctance to do as he told him, Nolan added, "I swear I'll shoot her."

Nolan pointed the shotgun directly at Rina. Shane glanced at her, desperate to see that she was all right. The sight of her caught at his heart. She was standing up so proud and straight to Nolan's crazed threats. If he did as the old man said and threw down his gun, Nolan would probably shoot them both.

But Shane knew without a doubt that if he didn't do what the old man said, he'd surely kill Rina.

Swearing under his breath, Shane tossed the pistol down at Nolan's feet.

Twenty

Nolan quickly scooped up Shane's pistol from the ground, tucking it into the waist of his baggy pants. He patted the handle of the gun.

"Now, that there makes me feel a whole heap better. Thank you, Delaney," he sneered.

Easing his shotgun into the crook of his arm, he put both hands on it before turning to Rina. He aimed the barrel at her chest.

"Ya gots two choices, missy. Give me the recipe, or watch him die."

Nolan pointed the shotgun at Shane. His gnarled hands shook, and the barrel wavered. The action was even more threatening for its unsteadiness.

Rina's knees buckled beneath her, and she almost fell. Shane dead? No! her heart screamed in denial. She couldn't stand by and let that happen.

If'n what Pa said about the secret Taylor whiskey recipe was true—that it didn't mean as much to him as her jumping the broom with Shane—then surely the recipe wasn't as important as Shane's life. Was it?

Nothing was as important as Shane Delaney's life. Nothing.

In a clear voice, she began to recite the ingredients to the recipe. "A spoonful of lemon peel, blackberry juice—"

"Rina, don't," Shane ordered, trying to stop her from giving away the secret.

"Shut up, gamblerman." Nolan jabbed at Shane with the shotgun barrel.

Shane clenched his fist with the effort it took to hold himself in check. He wanted nothing more than to charge the old man. However, if he did, it could put Rina in even more danger than she was already in. For now, he'd bide his time. Old fool Gant would make a mistake, and when he did, Shane would be ready for him.

When Rina had recited the last of the recipe, Nolan grabbed her by the arm and jerked her forward.

"Go on, go get the fixin's. I know you keeps them around here." A feverish gleam lit his eyes.

Rina obeyed without hesitation. Crossing Nolan when he was sane was one thing, but crossing him when he was crazed like now was another. Pulling the bag out from the rocks where she'd last hidden it, she handed it to him, but he slapped the bag away.

"Go on. Mix it."

Holding tightly to the shotgun, he kept it

pointed at her while she measured and stirred up a fresh batch for the still.

As soon as she'd finished, Nolan grabbed the mixture away from her and slowly, step by step, backed to the still. Watching him pile more wood under the copper pot, Rina remembered what her pa had said about Nolan not having "the sense of a flea."

If'n he kept adding to the fuel, the whiskey still was likely to blow sky high.

"Nolan—"

"Shut up," he screamed, kicking a pile of pine cones into the leaping flames.

"Nolan, that fire's hottening up way too fast."

"Shut up!" He nudged more pine needles toward the pine cones and wood feeding the fire.

"Nolan," she tried again.

"I won't listen to your lies." He raised his arms, putting his hands over his ears. "No."

"Rina," Shane whispered as loud as he dared.

She glanced at him, and he motioned her to back away from the still. Obeying immediately, she eased one slipper-clad foot backward, she shifted to her other foot and widened the distance between her and Nolan.

Inch by agonizing inch, she crept backwards. Glancing at the whiskey still, she could tell it was getting far too hot.

It was gonna blow at any moment.

As Nolan looked back over his shoulder at the still, Shane lunged forward, grabbing Rina by the hand. He jerked her toward him and took off running, pulling her along behind him.

Afraid of hearing Nolan's shotgun blast firing at them even before the still could explode, Shane headed for the shelter of the trees. A rumble shook the ground beneath their feet, giving a last warning.

Shane pulled Rina to him and yelled, "Get down!"

Shoving her to the ground, he dove after her, trying to cover her body protectively with his. An ear-splitting explosion rocked the clearing.

Once again, debris rained down in an arch from the still. Shane covered his head with his arms and prayed Rina would be safe beneath him.

After several seconds, he raised his head and peered behind them. A sunken hole filled with twisted, charred metal was all that was left of the whiskey still. Two downed pine trees laid haphazardly over the rubble, and between the trunks lay the dead body of Nolan Gant.

"Shane?" Rina leaned up and glanced around his shoulder. At her first sight of Nolan's twisted body, she cried out.

Shane buried her head in his shoulder, turning her away from the sight.

"He'll never threaten you again, sweetheart," he whispered against her ear.

She shuddered in his arms. Tilting her head up, Shane covered her trembling lips with his. He kissed her until he felt the numbness leave her, and she began to respond to him, moving beneath him.

Drawing back, he broke off the kiss. "Are you all right? Do you think you can stand?"

Rina nodded. As he surged to his feet and held out his hand, she clasped it tightly. He swung her up into the sweet, safe haven of his embrace, wrapping his arms around her waist.

Holding her close, he turned and led her away from the smoldering rubble. When she started to turn her head to look back, he pressed her head against his shoulder. Instinctively, he steered her toward their field of wildflowers.

Over his shoulder, he saw Ben Taylor grinning and waving at him from the safety of the trail. Shane paused, waiting.

Instead of coming forward to join them, Ben motioned Shane on away from him. Grinning widely, Rina's pa nodded his approval.

Shane tightened his hold on Rina and set his course for their private haven. Once there amongst the colorful blooms, he turned her to face him and cupped her chin with his hand. He kissed her hard and thoroughly, trying to banish the horror she'd just been through.

Only when she was clinging to him and breathless did he release her. Linking her hands behind his neck, she glanced down at her torn dress, and her lower lip quivered.

Ragged tears marred the once shimmering blue cloth. One long, jagged rip ran the full length of her leg, from thigh to ankle. Tattered shreds of dirt-stained petticoat parted to reveal her honey-tanned legs.

"Look at me." She stepped away and threw her hands up in disgust. "I was trying so hard. I'm never gonna be a lady."

Shane silenced her with a firm kiss on her lips. Slipping his hand through the parted skirt, he ran his hand up her thigh.

"Rina, sweetheart, if you were any more of a lady, I couldn't stand it."

"Shane, I'm serious."

"So am I." He leaned back and linked his hands around her waist, holding her a willing prisoner. "Sweetheart, you've taught me that being a real 'lady' comes from inside. Believe me, you are more of a lady than I could ever dream of wanting. Or having. Or deserving."

He gently wiped a streak of soot from her cheek, then followed the trail left behind with his lips. When he reached the sensitive spot at the side of her throat, Rina arched against him.

Shane eased her onto the fragrant blossoms, following her down. Taking full advantage of his position, he thoroughly kissed the woman he loved more than life.

"Shane," Rina murmured against his lips.

He smothered what she'd been about to say with his kisses, not stopping until he had to raise his head to breathe.

"Shane," she tried again, "about—"

He kissed her into silence again. Her lips twitching into a half-smile under his, she gave up and returned his kisses, wrapping her arms around his neck. She curled her fingers into the thick hair at his nape.

He kissed the corner of her mouth and trailed nibbling kisses down along her chin.

"Marry me, Rina," he groaned against her neck.

When she didn't answer him immediately, he added, "Sweetheart, I've been such a fool. I'm sorry for hurting you. Believe me, nothing happened with that woman in New Orleans. It was all a set-up of hers so she could get her hands on Belle Rive."

He caught her shoulders in his hands. With a desperate groan, he rained kisses across her lips and chin.

"Nothing happened." He drew back to meet her gaze with a heartfelt look of love. "I could never make love to another woman when I love you so much it hurts."

A smile tipped the corners of Rina's mouth. "How's your stomach a-feel in', outlander?"

With a dead serious look, he said, "Wonderful."

Rina threw her arms around his neck and pulled his head down for a kiss.

"I do love you, Shane Delaney."

"And I love you more than life itself, sweetheart," he vowed.

After a thoroughly breath-robbing kiss, he raised up on his elbows and gazed down at her.

"You never answered my question."

"I didn't hear you *asking.*"

Shane smiled and carefully reworded his proposal. "Rina Taylor, *will* you marry me?"

"Yes!"

He gazed down at her, into her eyes that were warm and soft with love.

"Shane," Rina's voice was so low he could hardly hear her, and he had to lean closer.

"If'n you want that plantation home of yours, I'm a-willin' to leave the hills and move to New Orleans."

"Not on your life." He kissed the tip of her lightly freckled nose. "I've come to like it here. New Orleans holds nothing for me anymore."

"I'm glad." She wiggled beneath him, stirring his blood. "Does anything around *here* hold you?" she teased.

"Most definitely."

Shane eased one hand along her torn skirt, pulling it aside. A light tug opened the bodice as well, laying her silken skin bared to his gaze. He kissed and suckled her breasts, favoring first one and then the other with his ministrations.

"Umm," he murmured against the valley of her breasts. "We'll build a cabin of our own," he began making plans as only a true gambler could.

"Shane—"

"One riverboat trip a year—to close the deals on the Taylor whiskey sales."

"Shane?" Rina repeated.

"Yes, sweetheart?"

"Are you gonna lay there all day sweet-talking me, or are you gonna make love to me?"

He obliged her.

Dear Reader,

I hope that you have enjoyed *GAMBLER'S LADY*, and I hope that I have been able to bring a little love and laughter into your life.

My next book will be *MOONLIGHT MASQUERADE* where a Union officer, who moonlights as a thief on secret orders from the President, and a determined secessionist beauty both vie for a packet of secret papers, then for love. Look for it in August, 1994.

A Rebel myself, I was born in Missouri—south of the Mason-Dixon line. I married the man I fell in love with in high school and now live in northern California with my husband and our cocker spaniel. My husband and I have lived in five states, including Hawaii where I attended college.

When not absorbed in writing, I love to spend time with my husband backpacking in the Sierras or traveling together.

I love writing romances, and I believe love lasts forever. I hope my books impart the reality of love to you, my readers.

I'd love to hear from you. Write to me in care of Zebra Books. Please include a self-addressed stamped envelope if you wish a response.

Joyce Adams

SURRENDER TO THE SPLENDOR OF THE ROMANCES OF F. ROSANNE BITTNER!

CARESS	(3791, $5.99/$6.99)
COMANCHE SUNSET	(3568, $4.99/$5.99)
ECSTASY'S CHAINS	(2617, $3.95/$4.95)
HEARTS SURRENDER	(2945, $4.50/$5.50)
LAWLESS LOVE	(3877, $4.50/$5.50)
PRAIRIE EMBRACE	(3160, $4.50/$5.50)
RAPTURE'S GOLD	(3879, $4.50/$5.50)
SHAMELESS	(4056, $5.99/$6.99)
SIOUX SPLENDOR	(3231, $4.50/$5.50)
SWEET MOUNTAIN MAGIC	(2914, $4.50/$5.50)

Available wherever paperbacks are sold, or order direct from the Publisher. Send cover price plus 50¢ per copy for mailing and handling to Penguin USA, P.O. Box 999, c/o Dept. 17109, Bergenfield, NJ 07621.Residents of New York and Tennessee must include sales tax. DO NOT SEND CASH.

EVERY DAY WILL FEEL LIKE FEBRUARY 14TH!

Zebra Historical Romances
by Terri Valentine

LOUISIANA CARESS   (4126-8, $4.50/$5.50)

MASTER OF HER HEART   (3056-8, $4.25/$5.50)

OUTLAW'S KISS   (3367-2, $4.50/$5.50)

SEA DREAMS   (2200-X, $3.75/$4.95)

SWEET PARADISE   (3659-0, $4.50/$5.50)

TRAITOR'S KISS   (2569-6, $3.75/$4.95)

Available wherever paperbacks are sold, or order direct from the Publisher. Send cover price plus 50¢ per copy for mailing and handling to Penguin USA, P.O. Box 999, c/o Dept. 17109, Bergenfield, NJ 07621.Residents of New York and Tennessee must include sales tax. DO NOT SEND CASH.